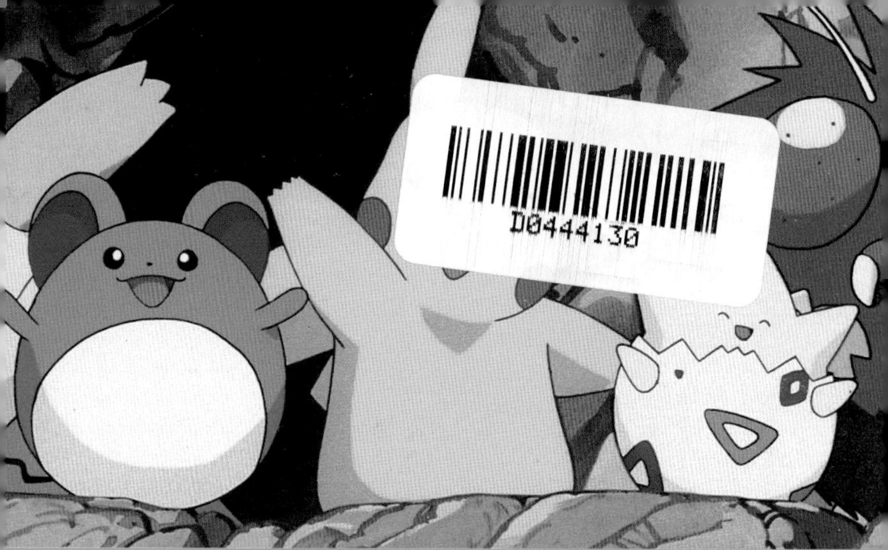

ALL THAT PIKACHU!

ANI-MANGA

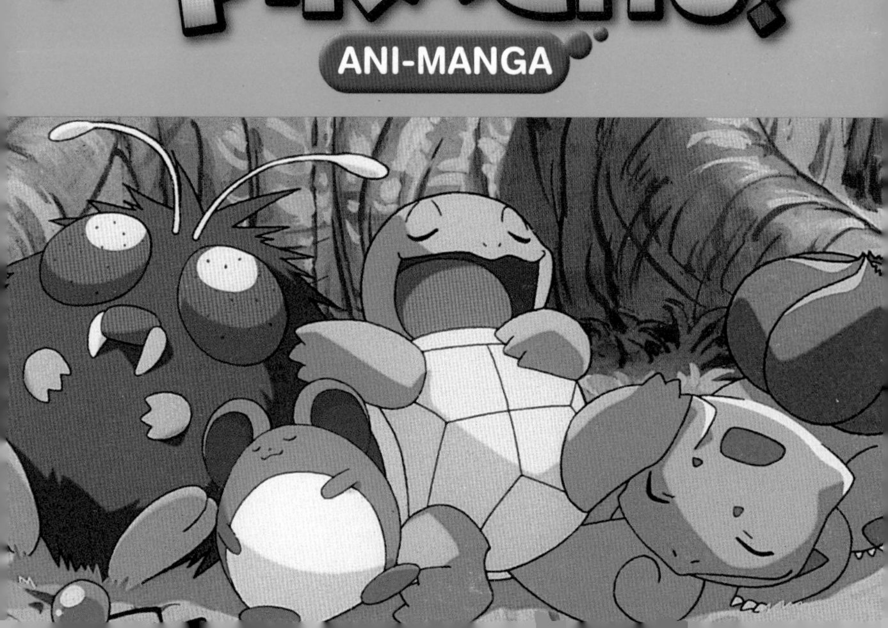

ALL THAT PIKACHU! ANI-MANGA

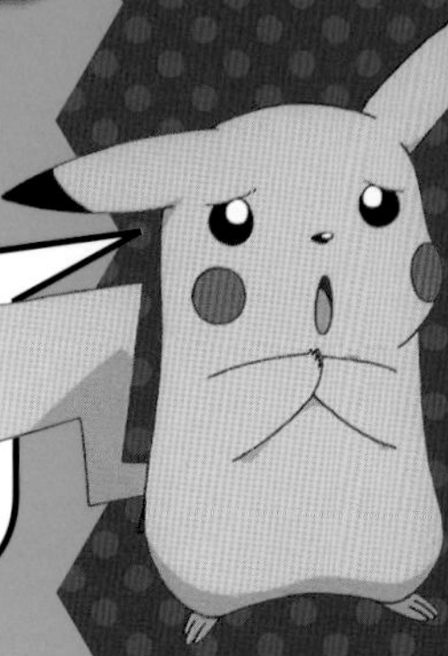

CONTENTS

ALL THAT PIKACHU! ANI-MANGA™

From the graphic novels *Pokémon The First Movie* and *Pokémon The Movie 2000* published by VIZ Media.

Story by Hideki Sonoda
Based on the concept by Tsunekazu Ishihara & Satoshi Tajiri

[VIZ GRAPHIC NOVEL Edition]
Translation/Kaori Kawakubo
Lettering/Dan Nakrosis
Graphics and Layout/tee graphics
Editor/Jason Thompson

[ALL THAT PIKACHU! Edition]
Design/Izumi Hirayama
Managing Editor/Masumi Washington

Editor in Chief/Alvin Lu
Sr. Director of Acquisitions/Rika Inouye
Sr. VP of Marketing/Liza Coppola
Exec. VP of Sales & Marketing/John Easum
Publisher/Hyoe Narita

First published by Shogakukan Inc. in Japan as "Pocket Monsters Gekijoban: Mewto no Gyakushu/Pikachu no Natsuyasumi" and "Pocket Monsters Gekijoban: Lugia no Bakutan/Pikachu Tankentai".

Printed in China

Published by VIZ Media, LLC
P.O. Box 77010
San Francisco, CA 94133

First printing, August 2006

vizkids
VIZ media™

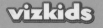

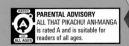

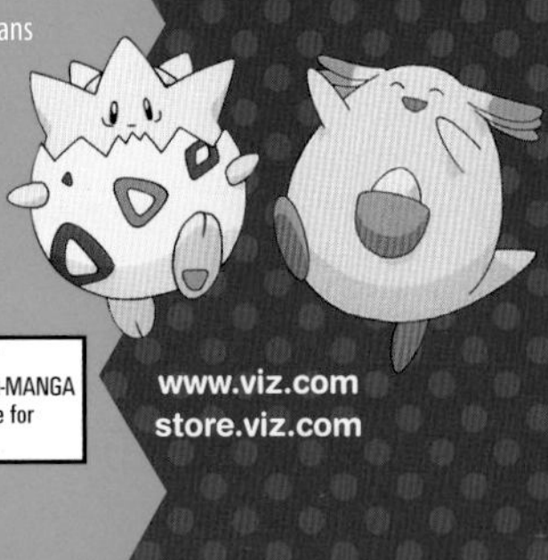

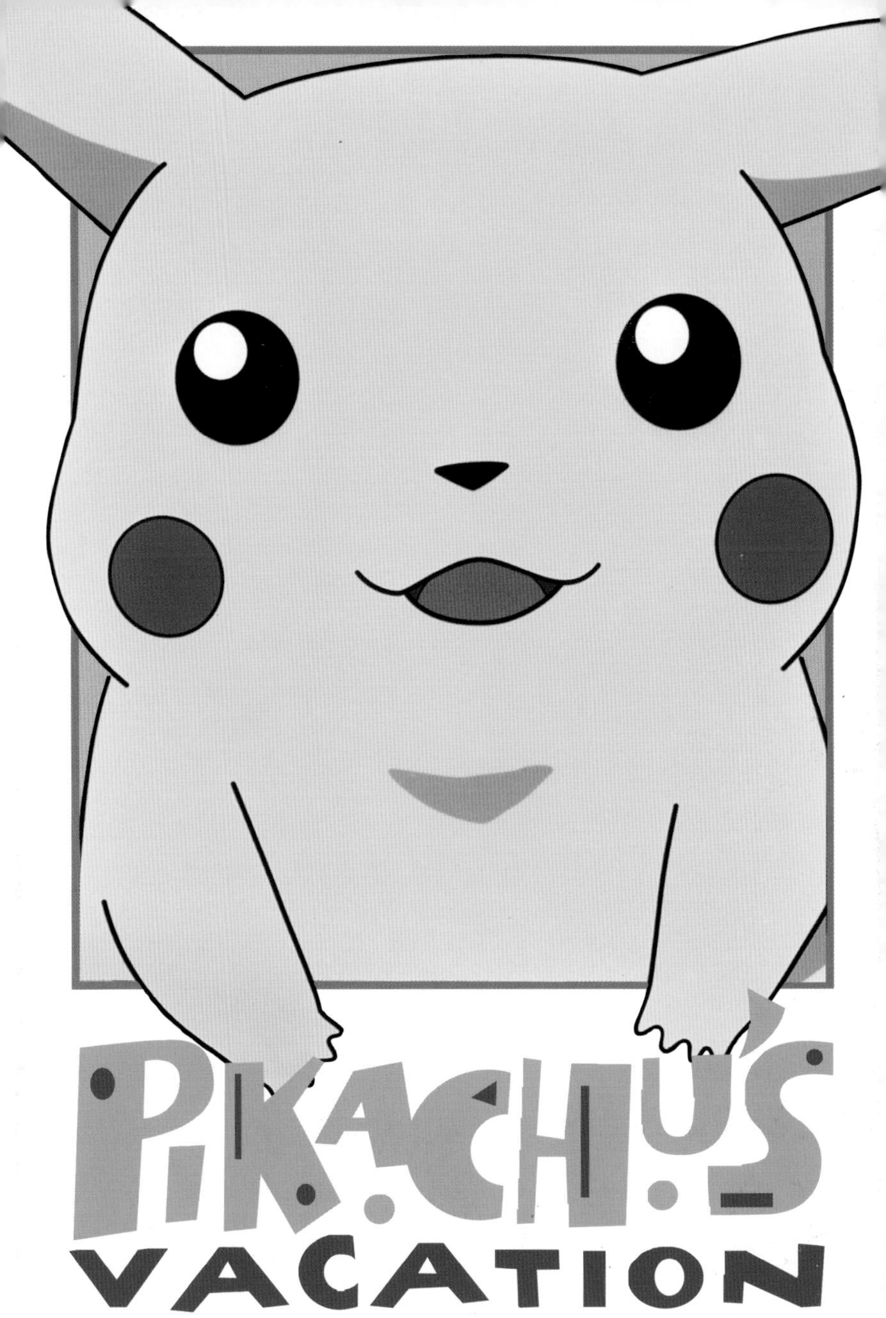

PIKACHU'S VACATION

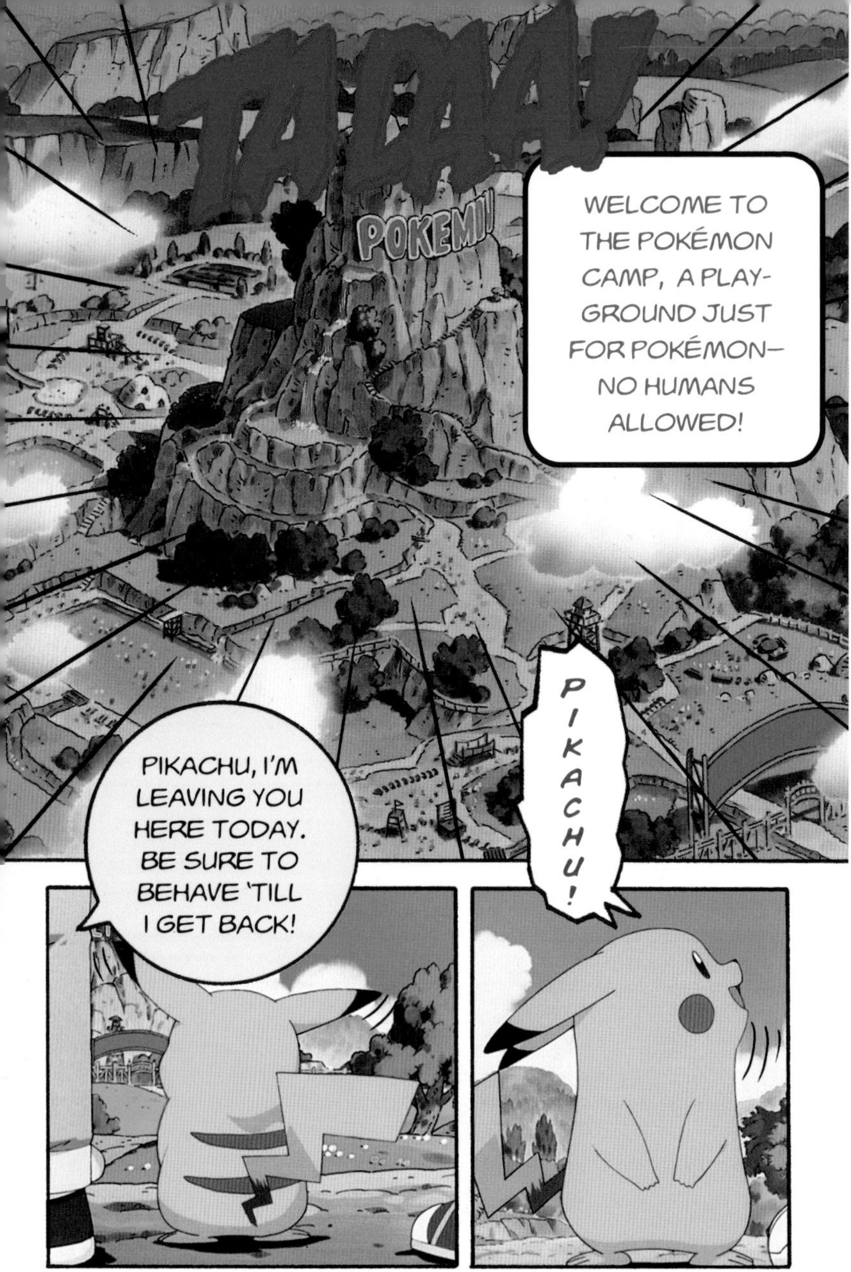
TADAA!
POKEMI!!
WELCOME TO THE POKÉMON CAMP, A PLAY-GROUND JUST FOR POKÉMON—NO HUMANS ALLOWED!
PIKACHU, I'M LEAVING YOU HERE TODAY. BE SURE TO BEHAVE 'TILL I GET BACK!
PIKACHU!

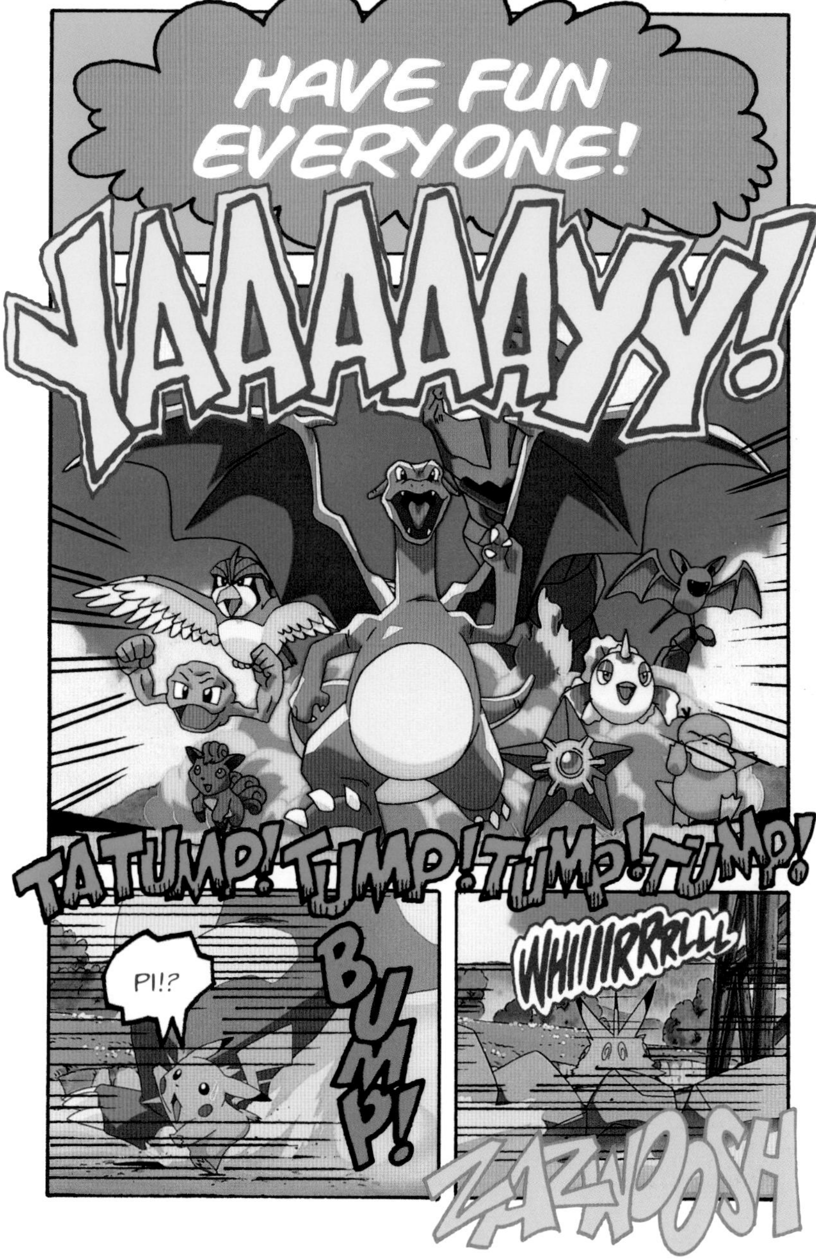

HAVE FUN EVERYONE!
YAAAAYY!
TATUMP! TUMP! TUMP! TUMP!
PI!?
BUMP!
WHIIIIRRRLLL
ZAZWOOSH

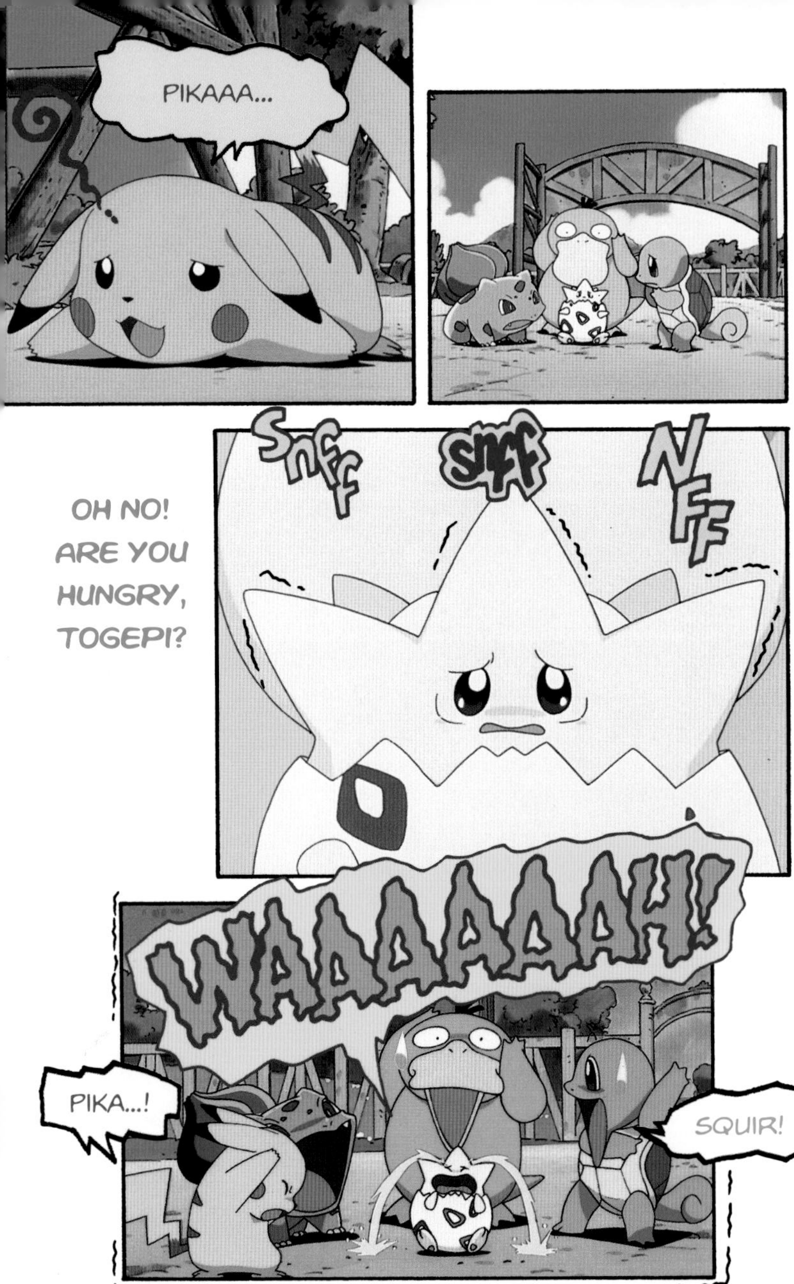
PIKAAA...
Sniff
sniff
NFF
OH NO! ARE YOU HUNGRY, TOGEPI?
WAAAAAH!
PIKA...!
SQUIR!

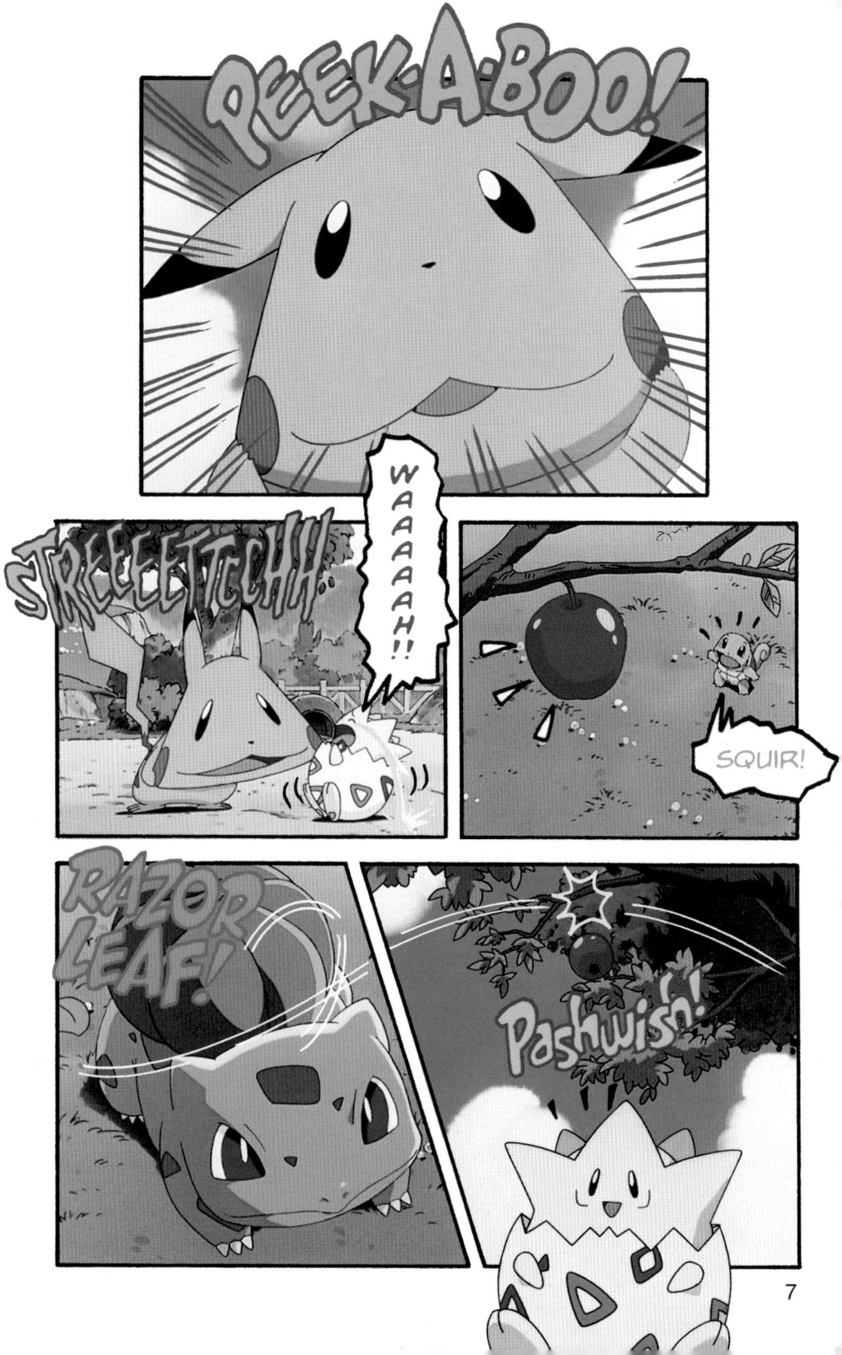
PEEK-A-BOO!
WAAAAAAH!!
STREEEETTCHH
SQUIR!
RAZOR LEAF!
Pashwish!

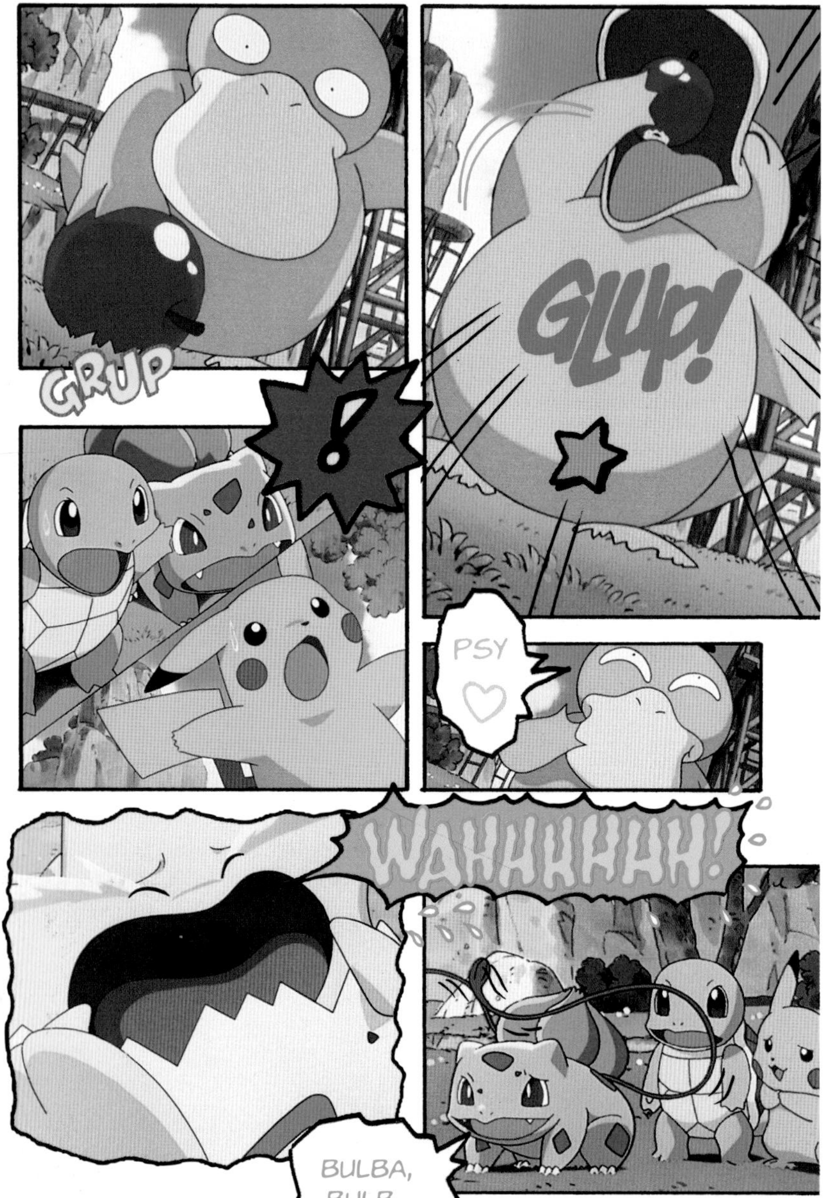

GRUP
GLUP!
!
PSY ♡
WAHHHHAH!
BULBA, BULB...

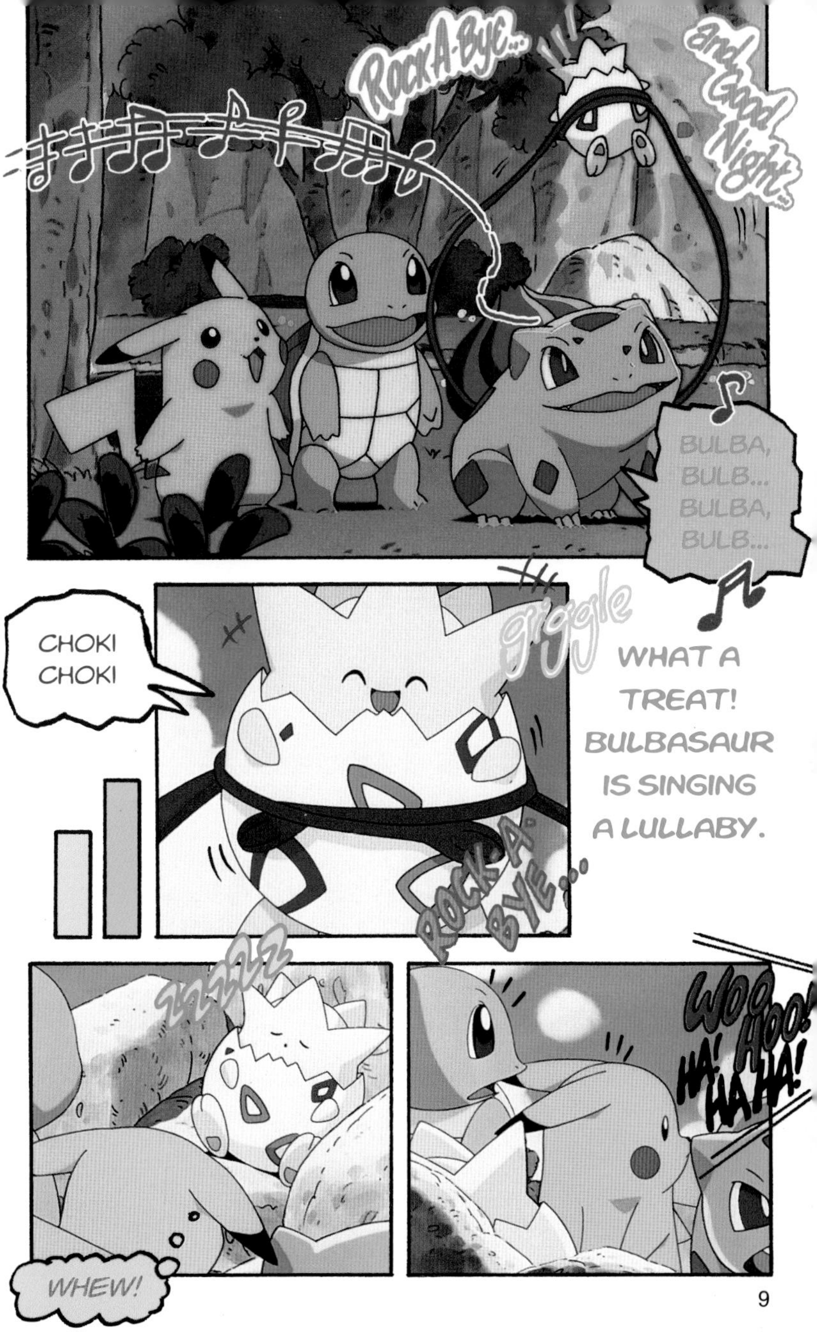
Rock-A-Bye...
and Good Night...
BULBA, BULB... BULBA, BULB...
CHOKI CHOKI
giggle
WHAT A TREAT! BULBASAUR IS SINGING A LULLABY.
ROCK-A-BYE...
ZZZZZZ
WHEW!
WOO HOO! HA HA! HA HA!

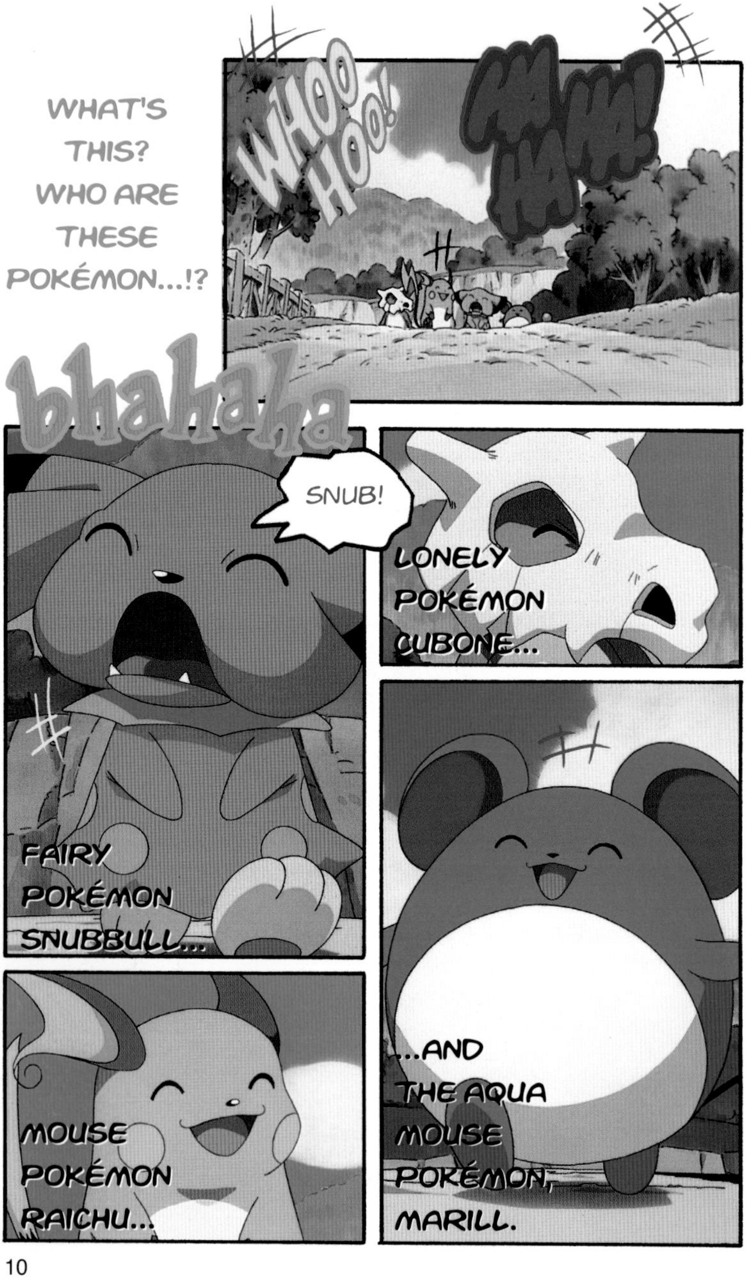

WHAT'S THIS? WHO ARE THESE POKÉMON...!?
WHOO HOO!
HA HA HA!
bhahaha
SNUB!
FAIRY POKÉMON SNUBBULL...
LONELY POKÉMON CUBONE...
MOUSE POKÉMON RAICHU...
...AND THE AQUA MOUSE POKÉMON, MARILL.

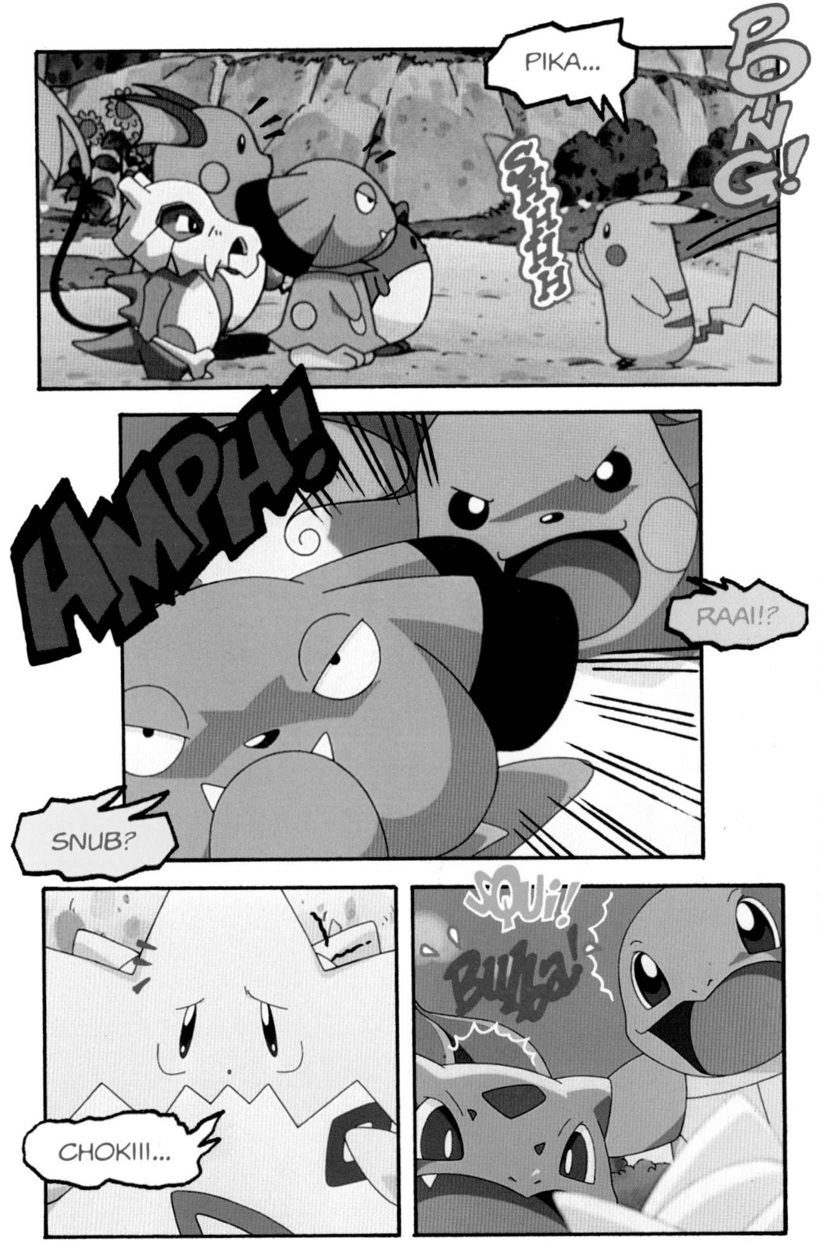

PIKA...
BOING!
AMPH!
RAAI!?
SNUB?
CHOKIII...
SQUI!
BULBA!

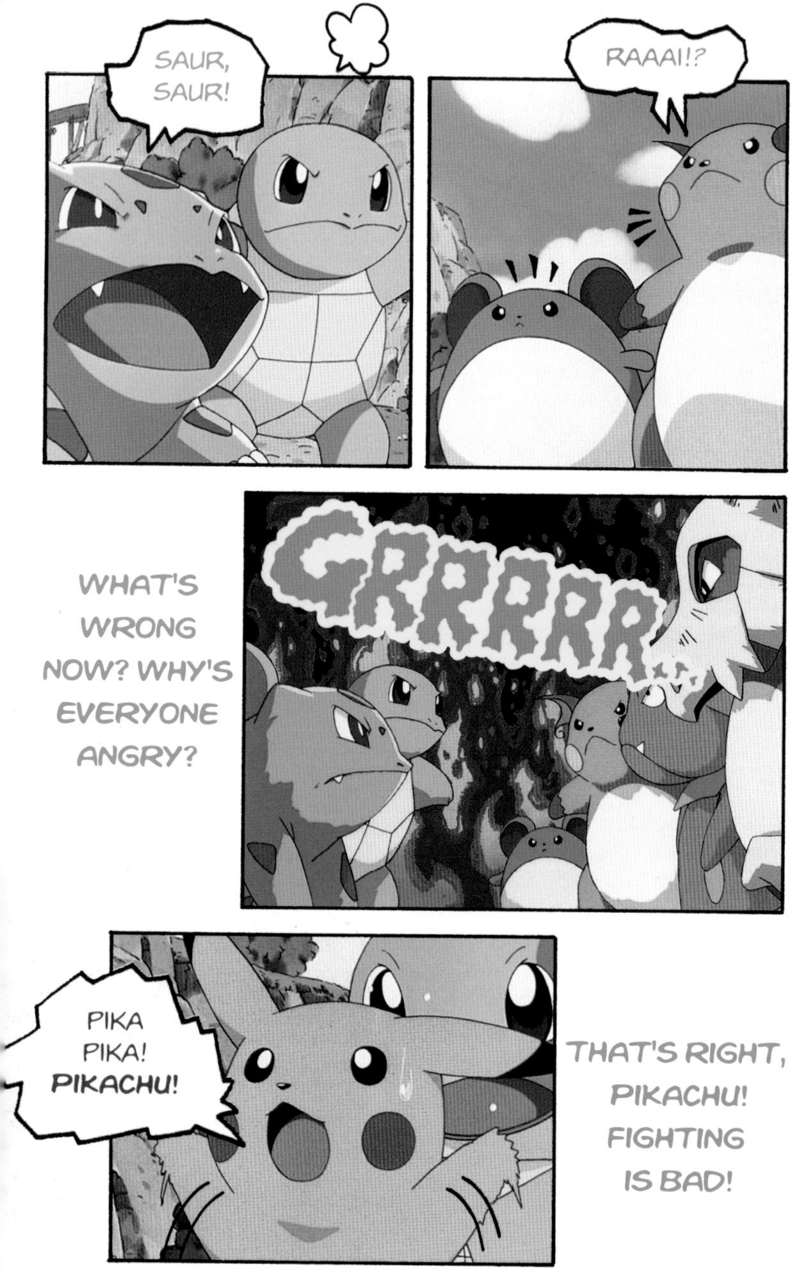
SAUR, SAUR!
RAAAI!?
GRRRRR...
WHAT'S WRONG NOW? WHY'S EVERYONE ANGRY?
PIKA PIKA! **PIKACHU!**
THAT'S RIGHT, PIKACHU! FIGHTING IS BAD!

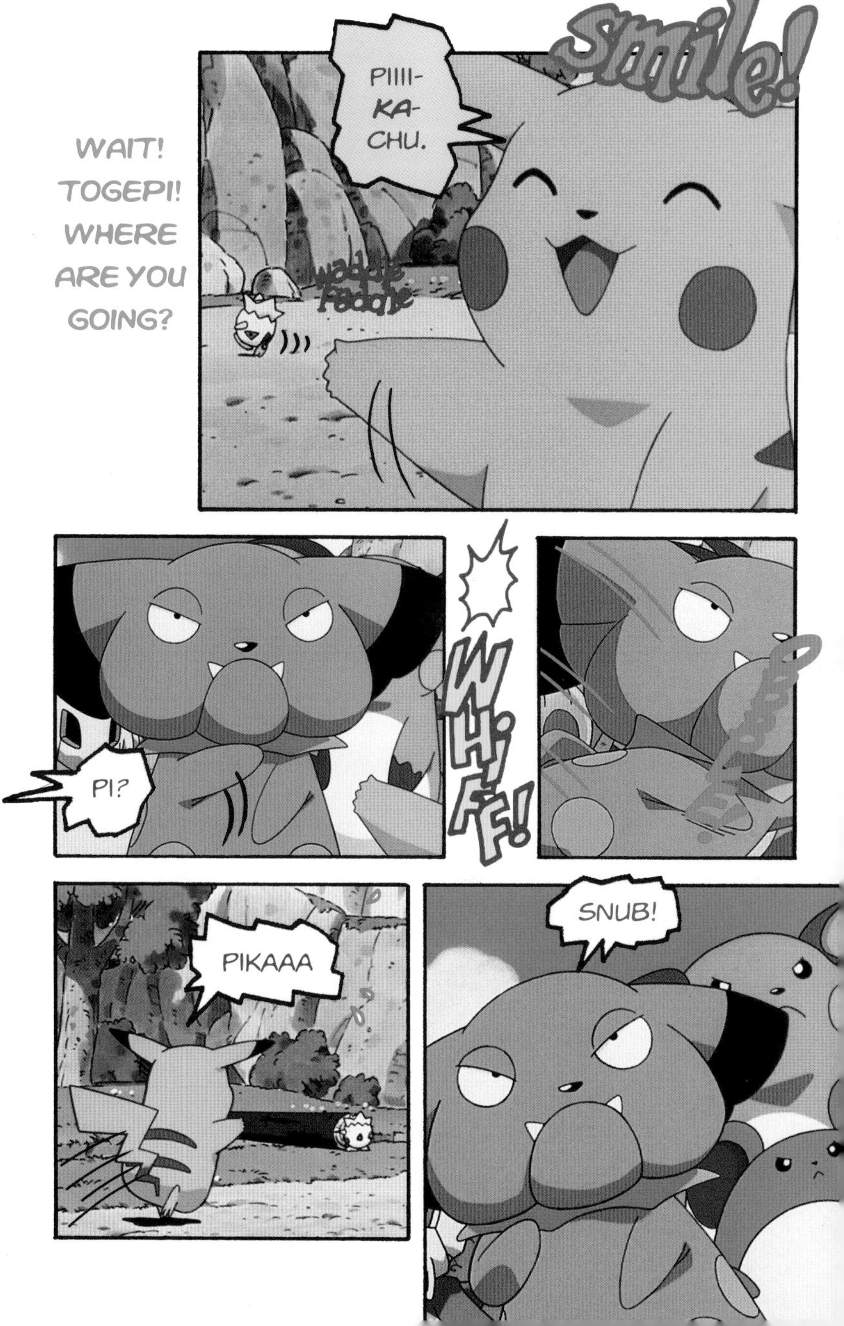
SMILE!
PIIII-KA-CHU.
WAIT! TOGEPI! WHERE ARE YOU GOING?
WADDLE WADDLE
PI?
WHIFF!
PIKAAA
SNUB!

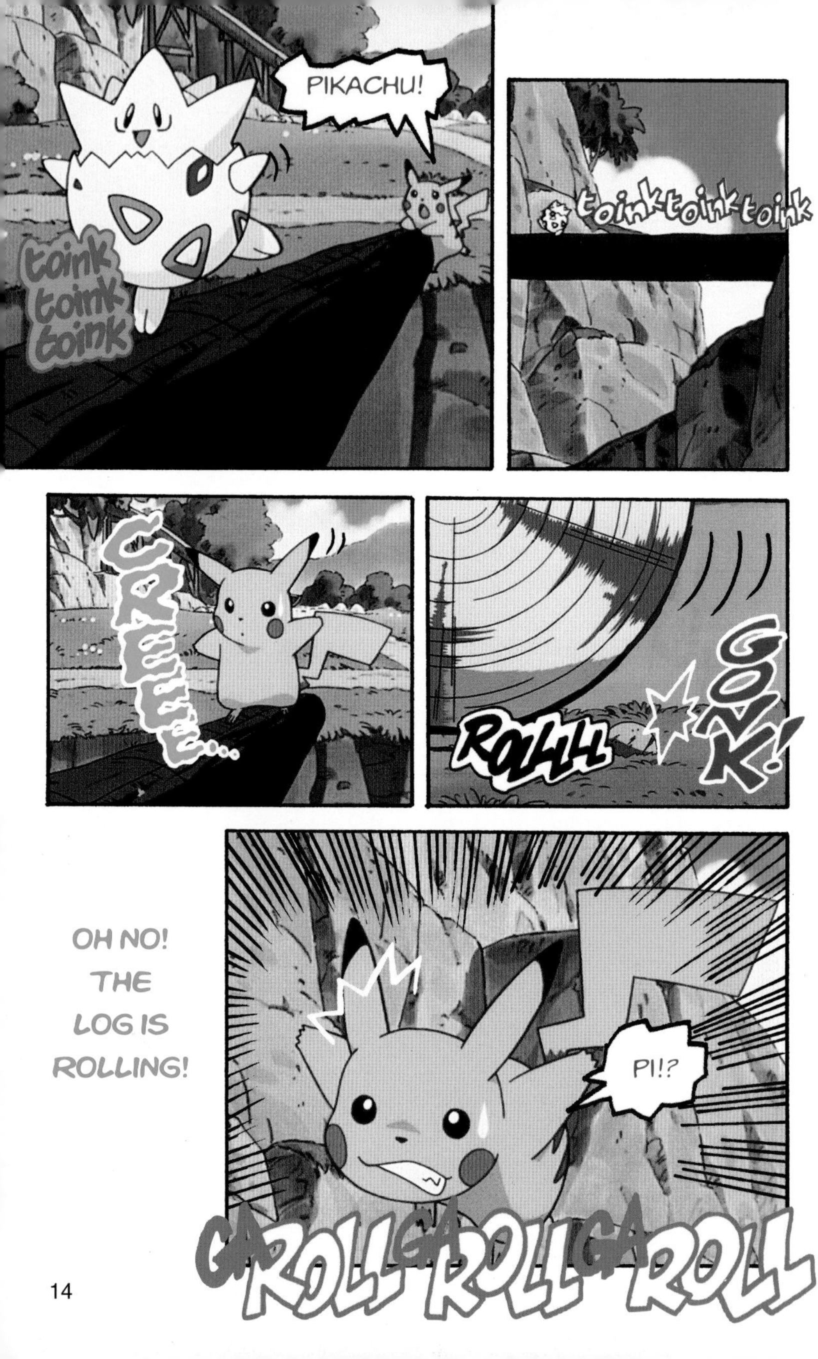
PIKACHU!
toink toink toink
toinktoinktoink
CREEEE...
ROLLLL
GONK!
OH NO! THE LOG IS ROLLING!
PI!?
GAROLL GAROLL GAROLL

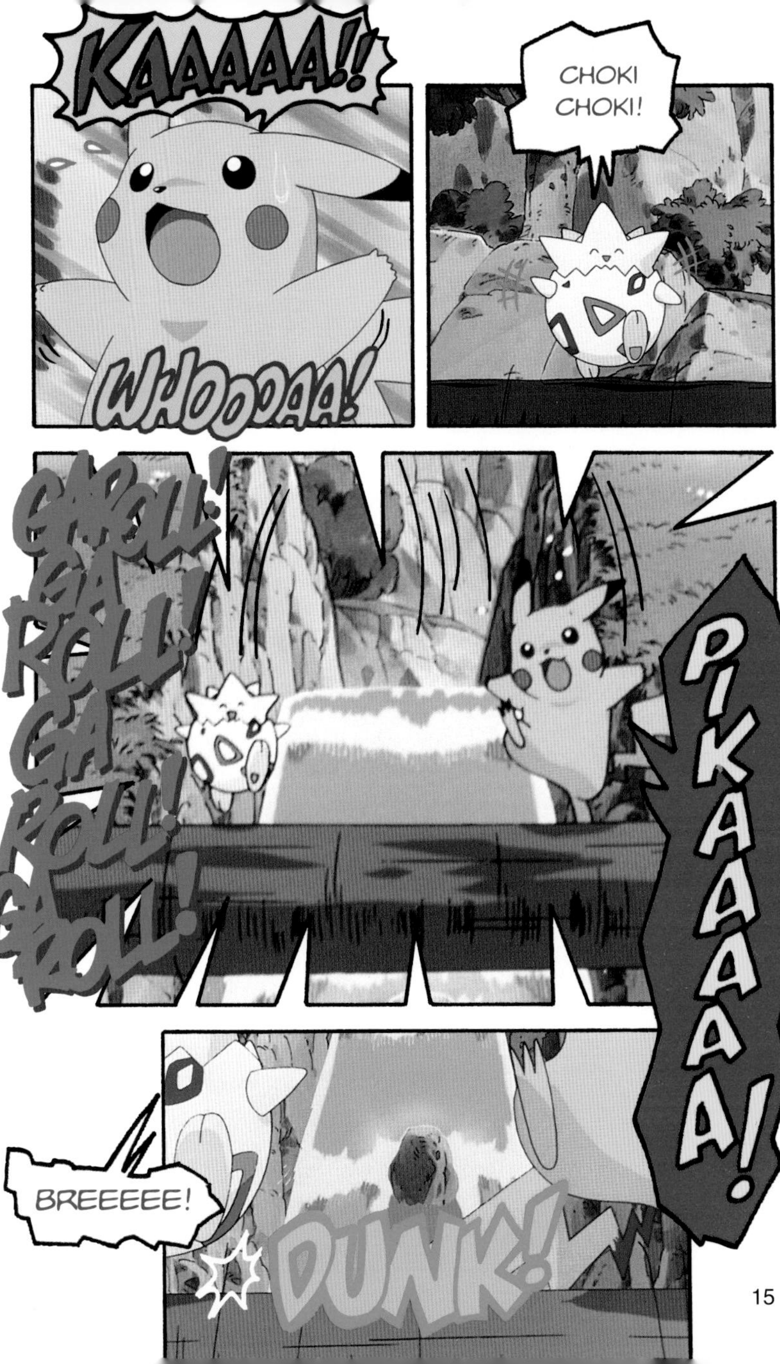
KAAAAA!!
WHOOOAA!
CHOKI CHOKI!
GAROLL! GA ROLL! GA ROLL! GA ROLL!
PIKAAAAA!
BREEEEEE!
DUNK!

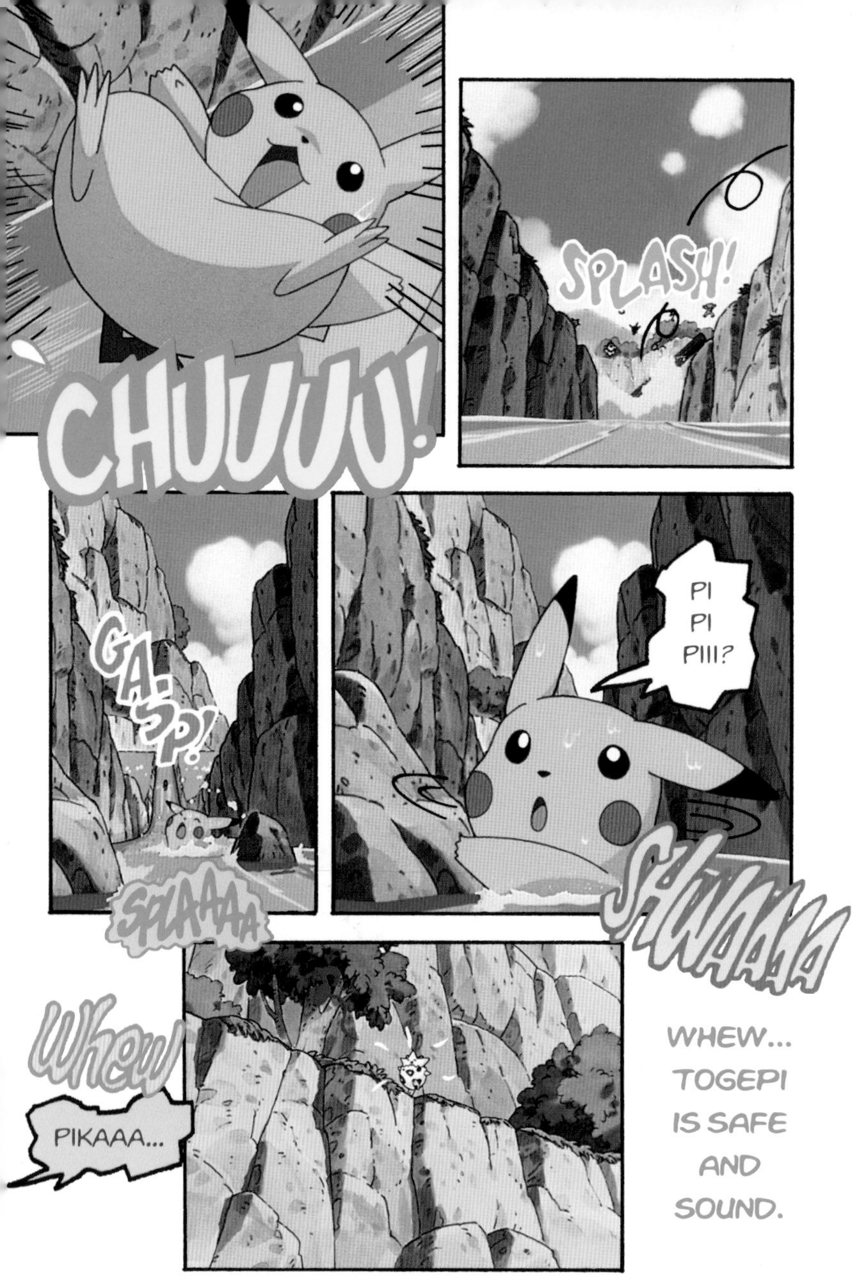
CHUUUU!
SPLASH!
GASP!
SPLAAAA
PI
PI
PIII?
SHWAAAA
WHEW... TOGEPI IS SAFE AND SOUND.
Whew
PIKAAA...

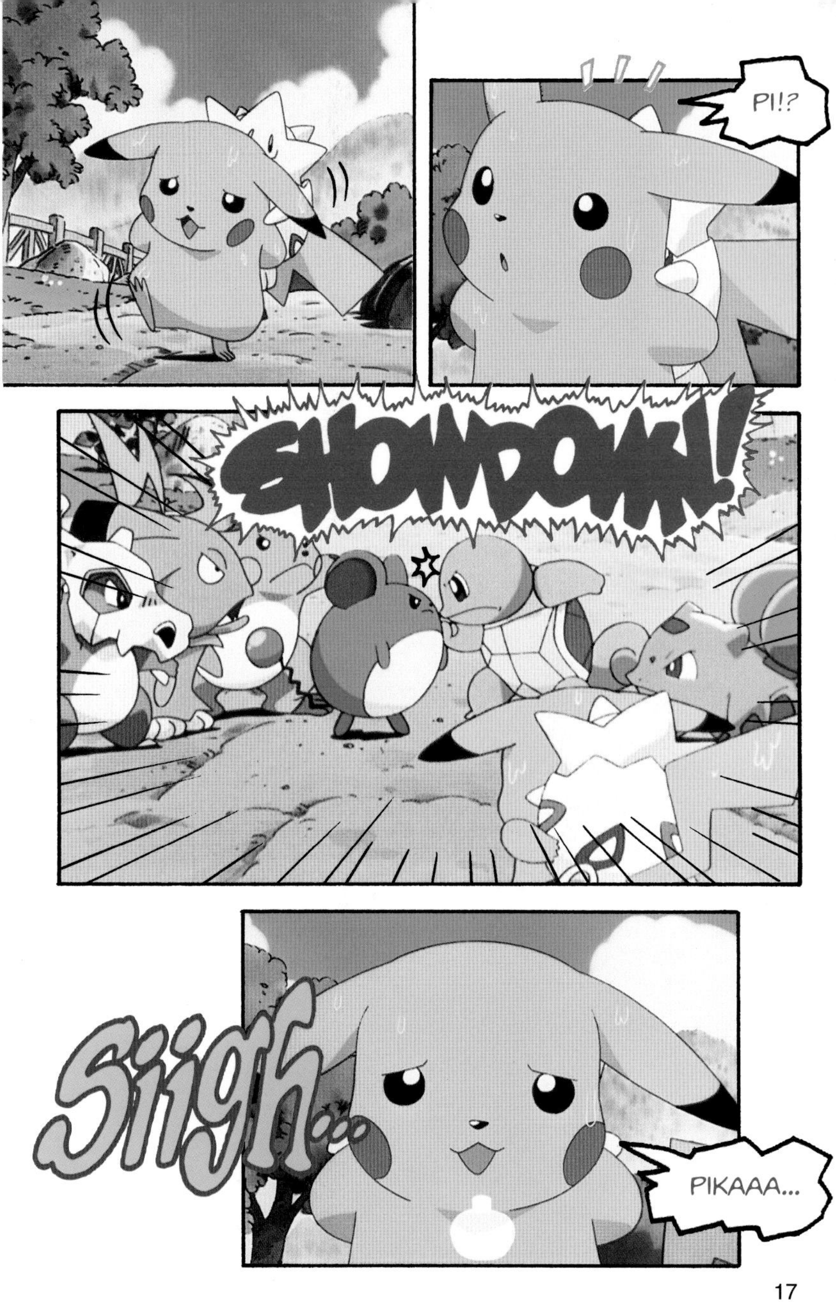
PI!?
SHOWDOWN!
Siigh...
PIKAAA...

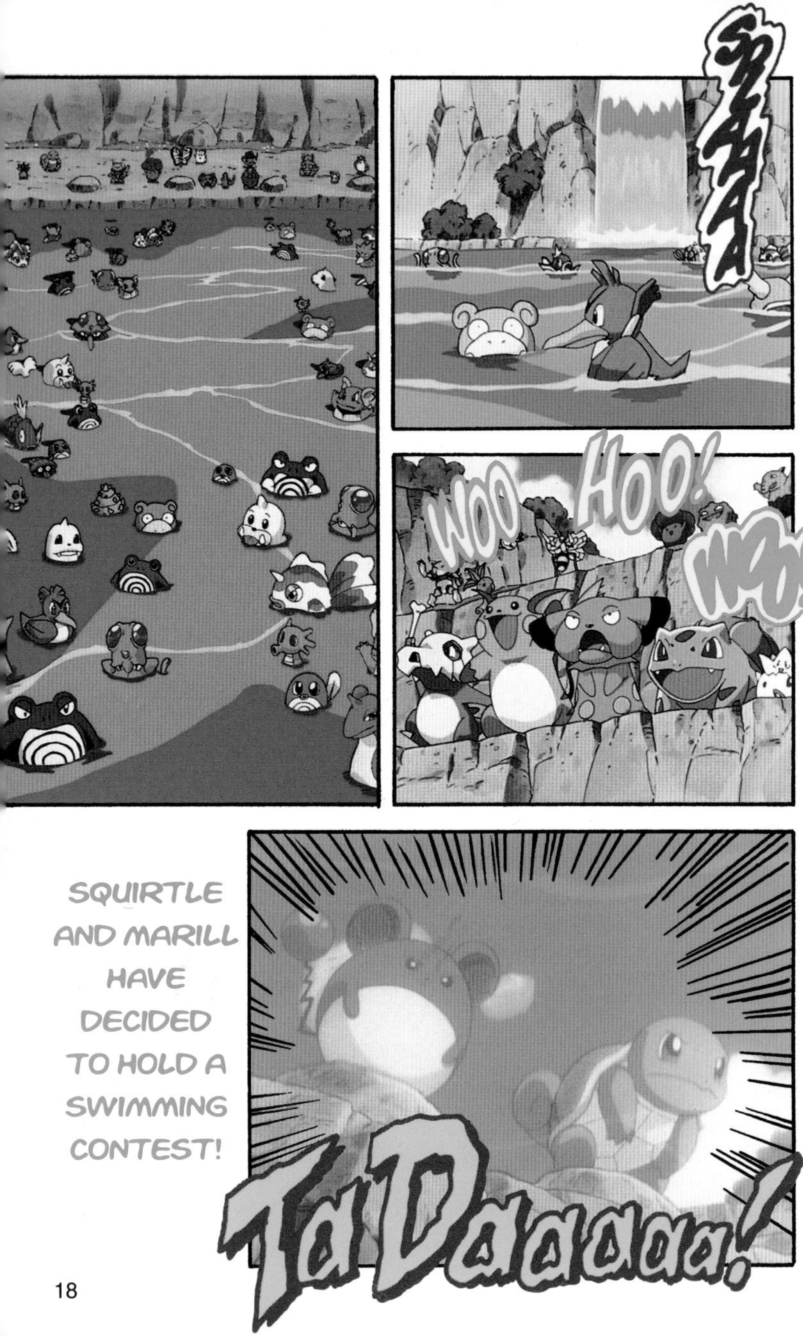
WOO HOO!
WOO!
SQUIRTLE AND MARILL HAVE DECIDED TO HOLD A SWIMMING CONTEST!
TaDaaaaa!

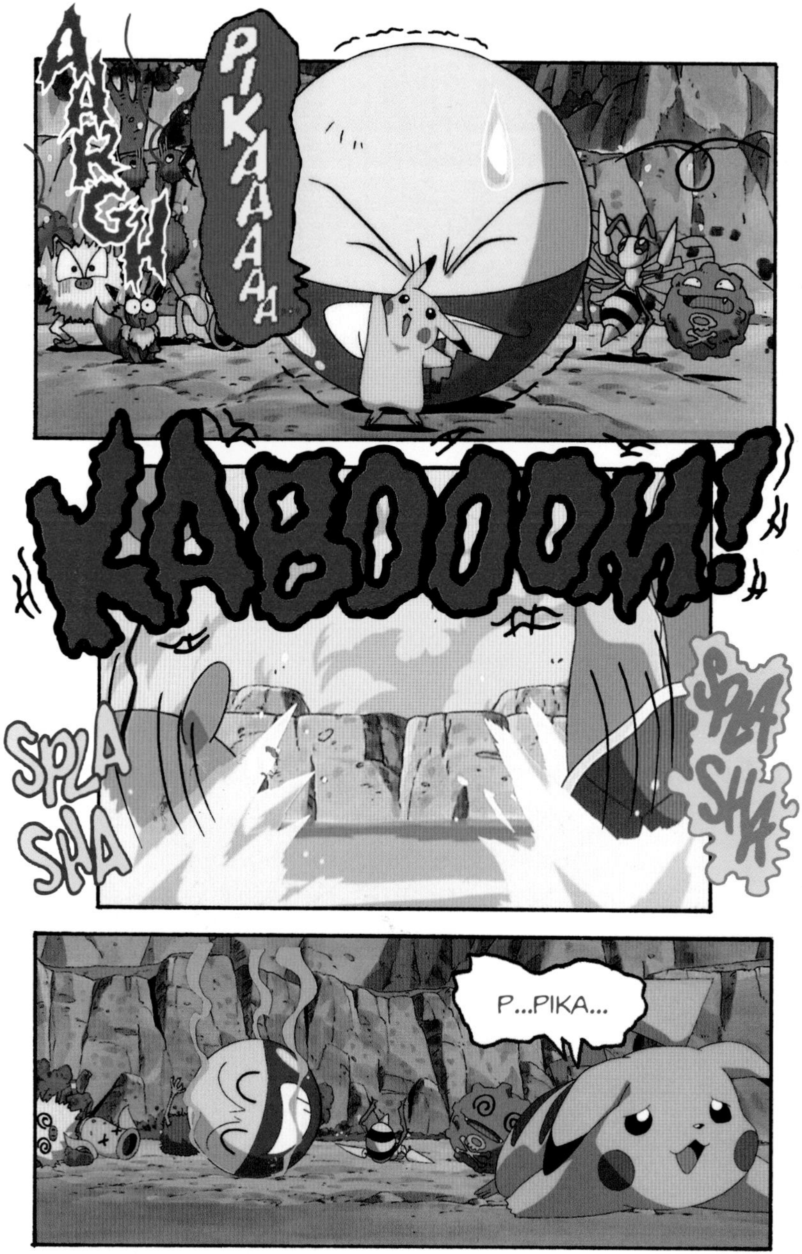
AARGH
PIKAAAAAA
KABOOOM!
SPLASHA
SPLASHA
P...PIKA...

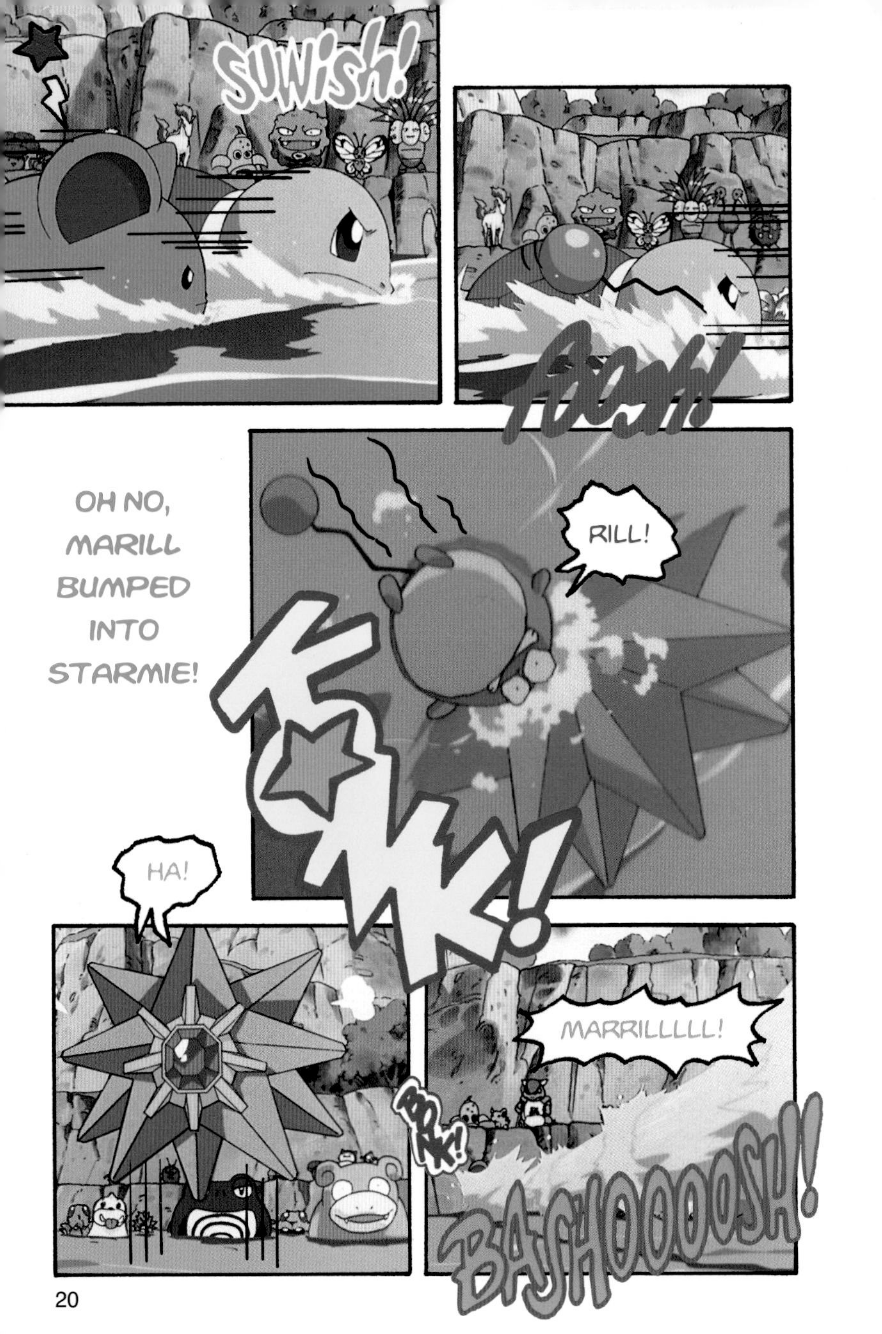
SWISH!
FOOSH!
OH NO, MARILL BUMPED INTO STARMIE!
RILL!
KONK!
HA!
BOINK!
MARRILLLLL!
BASHOOOOSH!

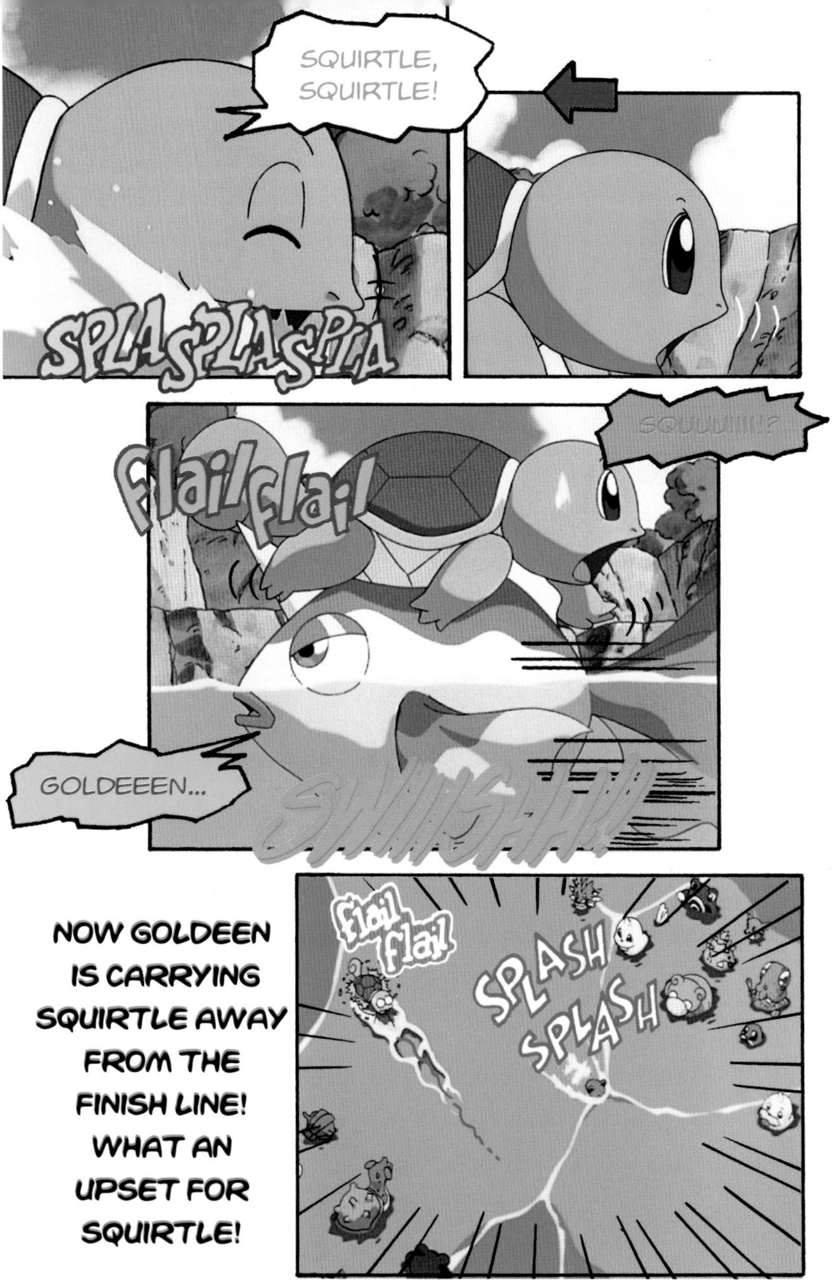
SQUIRTLE, SQUIRTLE!
SPLASPLASPLA
flail flail
GOLDEEEN...
NOW GOLDEEN IS CARRYING SQUIRTLE AWAY FROM THE FINISH LINE! WHAT AN UPSET FOR SQUIRTLE!
flail flail
SPLASH
SPLASH

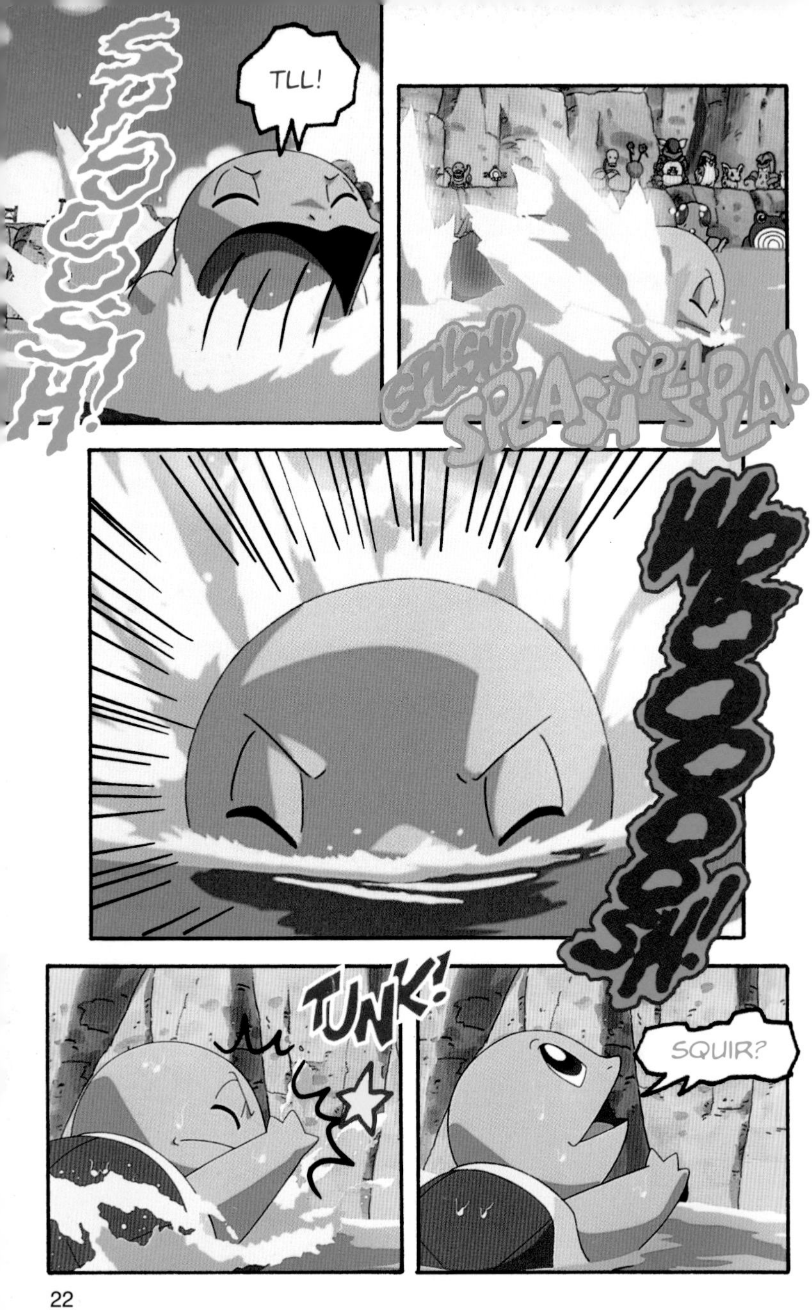
TLL!
SPOOOSH!
SPLISH! SPLASH SPL! SPLA!
WHOOOOSH!!
TUNK!
SQUIR?

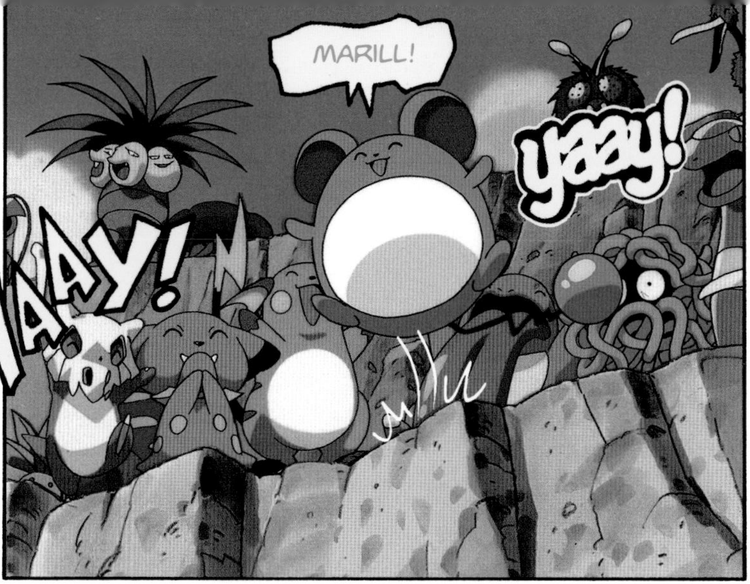
MARILL!
YAAY!
yaay!

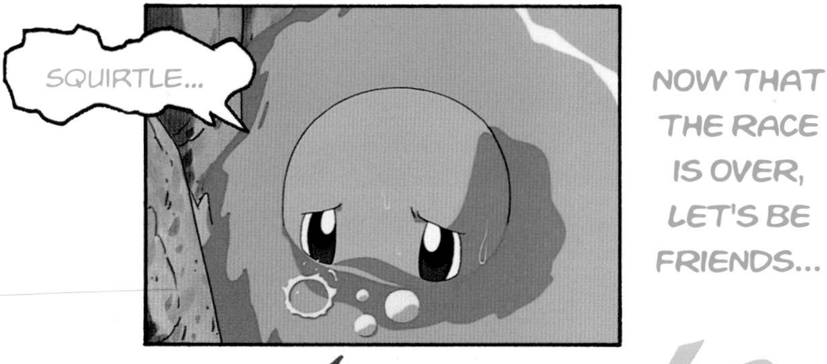
SQUIRTLE...
NOW THAT THE RACE IS OVER, LET'S BE FRIENDS...

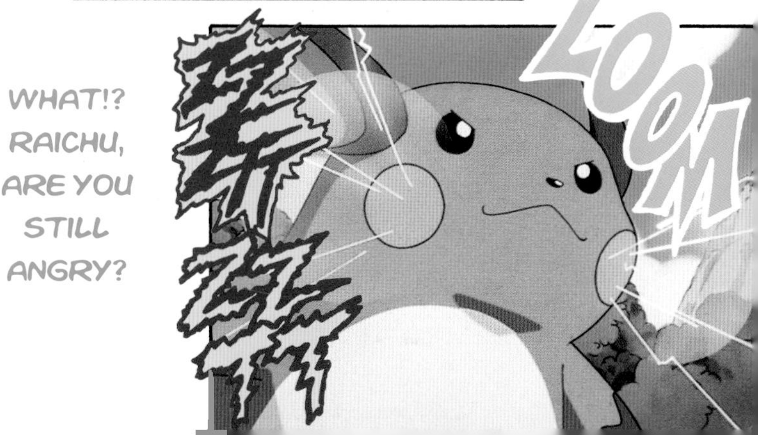
WHAT!? RAICHU, ARE YOU STILL ANGRY?
LOOM

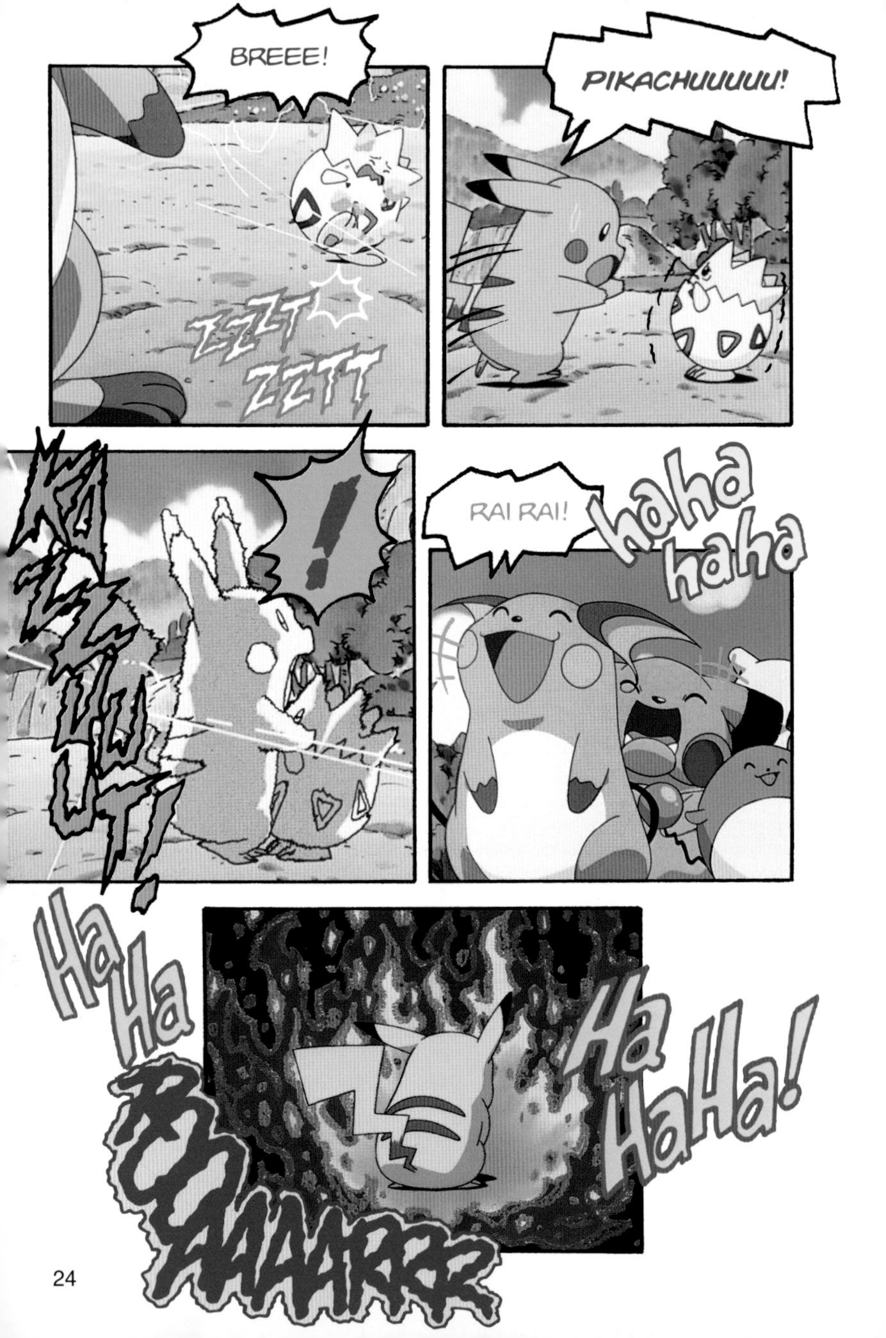
BREEE!
ZZZT
ZZTT
PIKACHUUUUU!
KAZZWUT!
!
RAI RAI!
haha
haha
HaHa
HaHa
HaHa!
BOAAARRR

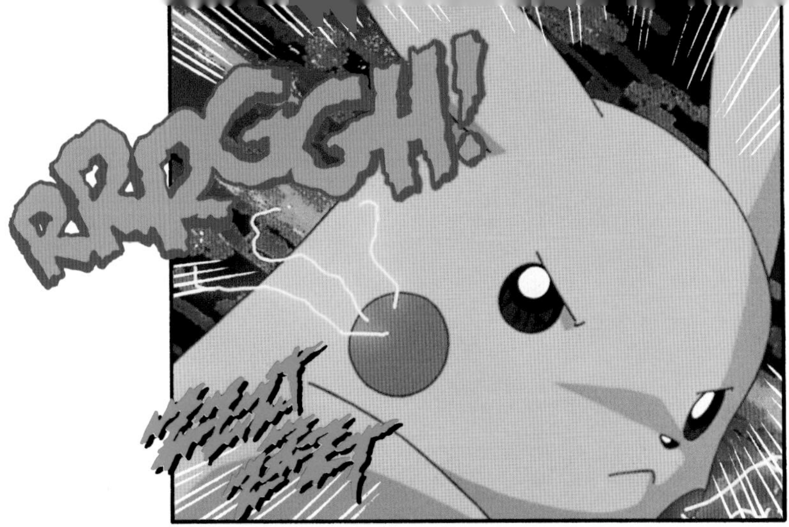

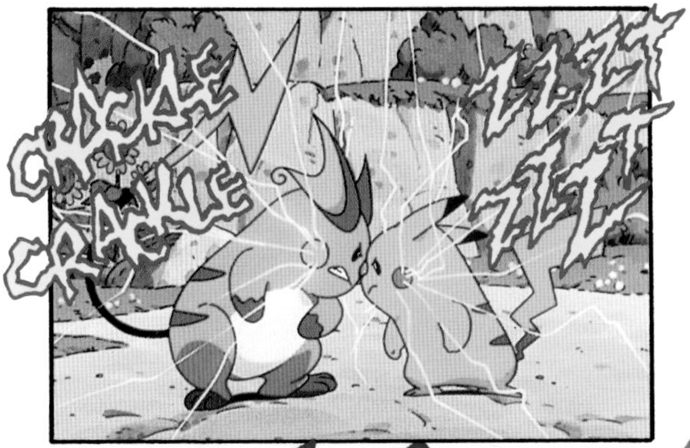
CRACKLE CRACKLE

OH NO!
PIKACHU!
FIGHTING
IS BAD!...
PIKACHU?...

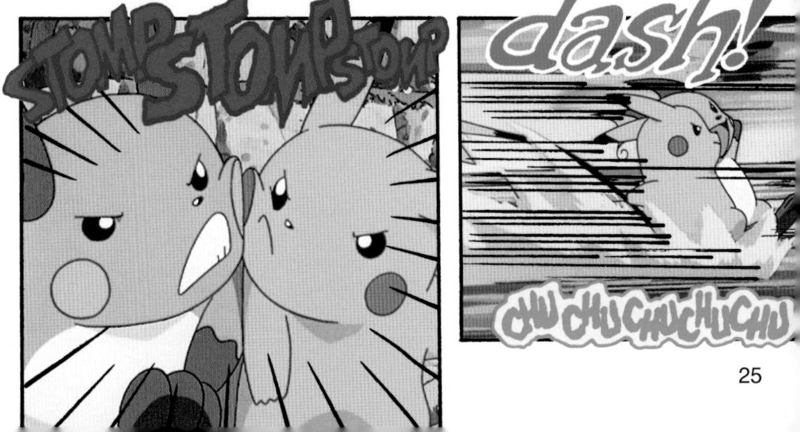
STOMP STOMP STOMP
dash!
CHUCHUCHUCHUCHU

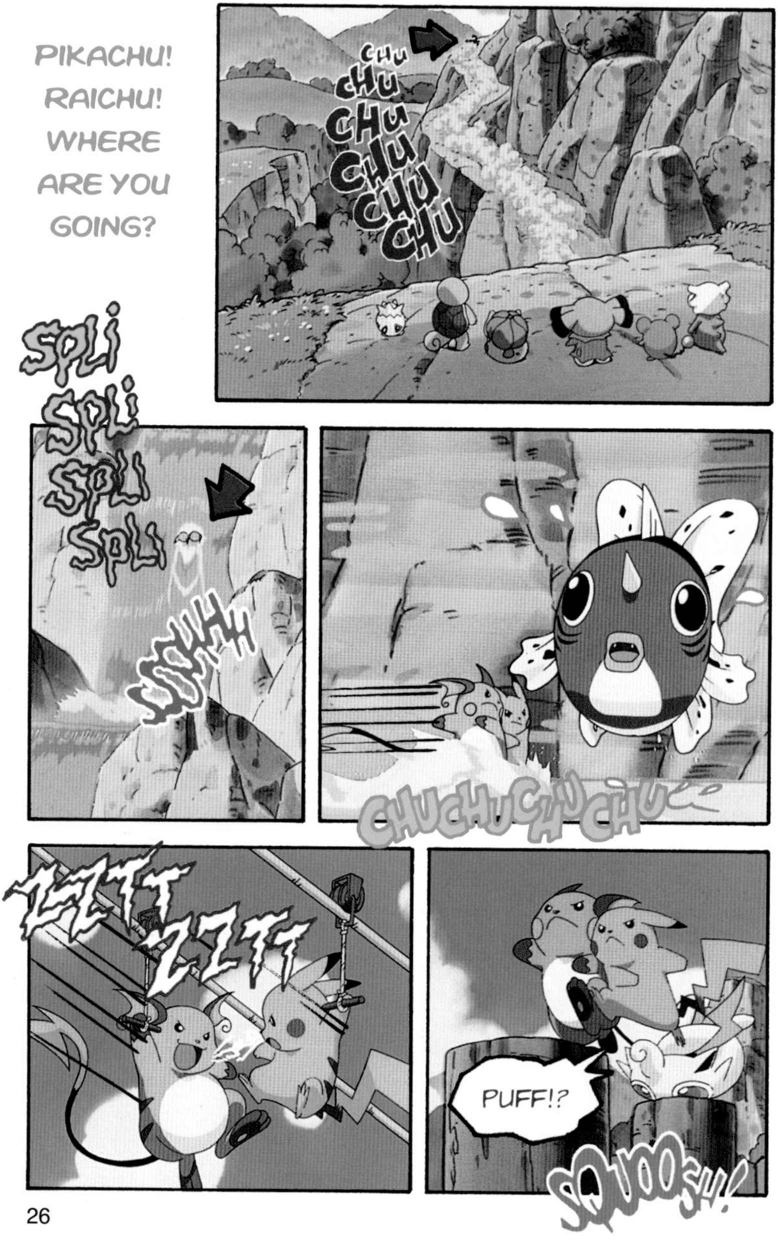
PIKACHU! RAICHU! WHERE ARE YOU GOING?
CHU CHU CHU CHU CHU CHU
SPLI SPLI SPLI SPLI
SSSHHH
CHUCHUCHUCHU
ZZTT ZZTT
PUFF!?
SQUOOSH!

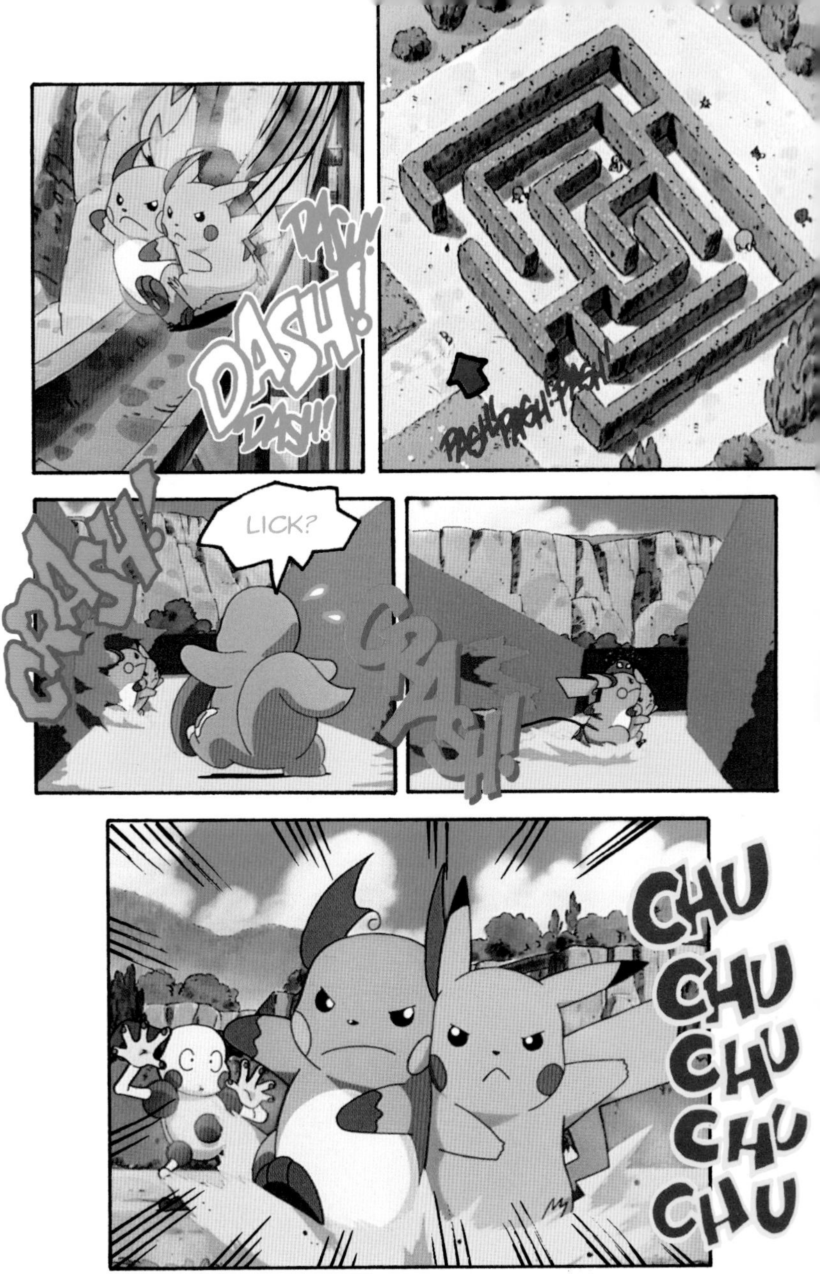
DASH!
DASH!
DASH!
DASH! DASH! DASH!
LICK?
CRASH!
CRASH!
CHU
CHU
CHU
CHU
CHU

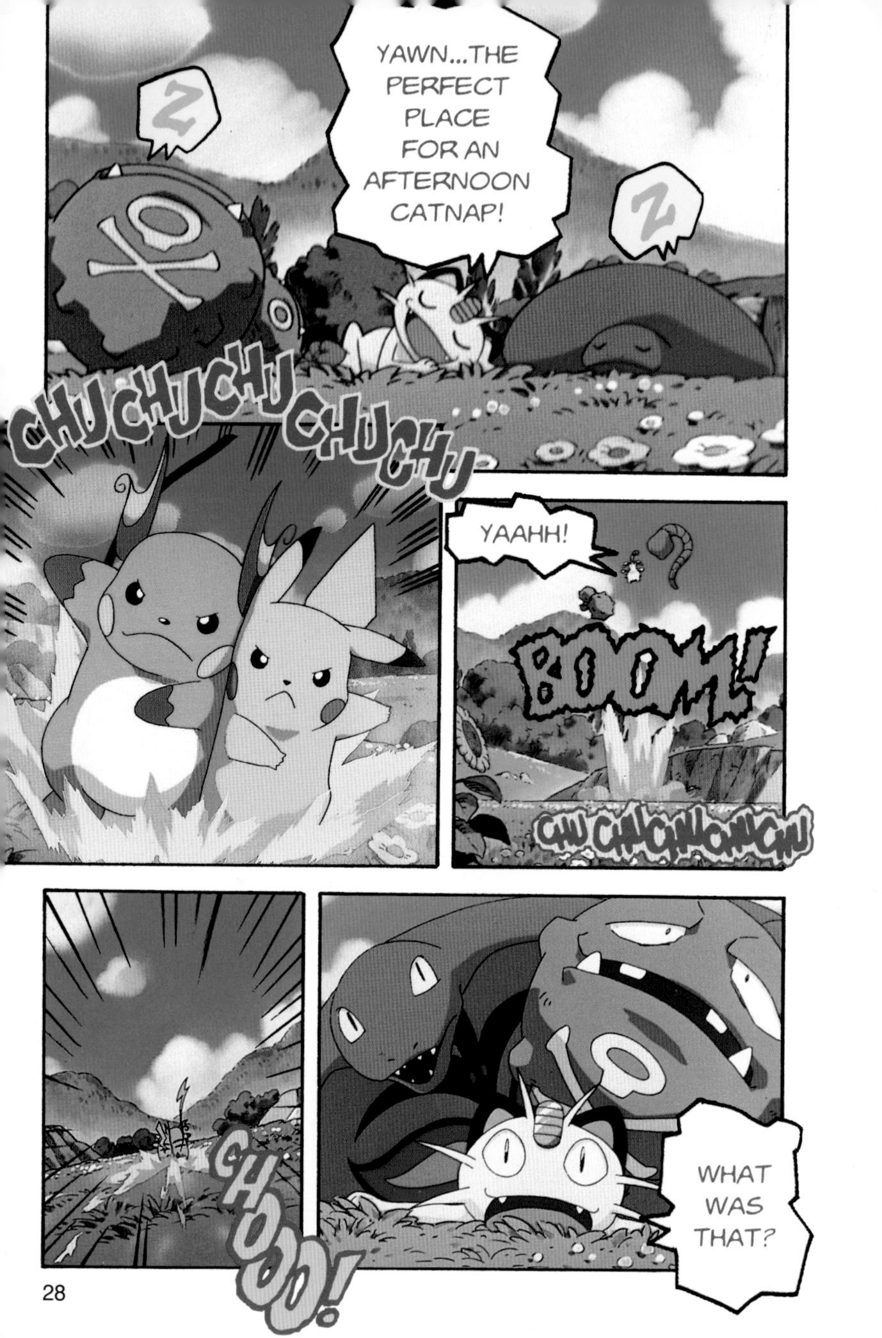
Z
YAWN...THE PERFECT PLACE FOR AN AFTERNOON CATNAP!
Z
CHUCHUCHUCHUCHU
YAAHH!
BOOM!
WHAT WAS THAT?
CHOOO!

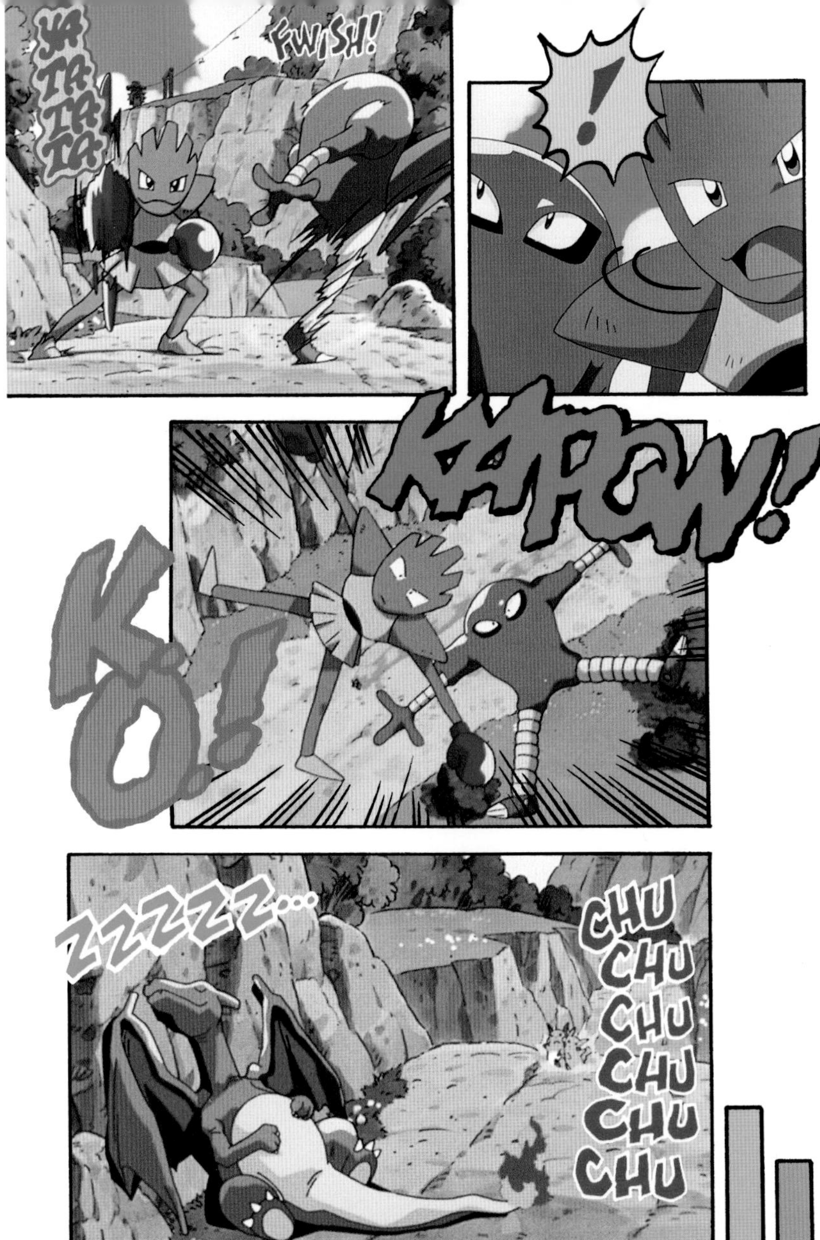
YA TA TA TA
FWISH!
!
KAPOW!
KO!
ZZZZZZ...
CHU CHU CHU CHU CHU CHU

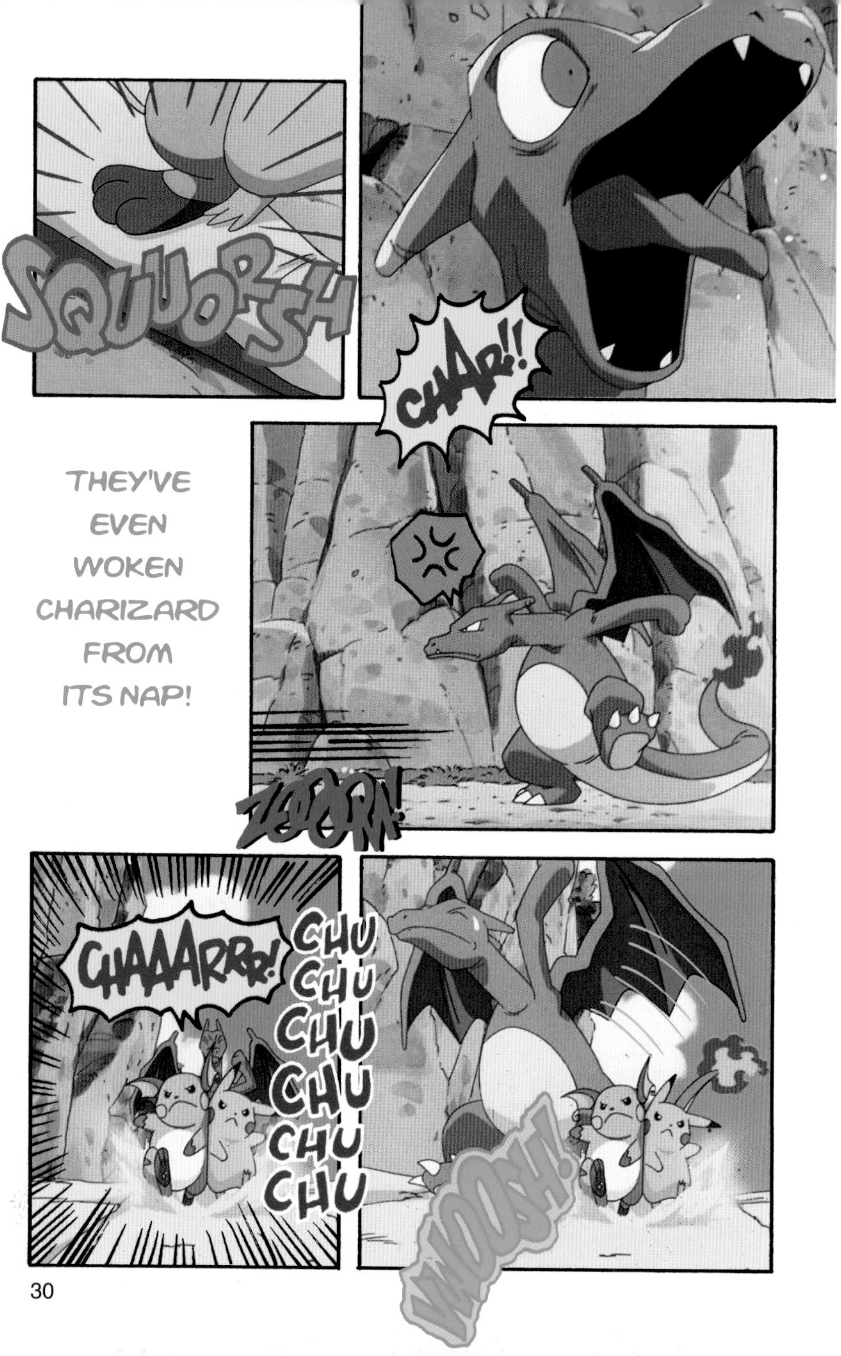
SQUUORSH
CHAR!!
THEY'VE EVEN WOKEN CHARIZARD FROM ITS NAP!
ZOOOM!
CHAAARRR!
CHU CHU CHU CHU CHU CHU
WHOOSH!

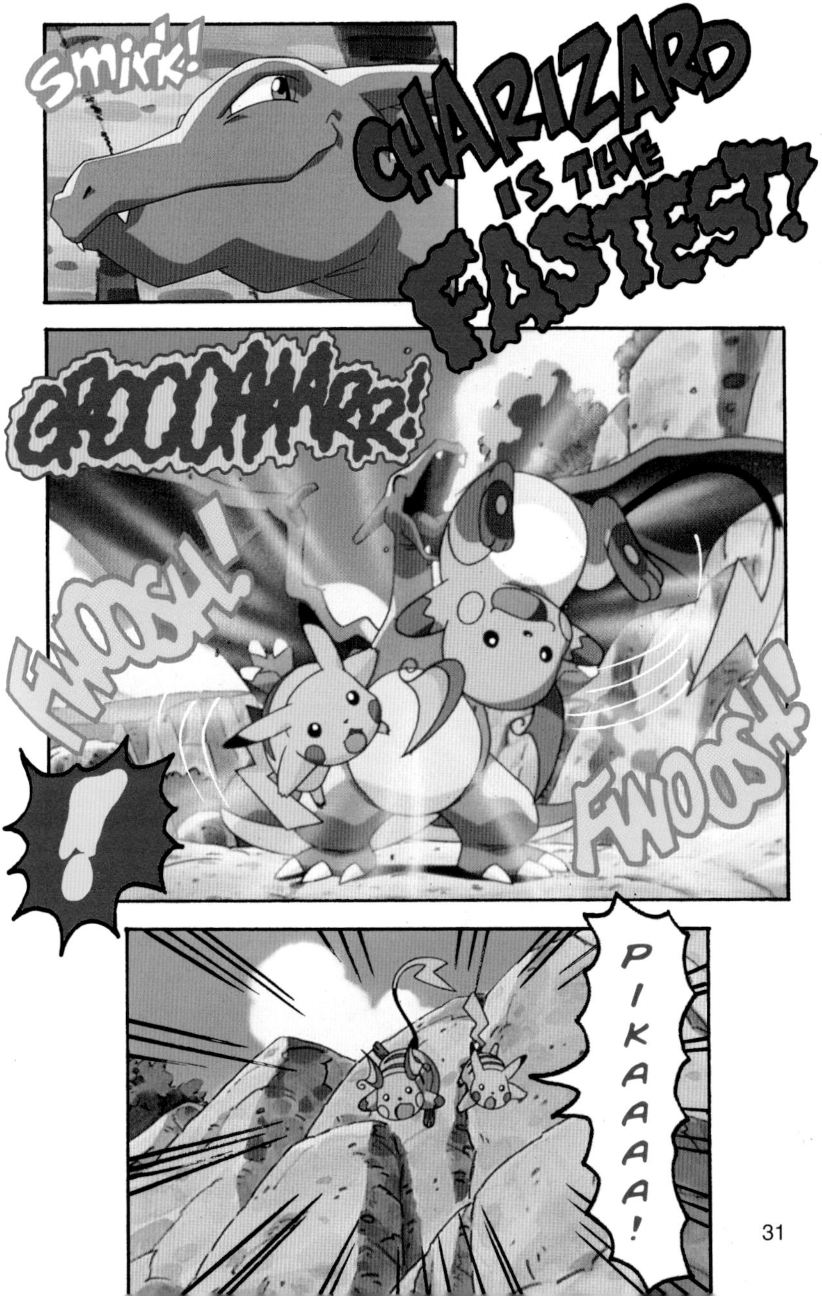
SMIRK!
CHARIZARD IS THE FASTEST!
GROOOAARR!
FWOOSH!
FWOOSH!
!
PIKAAAAAA!

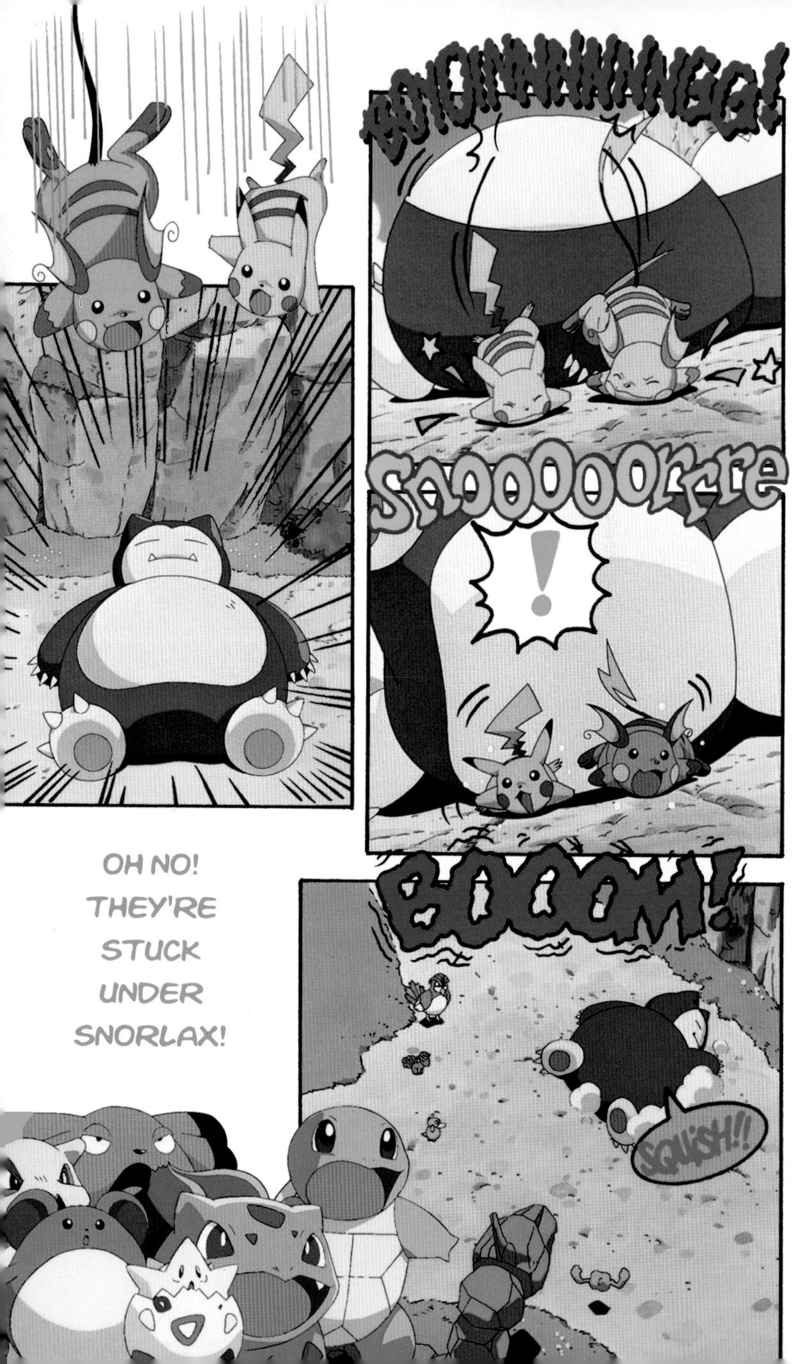
BOOOM!
SQUISH!!
OH NO! THEY'RE STUCK UNDER SNORLAX!

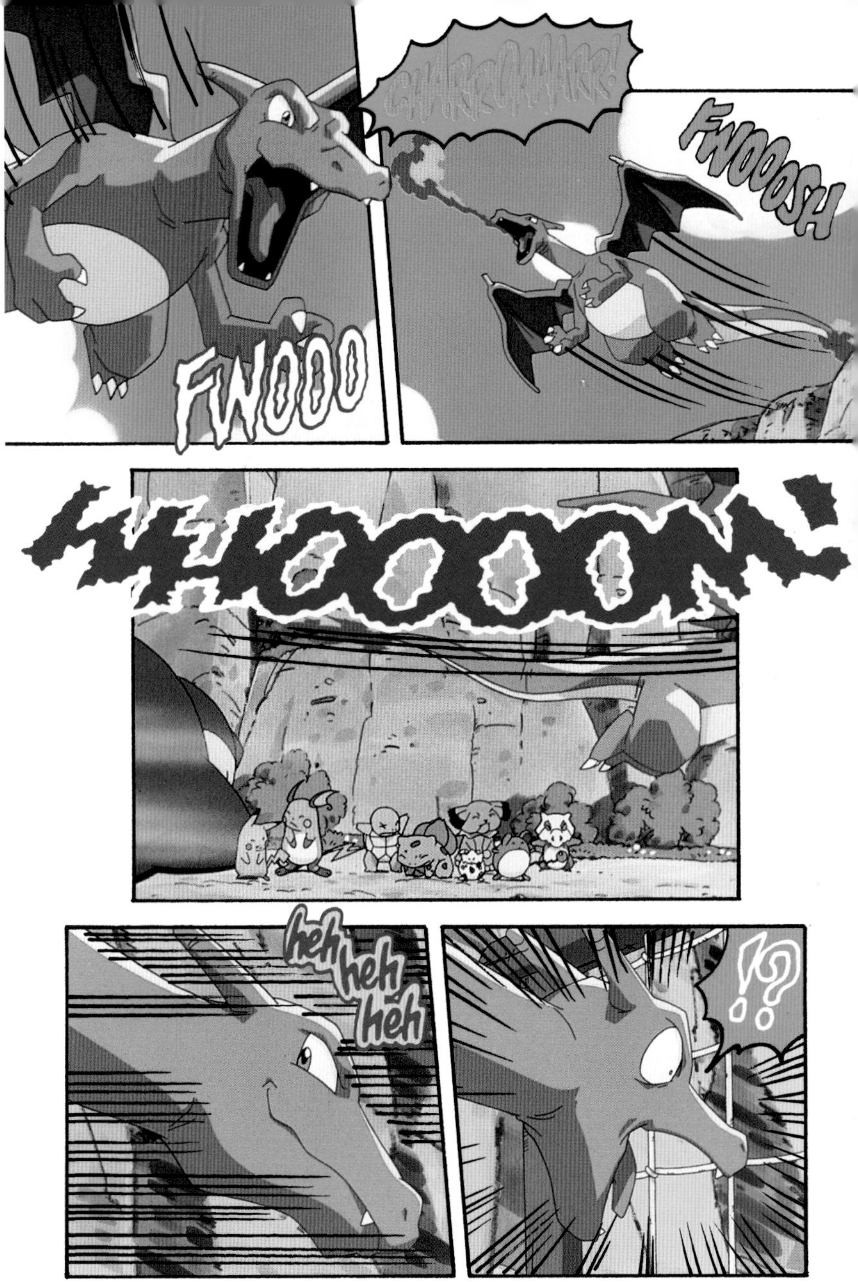

CHARRCHARR!
FWOOOSH
FWOOO
WHOOOOM!
heh heh heh
!?

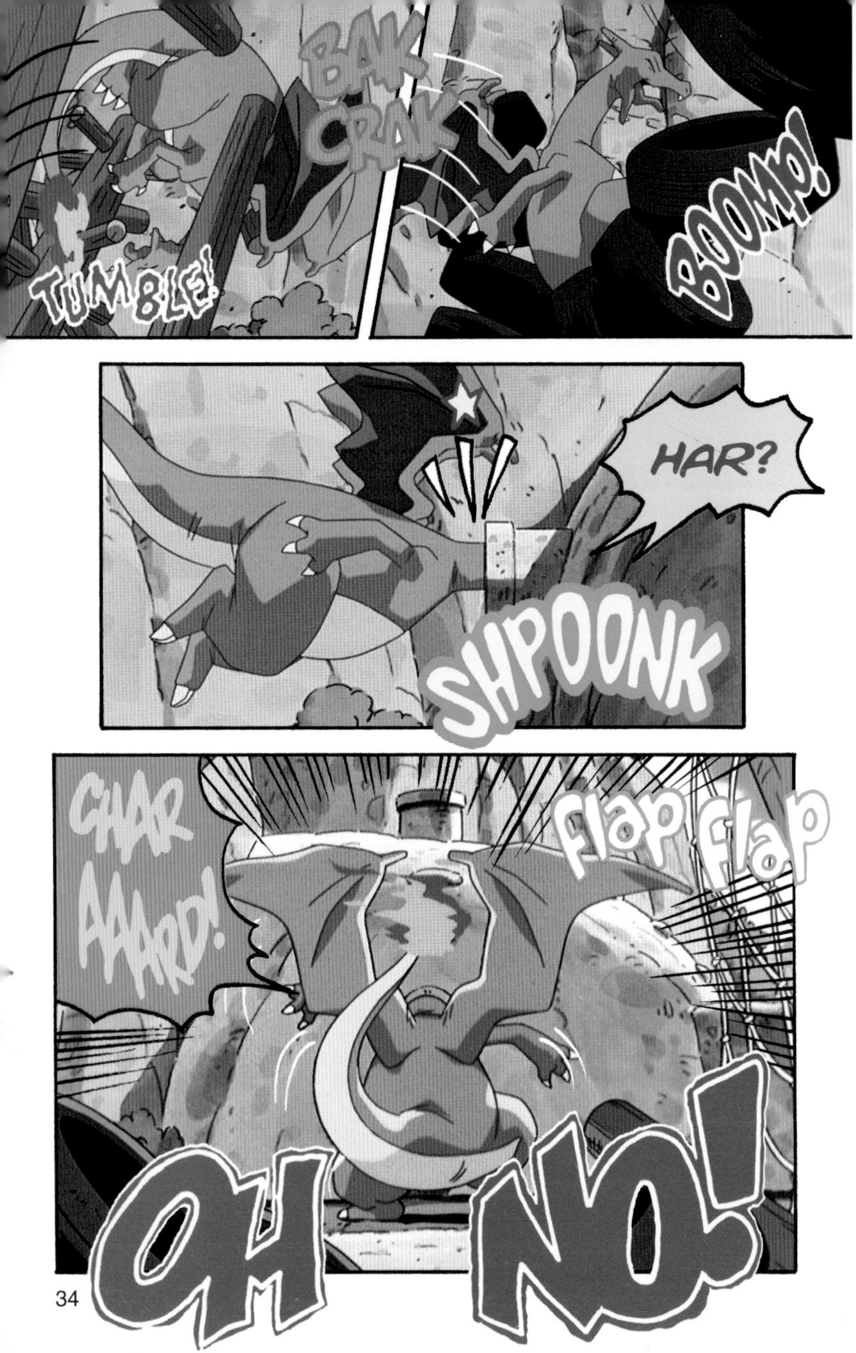
TUMBLE!
BAK
CRAK
BOOMP!
HAR?
SHPOONK
CHAR
AAARD!
flap flap
OH NO!

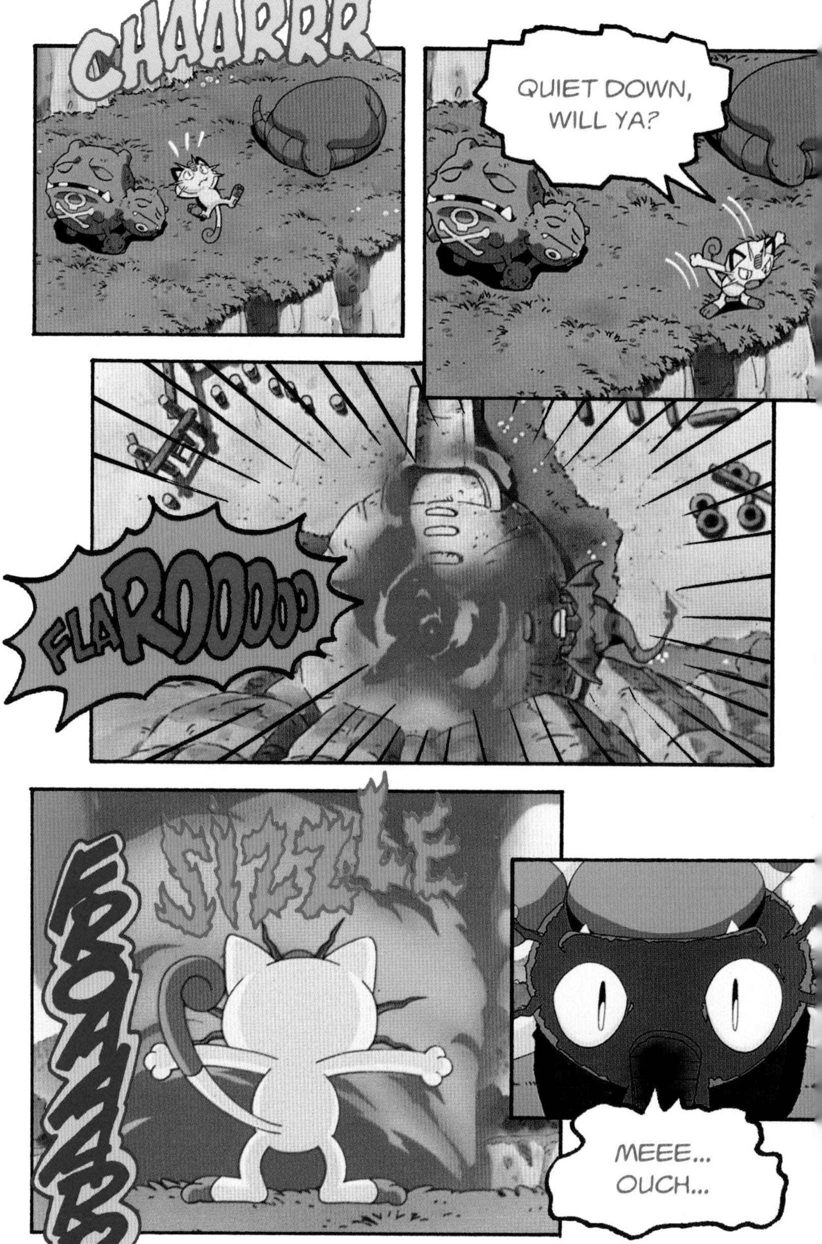
CHAARRR
QUIET DOWN, WILL YA?
FLAROOOOO
SIZZLE
MEEE... OUCH...

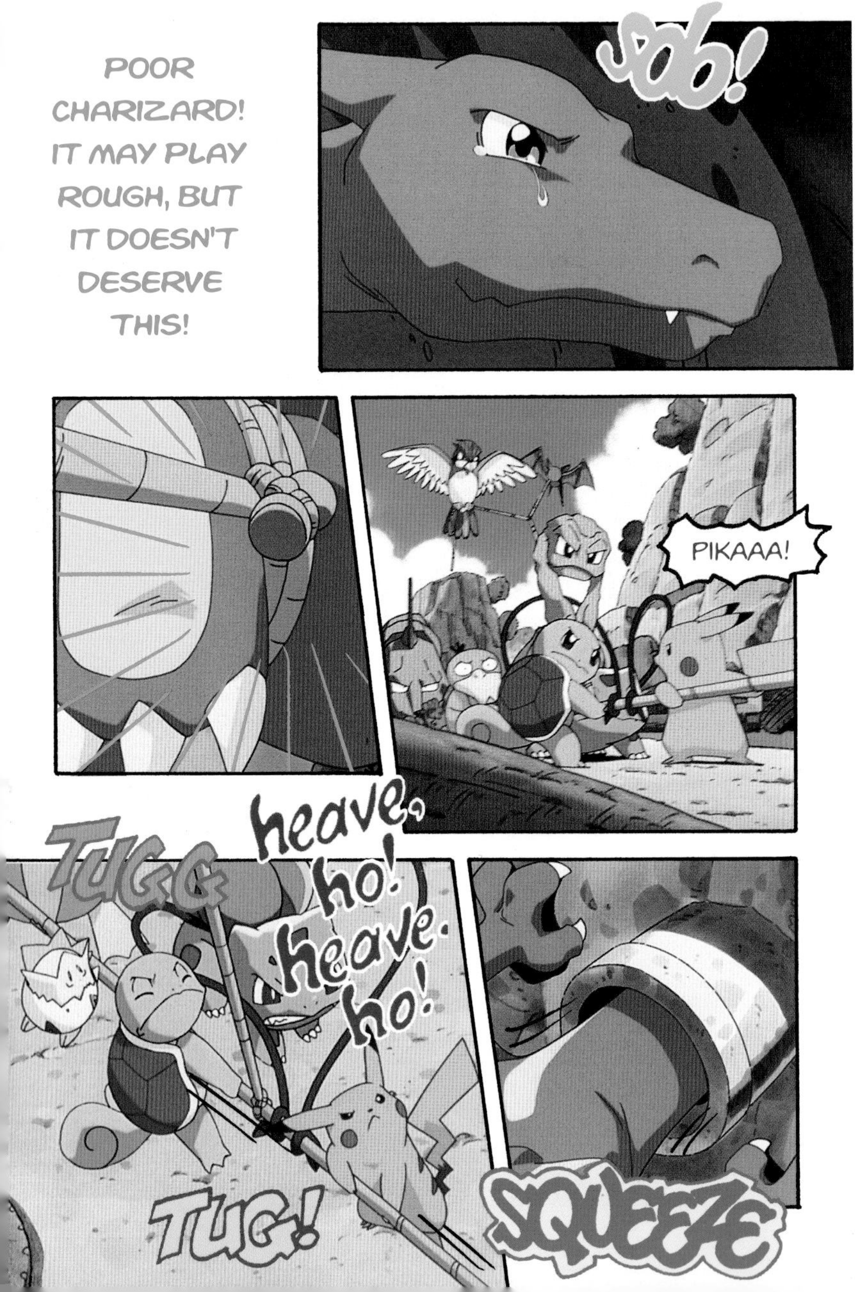
POOR CHARIZARD! IT MAY PLAY ROUGH, BUT IT DOESN'T DESERVE THIS!
SOB!
PIKAAA!
TUG
heave, ho! heave, ho!
TUG!
SQUEEZE

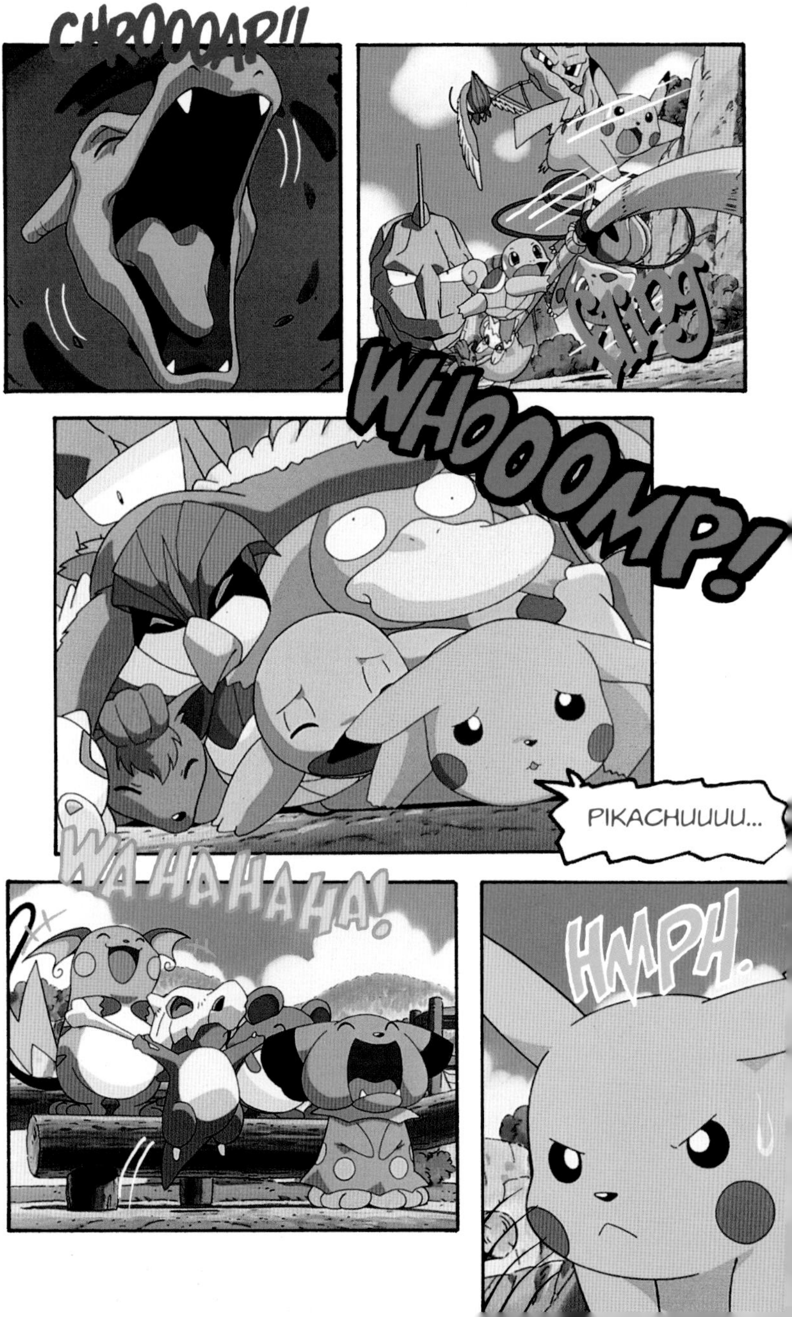
CHROOOAR!!
FLING
WHOOOOMP!
PIKACHUUUU...
WA HA HA HA HA!
HMPH.

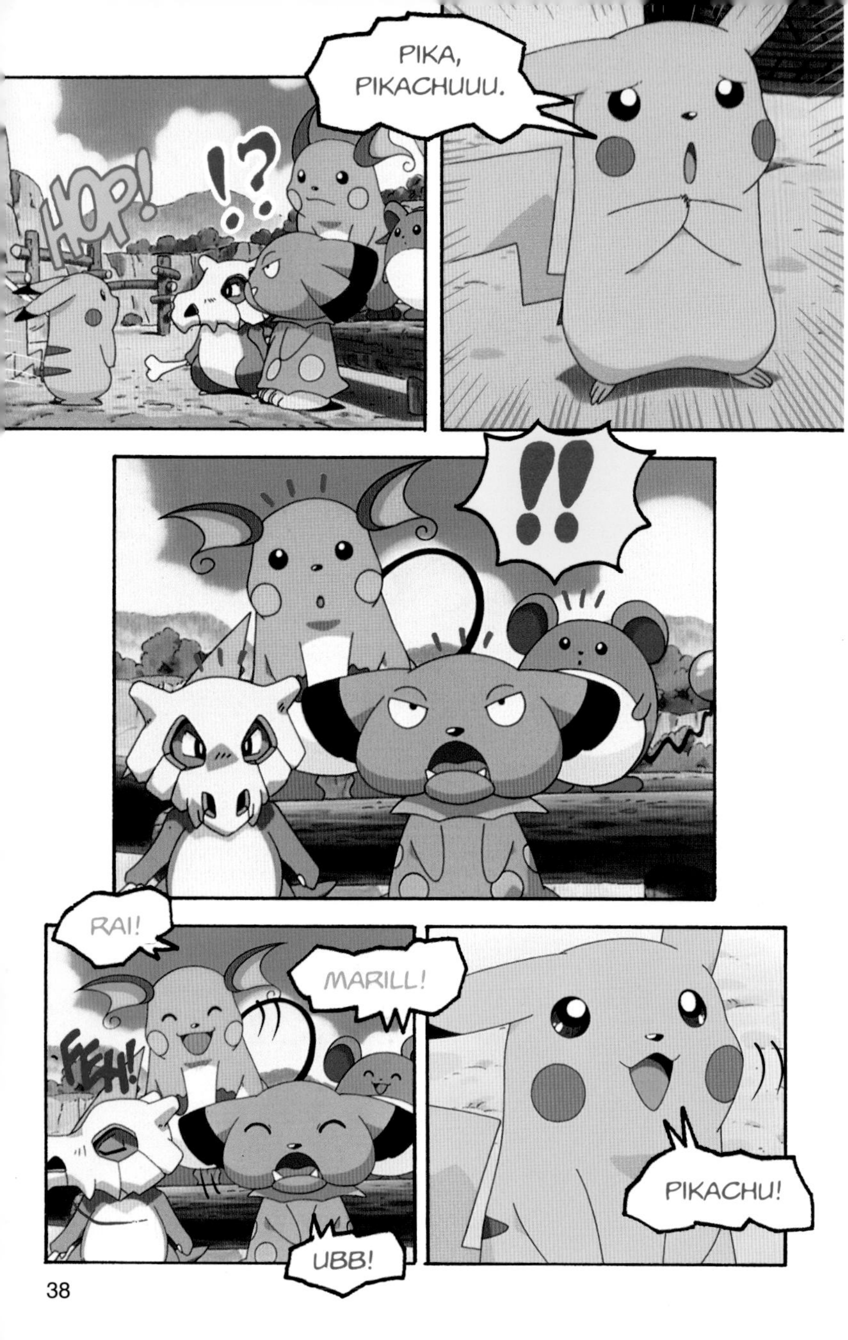
HOP!
!?
PIKA, PIKACHUUU.
!!
RAI!
MARILL!
FEH!
UBB!
PIKACHU!

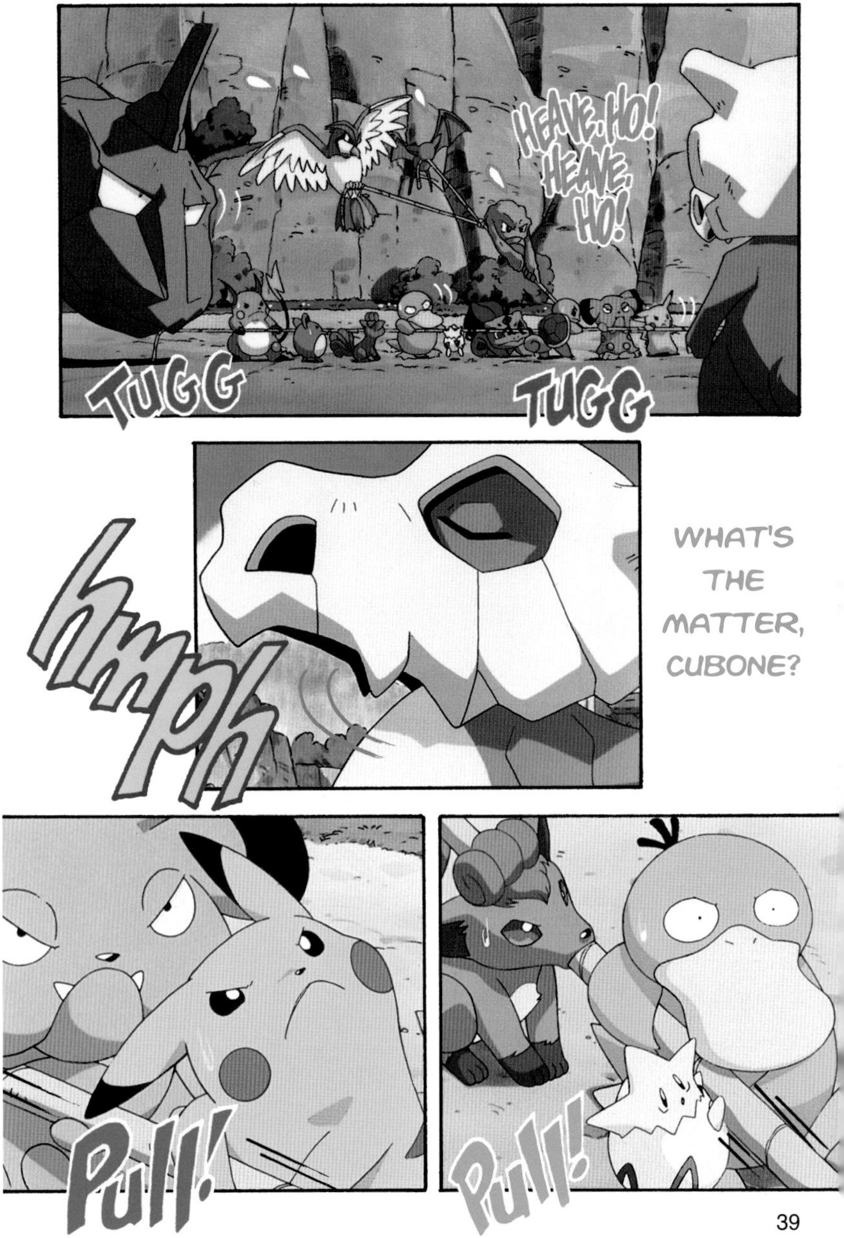
HEAVE, HO! HEAVE, HO!
TUGG
TUGG
hmph
WHAT'S THE MATTER, CUBONE?
Pull!
Pull!

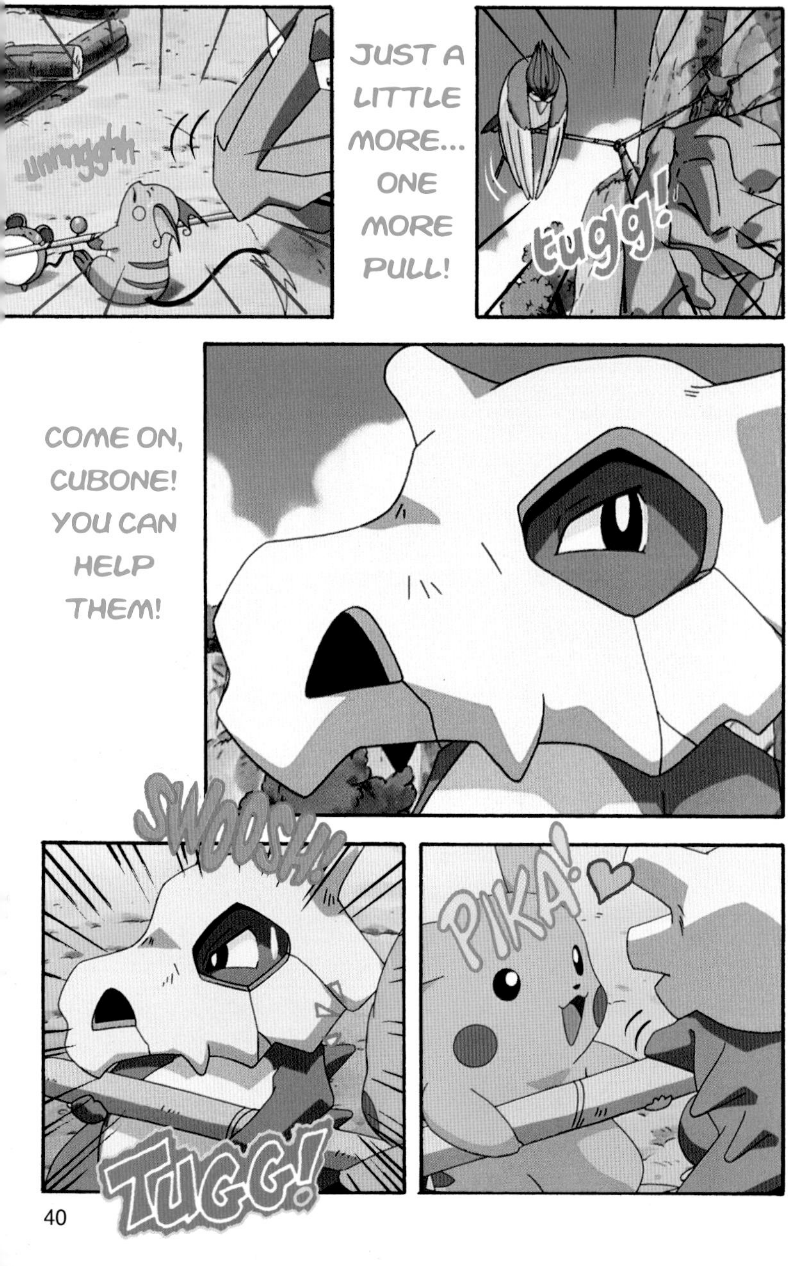
unnngghh
JUST A LITTLE MORE... ONE MORE PULL!
tugg!
COME ON, CUBONE! YOU CAN HELP THEM!
SWOOSH!
TUGG!
PIKA!

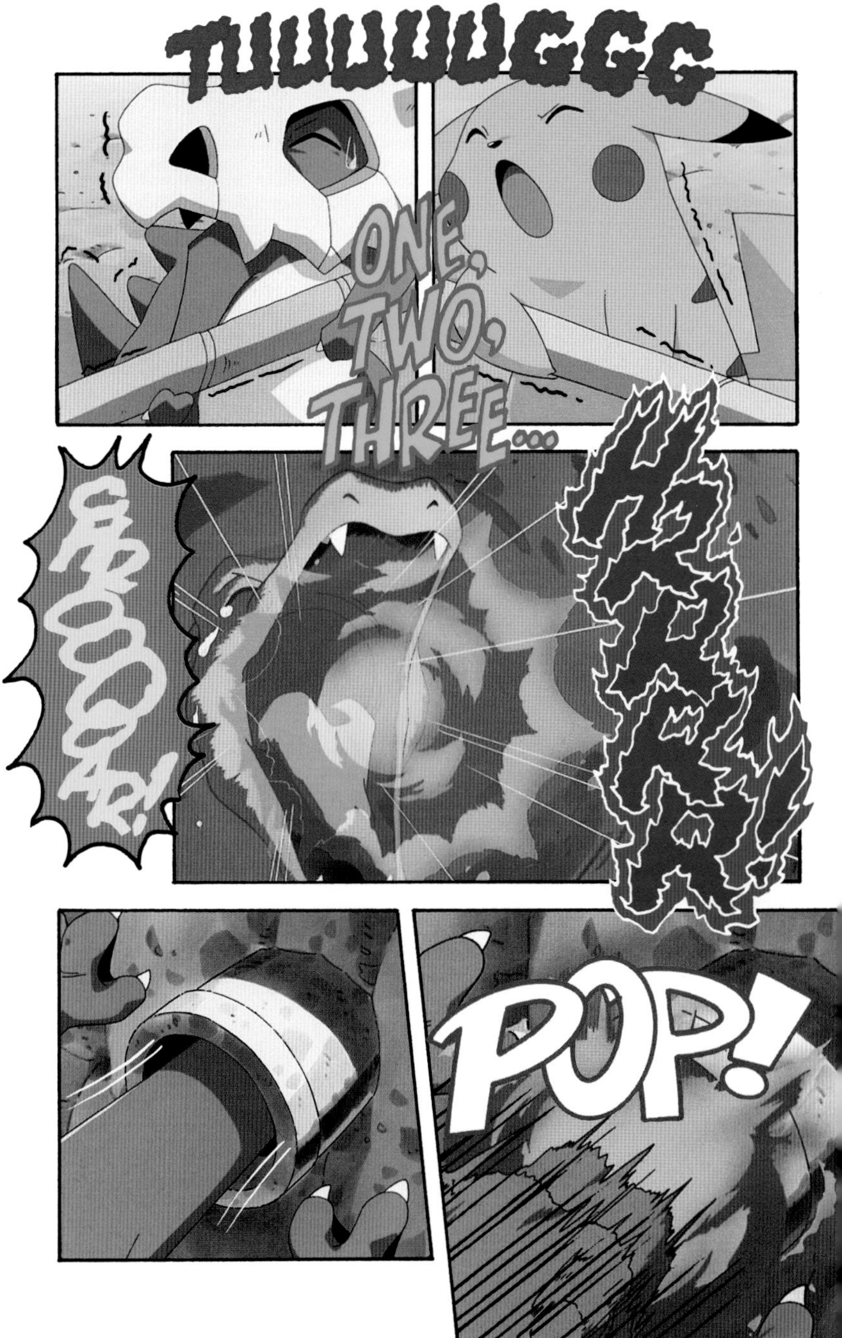
TUUUUUGGG
ONE, TWO, THREE...
GROOOAR!
HAAA!!
POP!

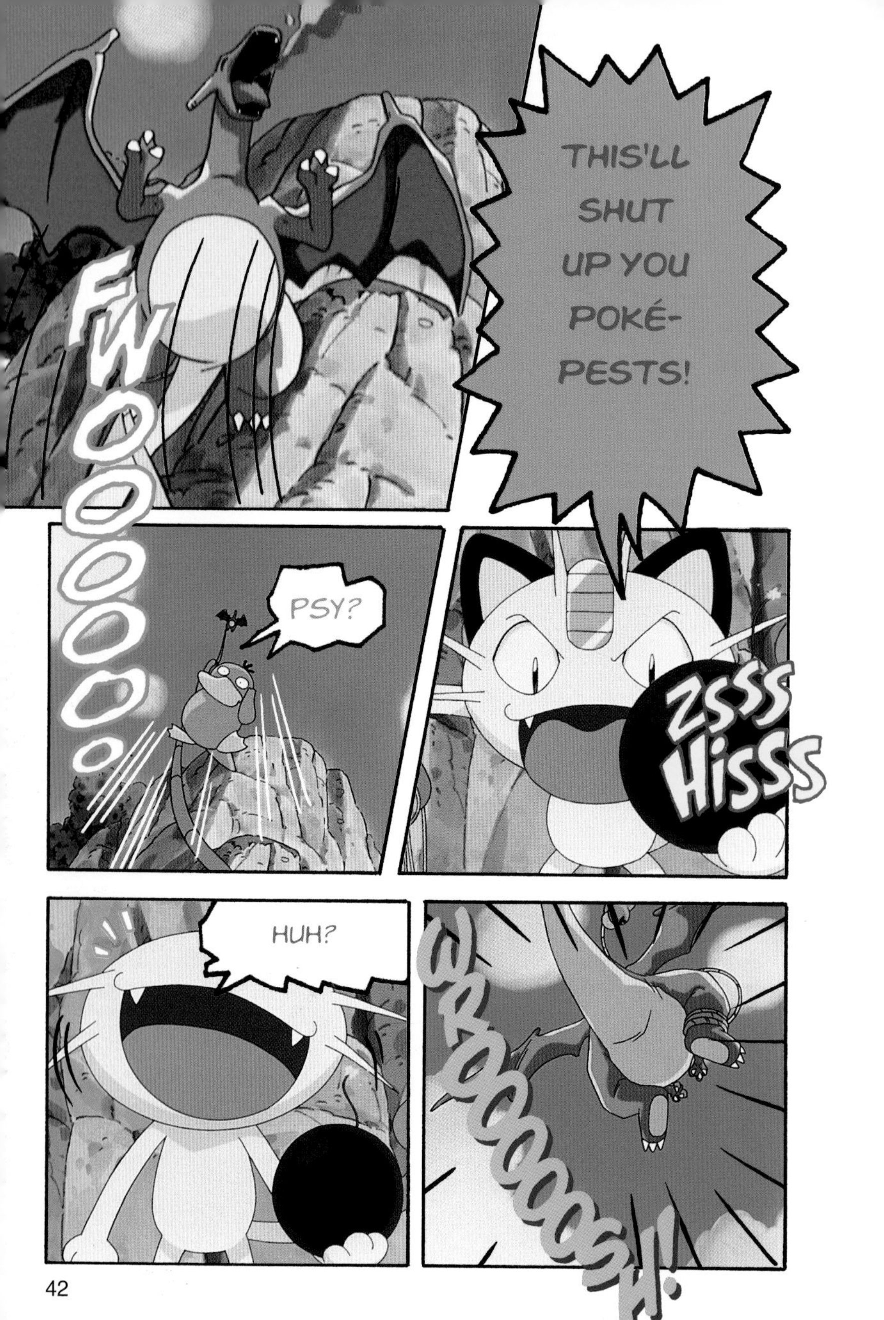
FWOOOOOOOOOO
THIS'LL SHUT UP YOU POKÉ-PESTS!
PSY?
ZSSS
HISSS
HUH?
!!
SWOOOOOOSH!!

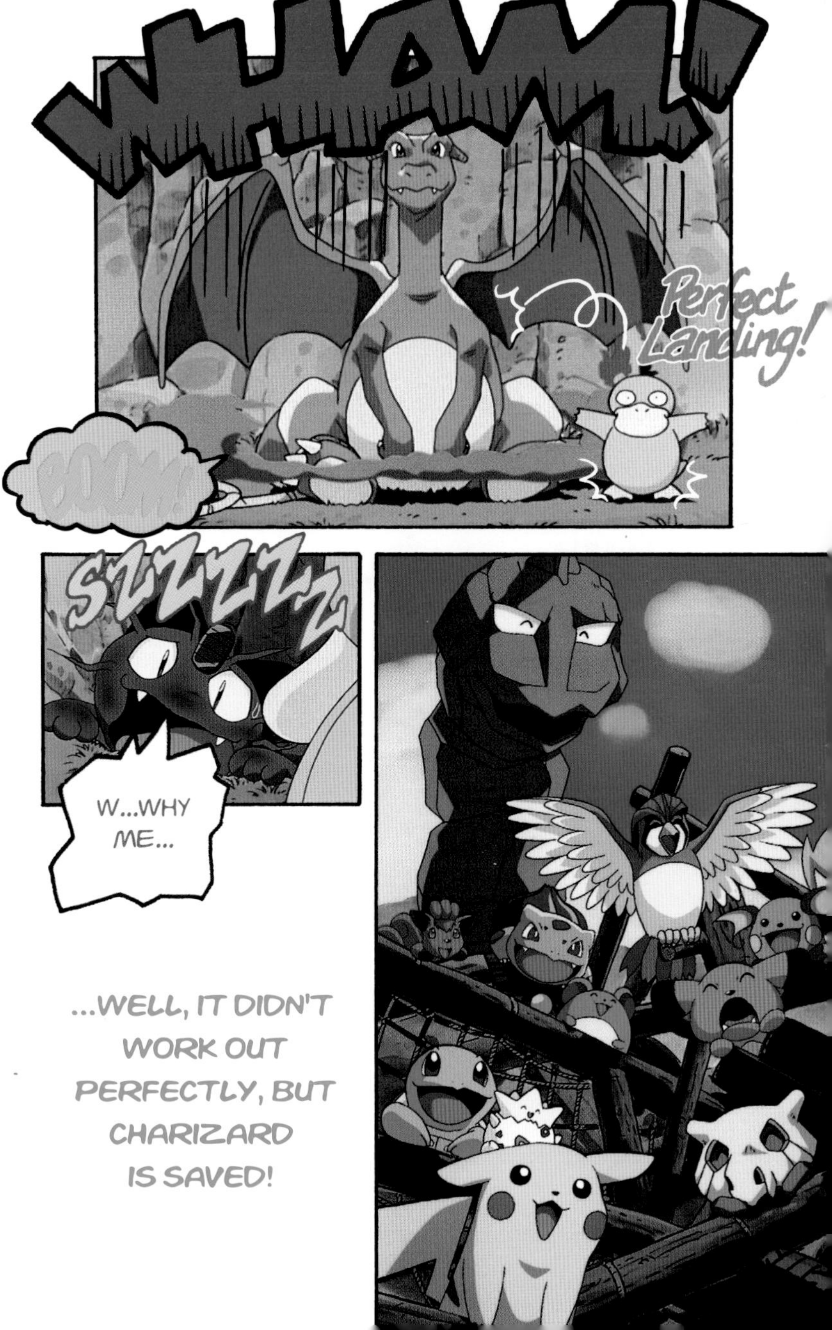
WHAM!
Perfect Landing!
BOOM!
SZZZZZ
W...WHY ME...
...WELL, IT DIDN'T WORK OUT PERFECTLY, BUT CHARIZARD IS SAVED!

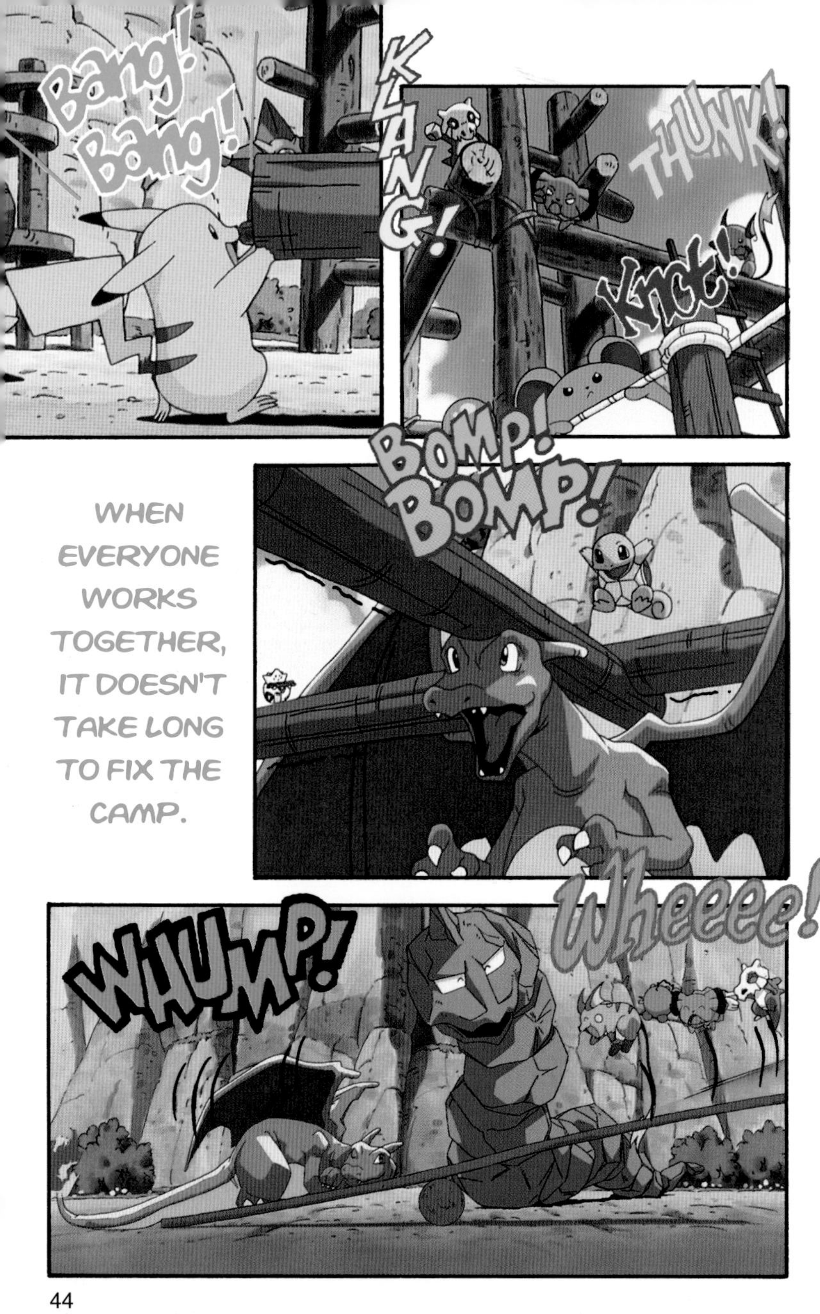
Bang! Bang!
KLANG!
THUNK!
Knck!
BOMP! BOMP!
WHEN EVERYONE WORKS TOGETHER, IT DOESN'T TAKE LONG TO FIX THE CAMP.
WHUMP!
Wheeee!

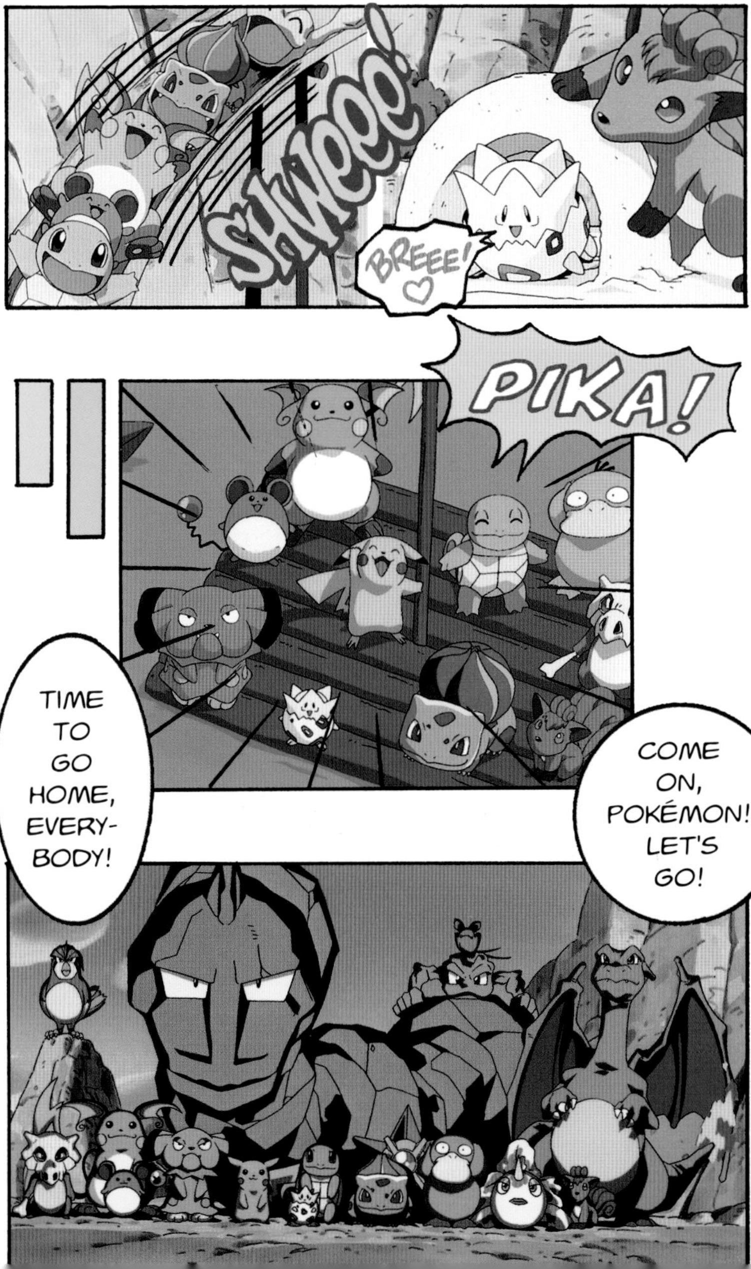
SHWEEE!
BREEEE! ♡
PIKA!
TIME TO GO HOME, EVERY-BODY!
COME ON, POKÉMON! LET'S GO!

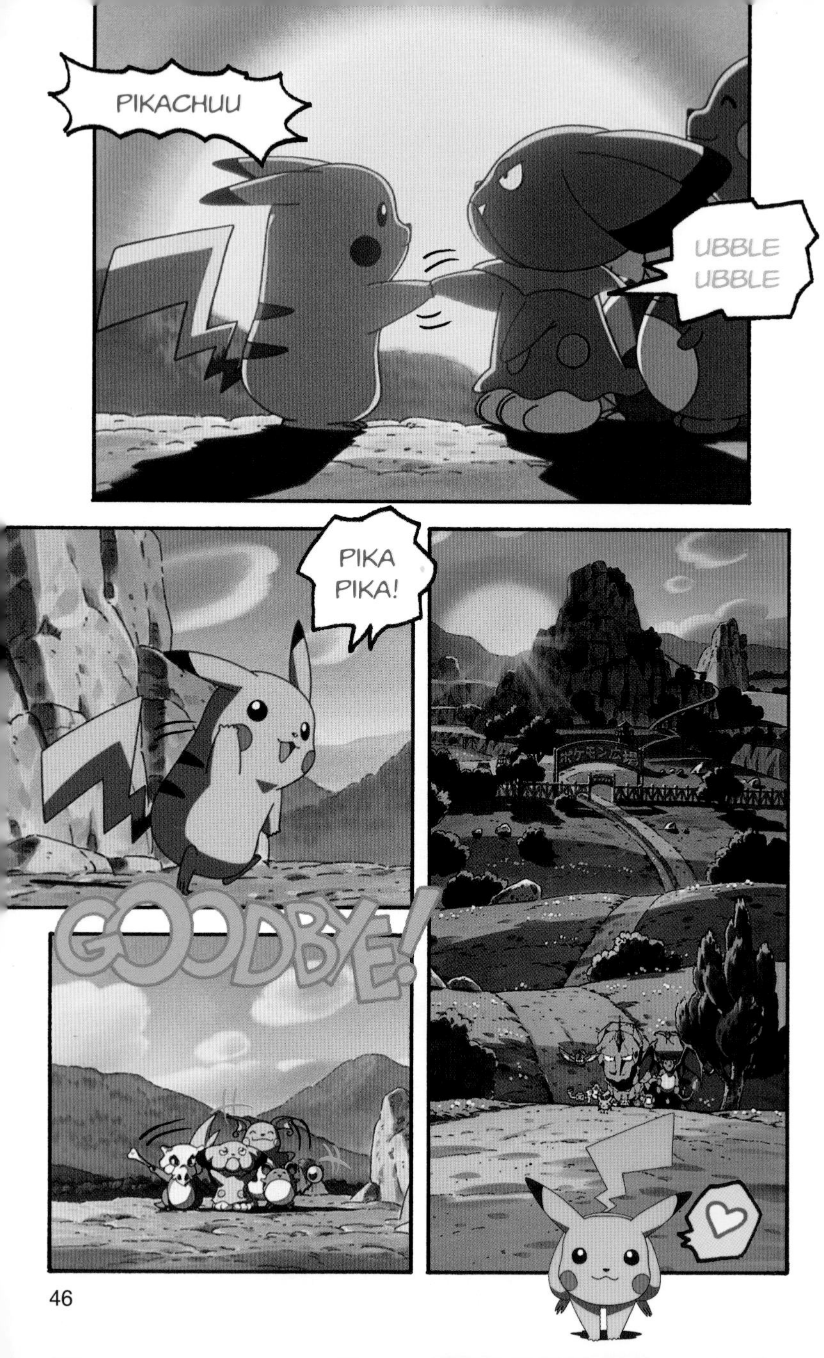
PIKACHUU
UBBLE UBBLE
PIKA PIKA!
GOODBYE!

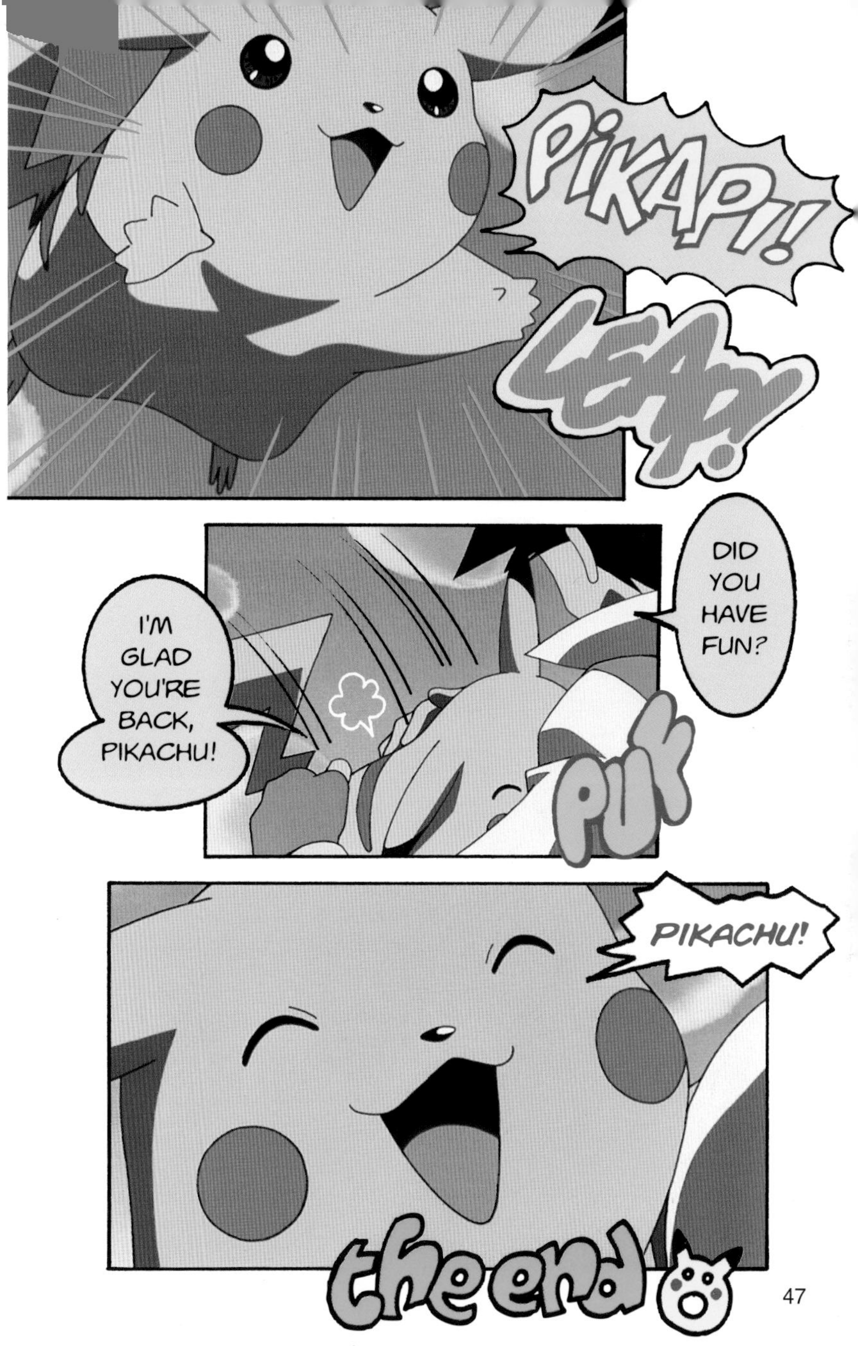
PIKAPI!
LEAP!
DID YOU HAVE FUN?
I'M GLAD YOU'RE BACK, PIKACHU!
PUK
PIKACHU!
the end

Pikachu's Vacation Pokédex

Pikachu

Mouse Pokémon

Height: 1´4˝
Weight: 13 lbs.

Pokémon No.
25

Pikachu and Ash have traveled together ever since Pallet Town. Pikachu is a very cute and reliable partner, and not quite the same as other Pikachu. Pikachu can use the attack, Thundershock. Keep taking care of Ash, okay, Pikachu?

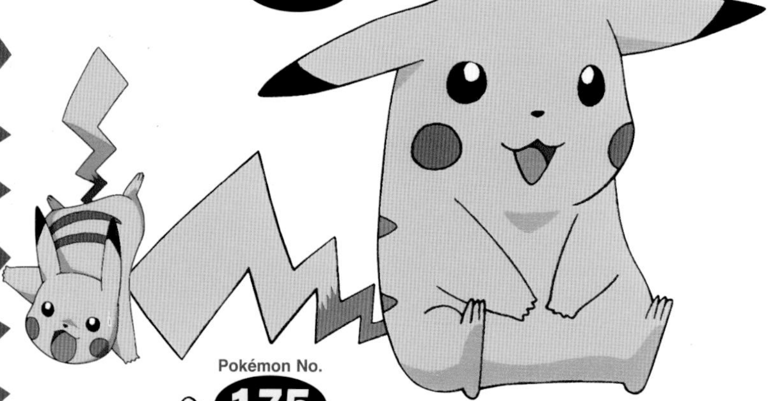

Pokémon No.
175

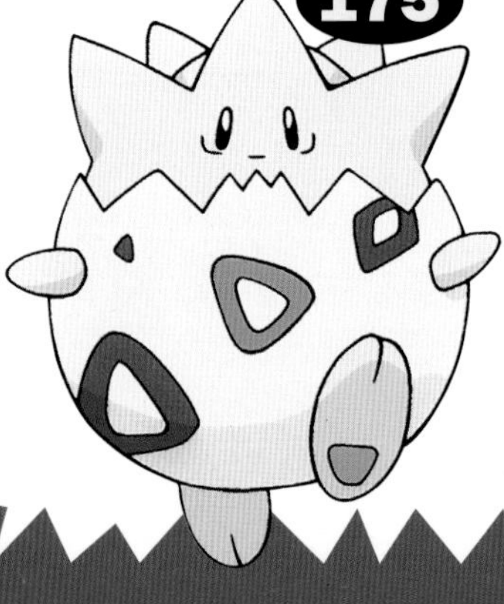

Togepi

Spike Ball Pokémon

Height: 1´ / Weight: 3 lbs.

By chance, Ash and friends found a mysterious Egg in a cave full of Pokémon fossils. Togepi is the Pokémon that hatched from this egg. Presently, Misty carries it on her journeys. What powers does it possess?

1

Bulbasaur
Seed Pokémon

Height: 2´4˝ / Weight: 15 lbs.

Ash caught this Pokémon in the Hidden Village. Bulbasaur is an extremely adept Pokémon that can use the attack, Solarbeam.

Squirtle
Tinyturtle Pokémon

Height: 1´8˝ / Weight: 20 lbs.

A water type Pokémon who was formerly the leader of a group of troublemakers. After becoming Ash's Pokémon, Squirtle calmed down.

Pokémon No.

7

Pokémon No.

95

Onix
Rock Snake Pokémon

Height: 28´10˝ / Weight: 463 lbs.

Brock's Rock-type Pokémon. It has one of the longest bodies of any known Pokémon.

Psyduck
Duck Pokémon

Pokémon No.

54

Height: 2´7˝ / Weight: 43 lbs.

Attached itself to Misty voluntarily. It is easygoing by nature, but it's also pretty out of it. This is frustrating to Misty.

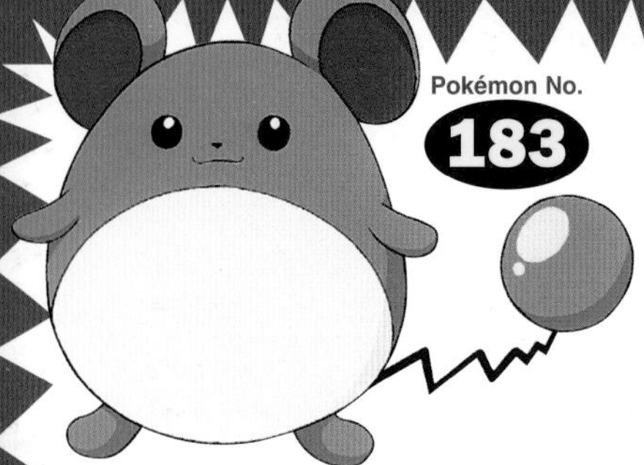

Pokémon No.
183

Marill
Aquamouse Pokémon

Height: 1´4˝ / Weight: 19 lbs.

Competed in a swimming race against Squirtle at the Pokémon camp. Marill seems to have an innocent and carefree personality.

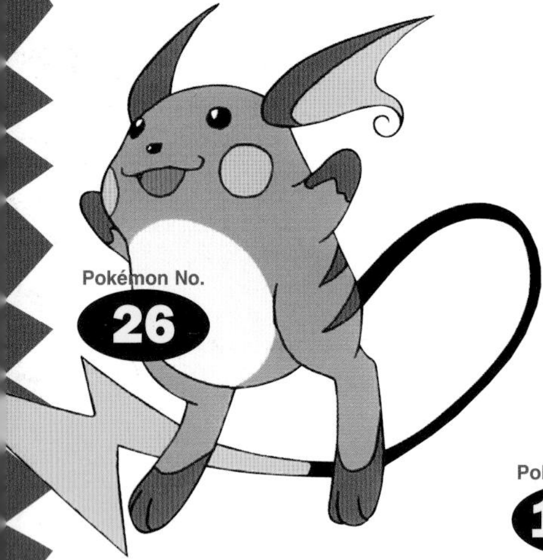

Pokémon No.
26

Raichu
Mouse Pokémon

Height: 2´7˝ / Weight: 66 lbs.

Raichu is the evolved form of Pikachu. Its electric Attack power is far more potent than Pikachu's.

Snubbull
Fairy Pokémon

Height: 2´ / Weight: 17 lbs.

Became pals with Pikachu and friends at the Pokémon Camp. Its expression looks fierce, but Snubbull's really a good friend.

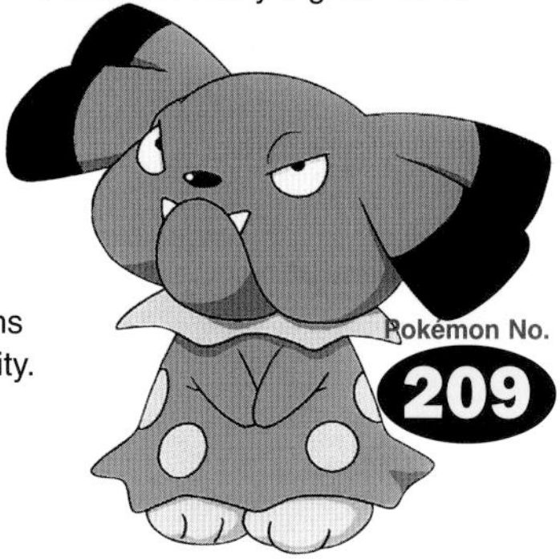

Pokémon No.
209

Cubone
Lonely Pokémon

Height: 1´4˝ / Weight: 14 lbs.

Cubone wears the bones of other Pokémon over its head, so no one has ever seen its face. It is a loner, but beneath its hard exterior, Cubone is actually quite caring.

Pokémon No.
104

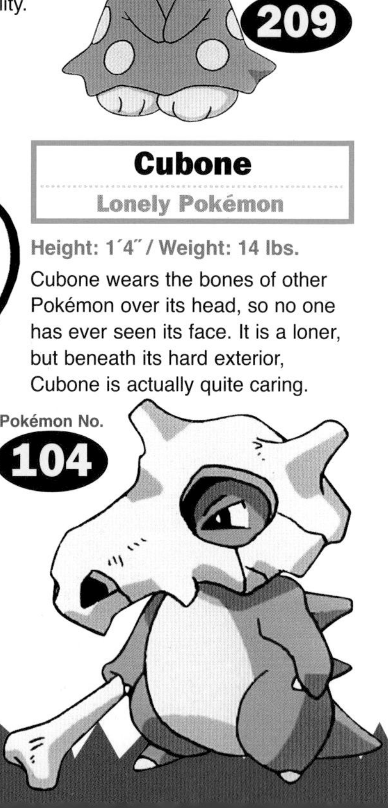

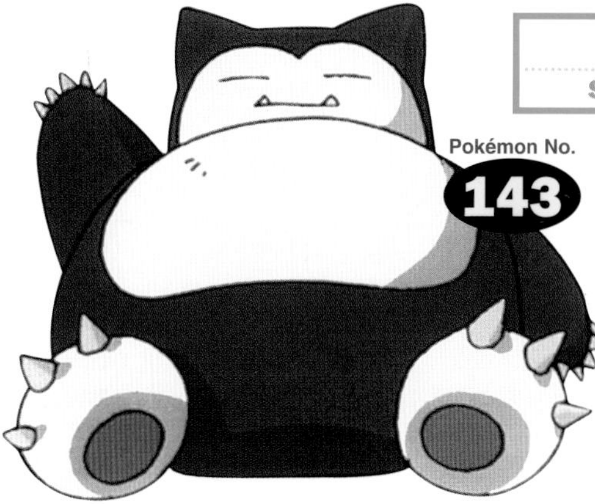

Snorlax

Sleeping Pokémon

Pokémon No.

143

Height: 6´11˝
Weight: 1014 lbs.

This Pokémon eats about 1000 lbs. of food a day. After eating, it falls asleep. It is possible to wake Snorlax with the Poké Flute, but once awake, it just resumes eating.

Pokémon No.

110

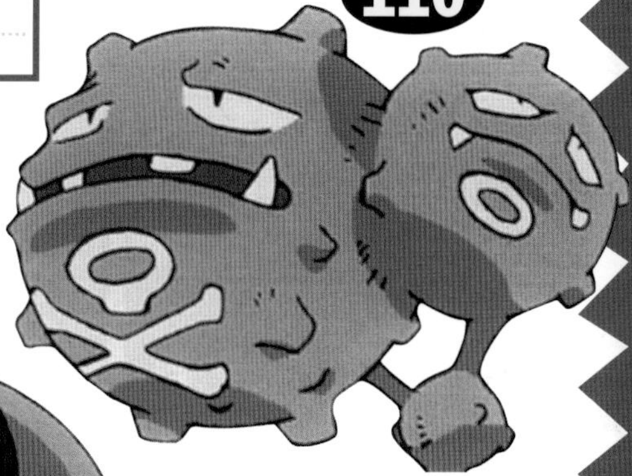

Weezing

Poison Gas Pokémon

Height: 3´11˝ / Weight: 21 lbs.

The evolved stage of Koffing, Weezing uses powerful poison gas attacks. Its appearance is scary, but it's not that mean, and is quite fond of its trainer James.

Pokémon No.

24

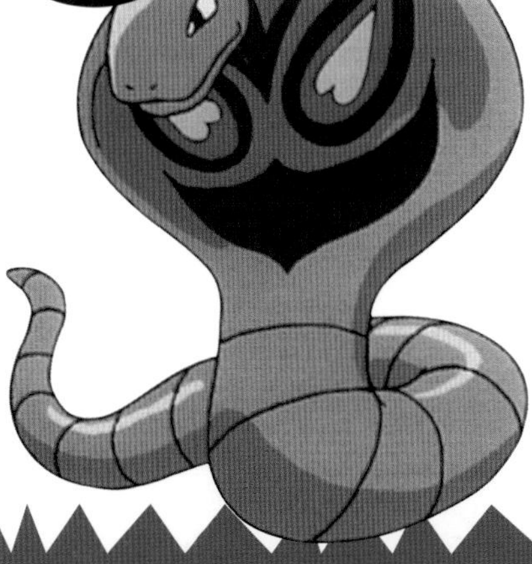

Arbok

Cobra Pokémon

Height: 11´6˝ / Weight: 143 lbs.

The evolved state of Ekans. The warning markings on its belly are different from area to area. Jessie's Arbok obeys her and (when she orders it) readily terrorizes Ash's Pokémon with attacks such as "Leer."

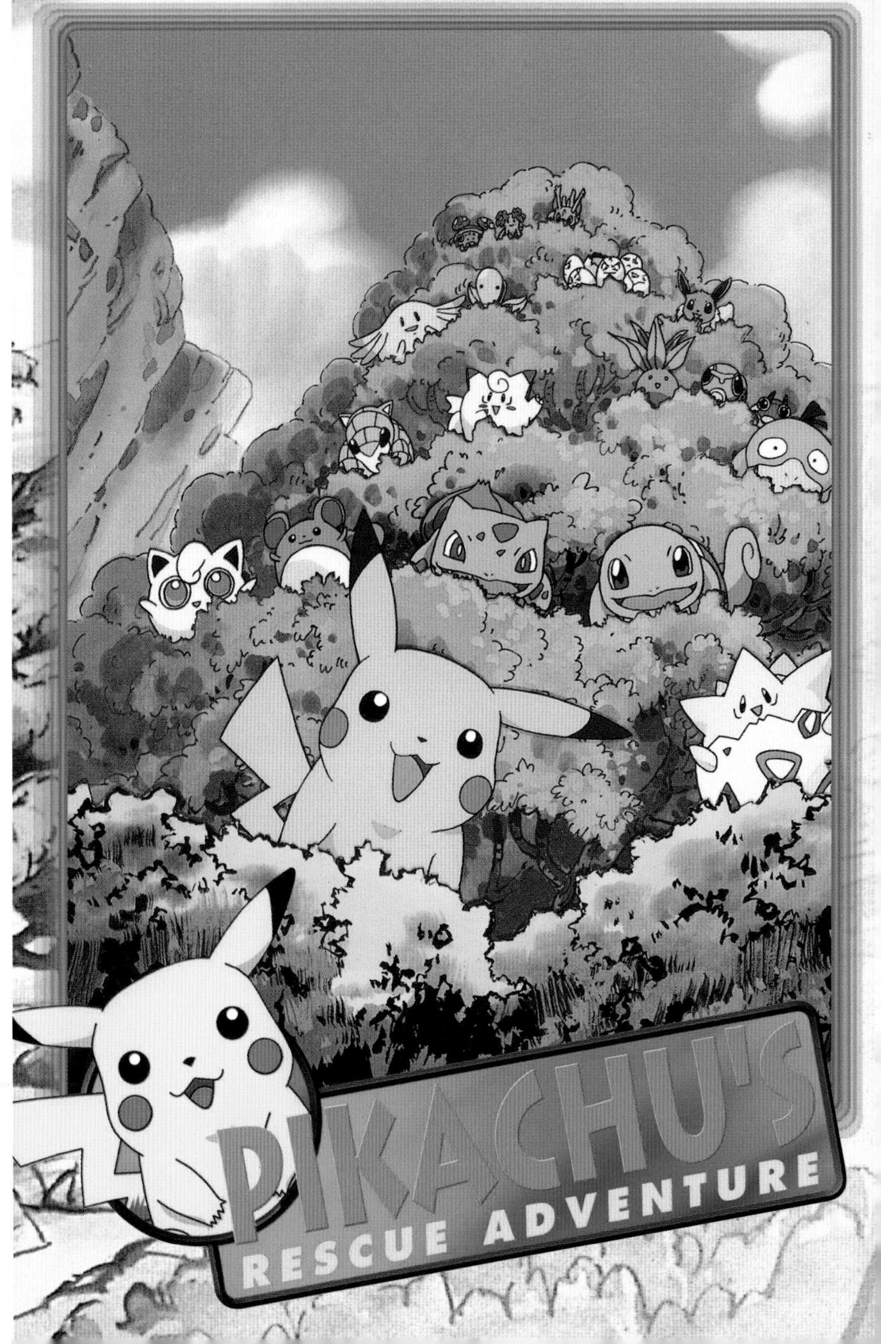
PIKACHU'S
RESCUE ADVENTURE

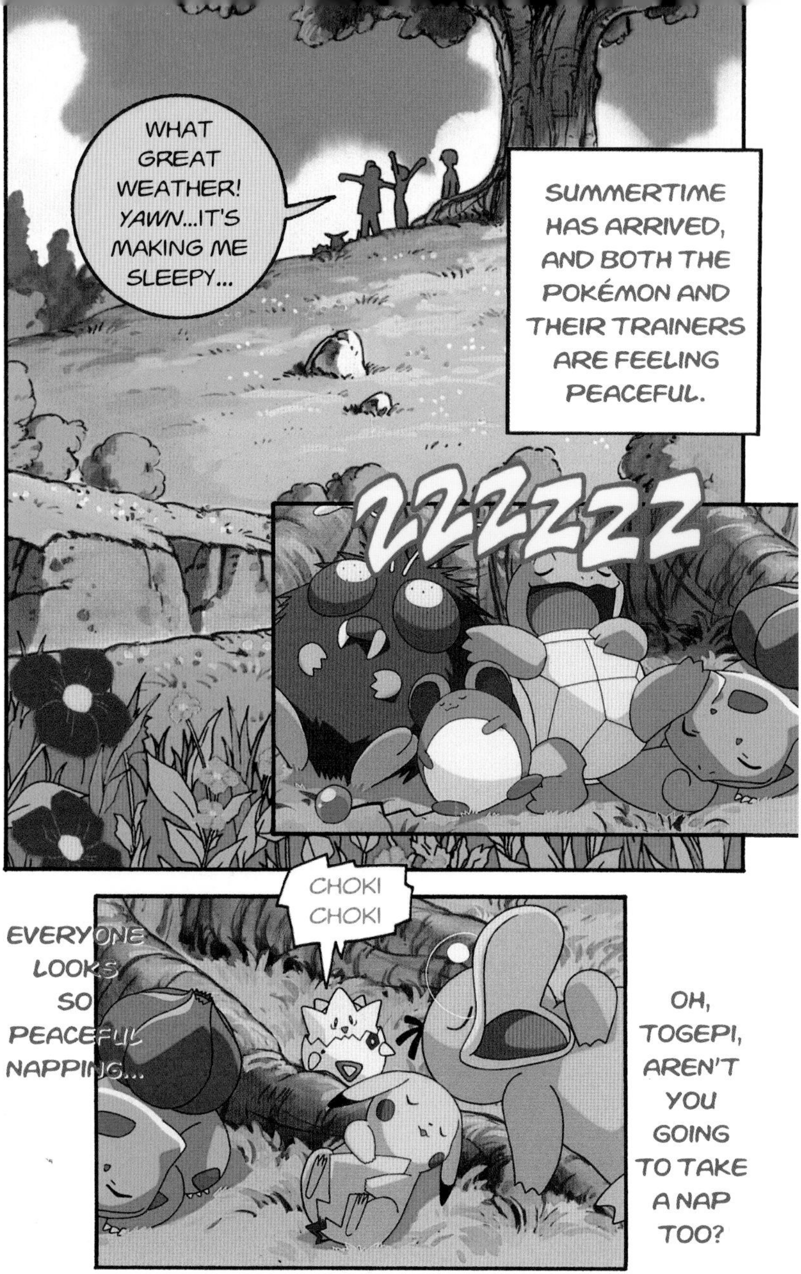

SUMMERTIME HAS ARRIVED, AND BOTH THE POKÉMON AND THEIR TRAINERS ARE FEELING PEACEFUL.
WHAT GREAT WEATHER! YAWN...IT'S MAKING ME SLEEPY...
ZZZZZZ
EVERYONE LOOKS SO PEACEFUL NAPPING...
CHOKI CHOKI
OH, TOGEPI, AREN'T YOU GOING TO TAKE A NAP TOO?

IT'S A SWARM OF LEDYBA! WHERE ARE THEY GOING?

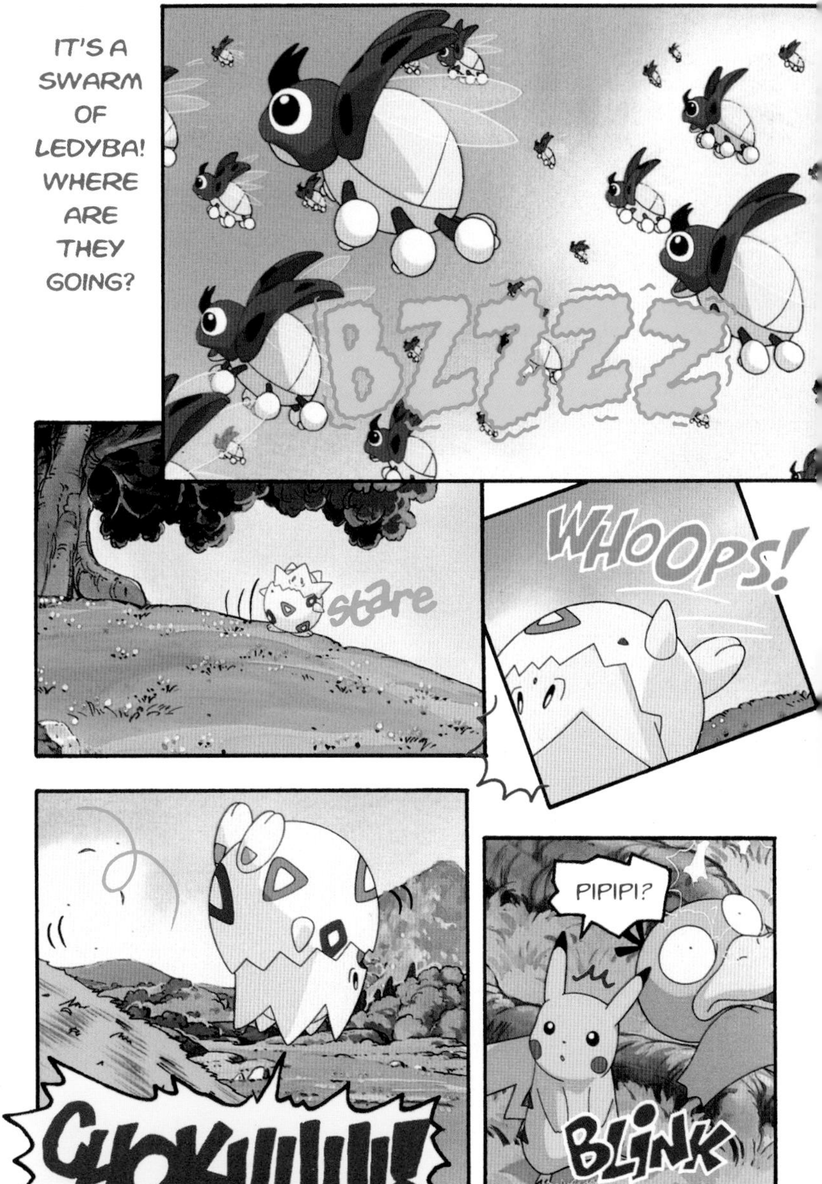
BZZZ
stare
WHOOPS!
CHOKIIIIII!
PIPIPI?
BLINK

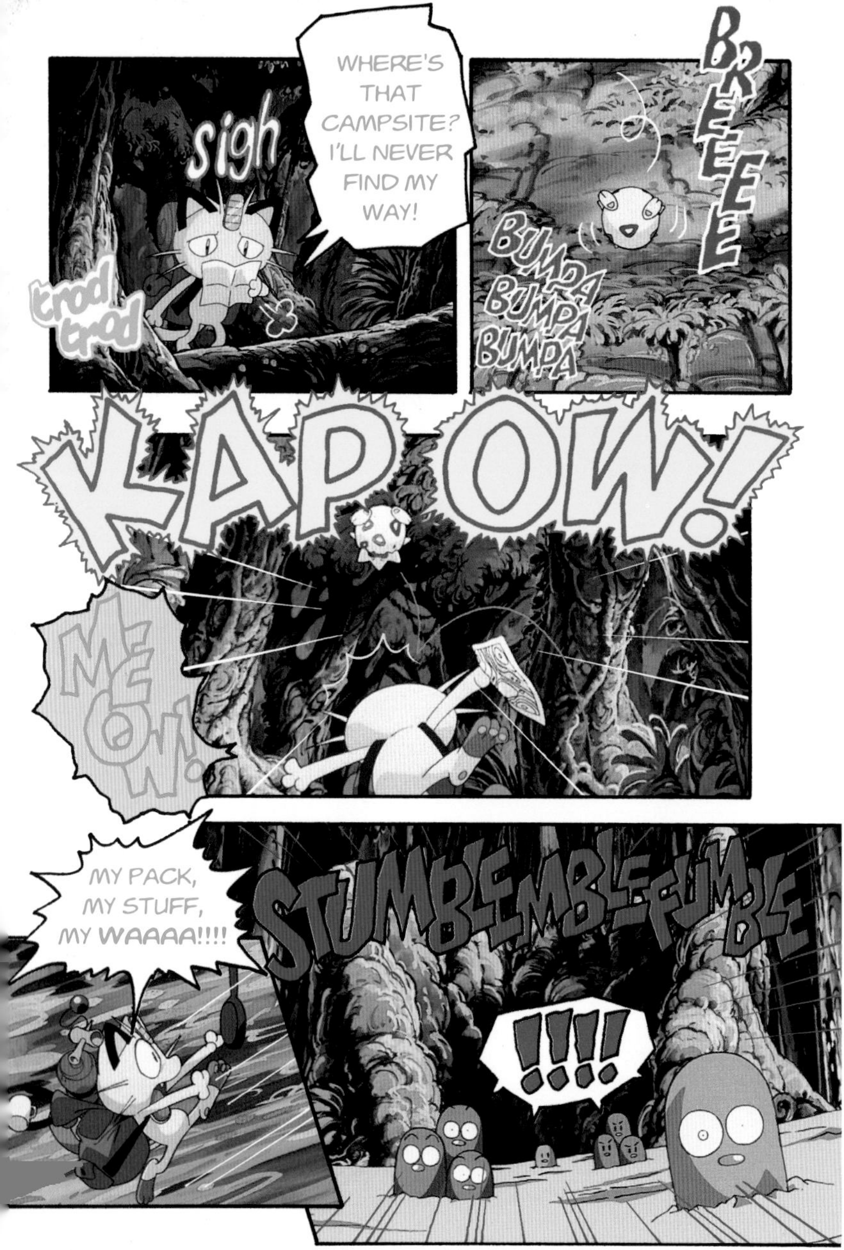
sigh
WHERE'S THAT CAMPSITE? I'LL NEVER FIND MY WAY!
trod trod
BREEEE
BUMPA BUMPA BUMPA BUMPA
KAPOW!
MEEOW!!
MY PACK, MY STUFF, MY WAAAA!!!!
STUMBLEMBLEFUMBLE
!!!!

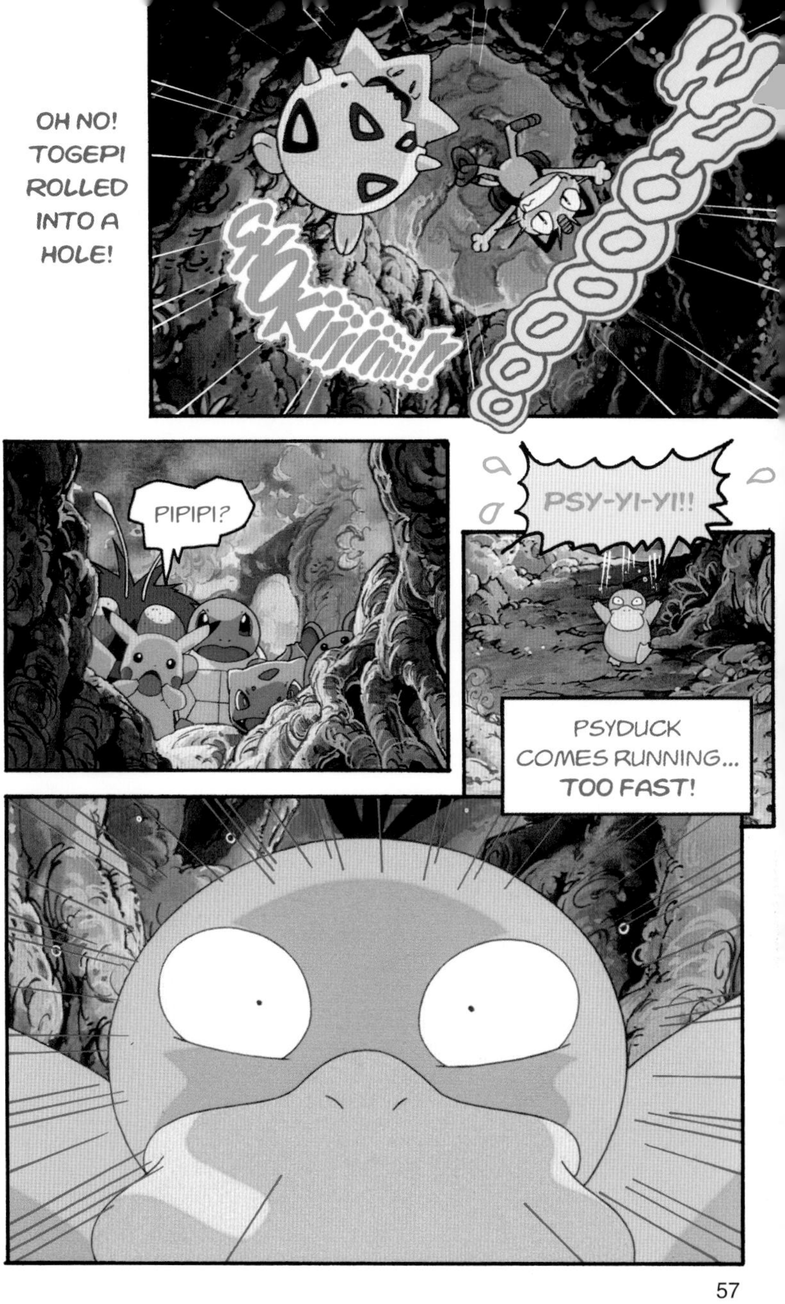
OH NO! TOGEPI ROLLED INTO A HOLE!
PIPIPI?
PSY-YI-YI!!
PSYDUCK COMES RUNNING... TOO FAST!

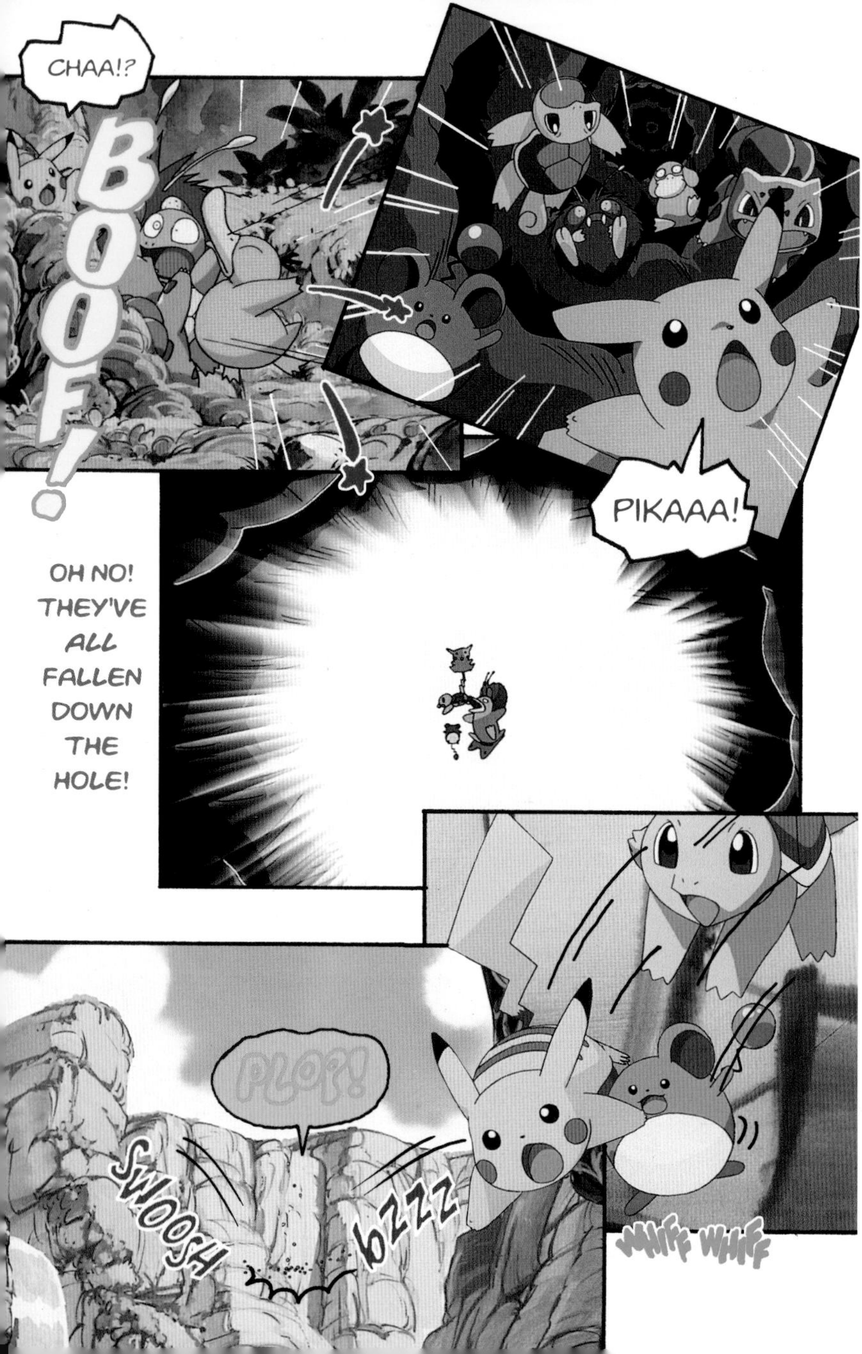
CHAA!?
BOOF!
PIKAAA!
OH NO! THEY'VE ALL FALLEN DOWN THE HOLE!
PLOP!
SWOOSH
bzzz
WHIFF WHIFF

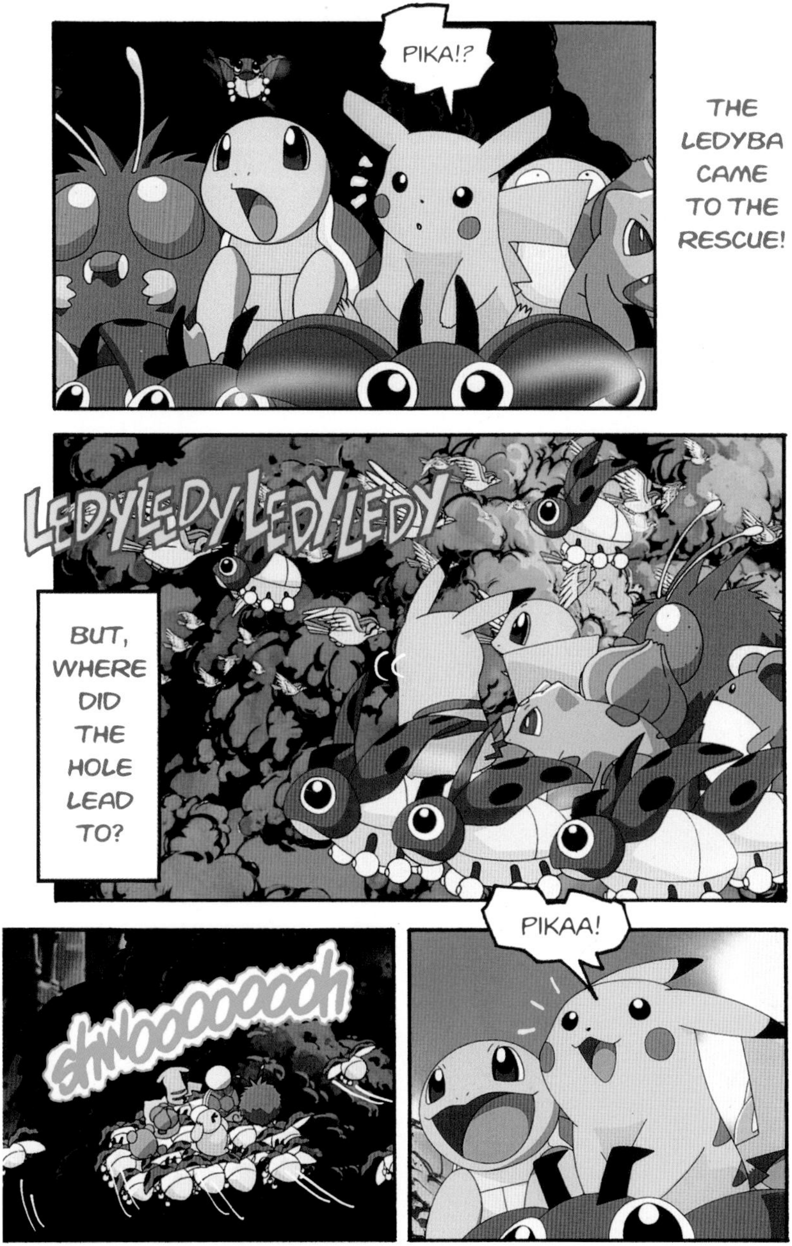
PIKA!?
THE LEDYBA CAME TO THE RESCUE!
LEDY LEDY LEDY LEDY
BUT, WHERE DID THE HOLE LEAD TO?
shwoooooooh
PIKAA!

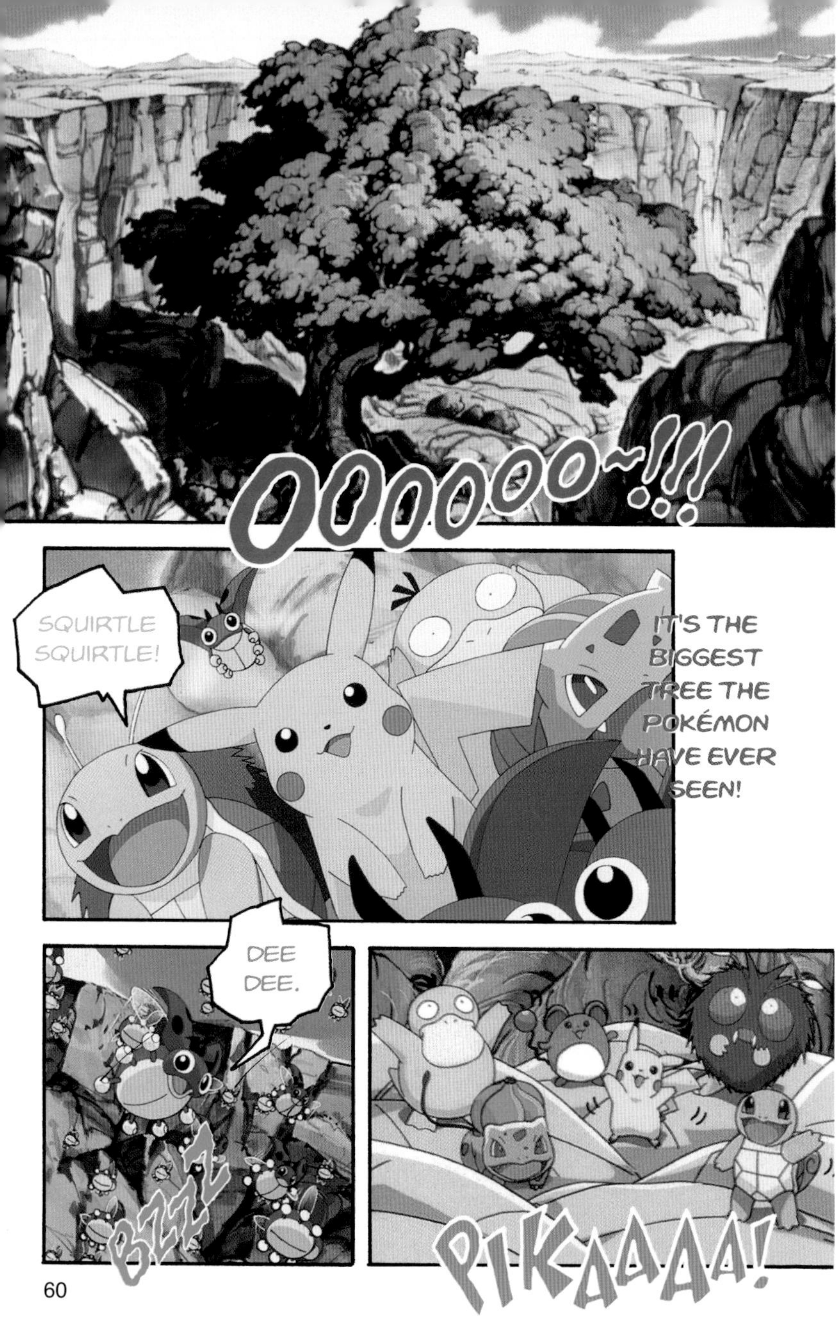
OOOOOO~!!!
SQUIRTLE SQUIRTLE!
IT'S THE BIGGEST TREE THE POKÉMON HAVE EVER SEEN!
DEE DEE.
BZZZ
PIKAAAA!

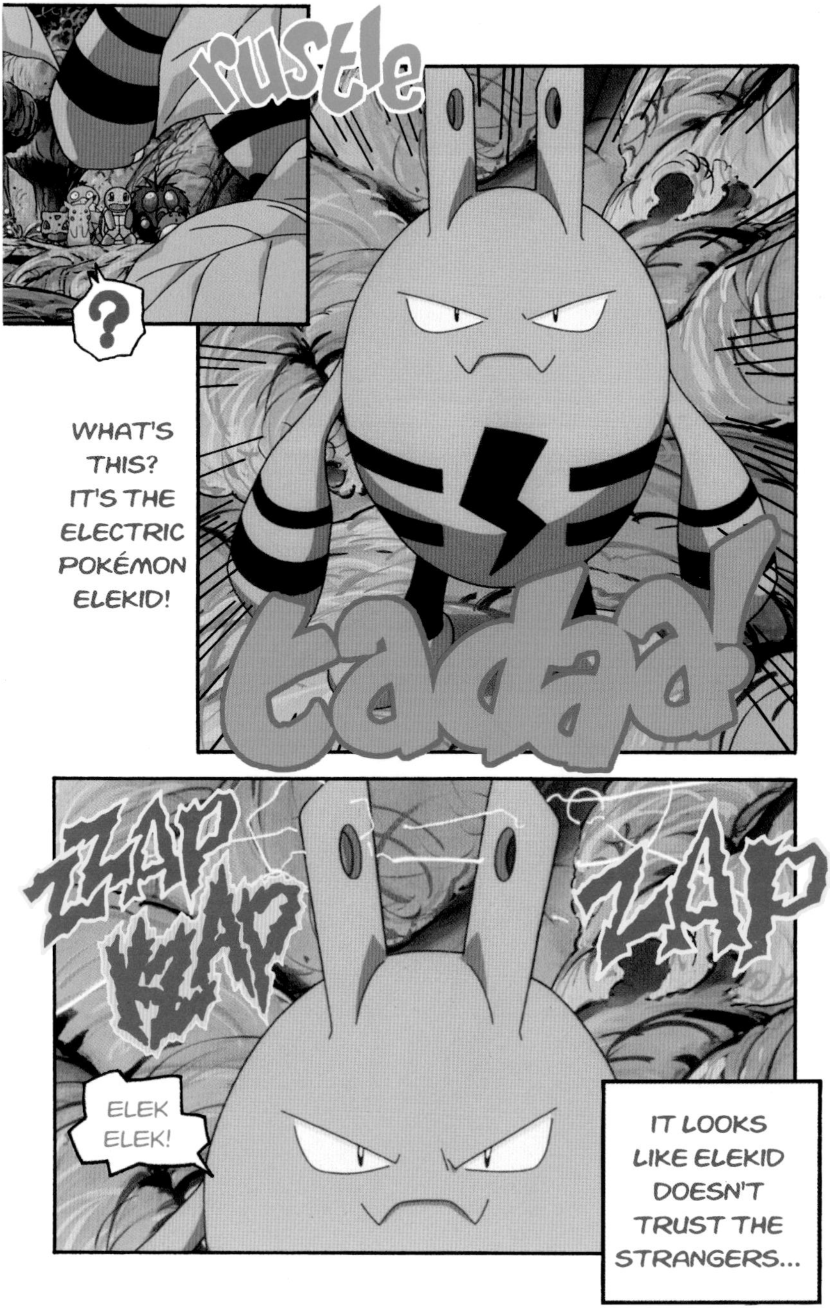
rustle
?
WHAT'S THIS? IT'S THE ELECTRIC POKÉMON ELEKID!
tada!
ZAP ZAP
ZAP
ELEK ELEK!
IT LOOKS LIKE ELEKID DOESN'T TRUST THE STRANGERS...

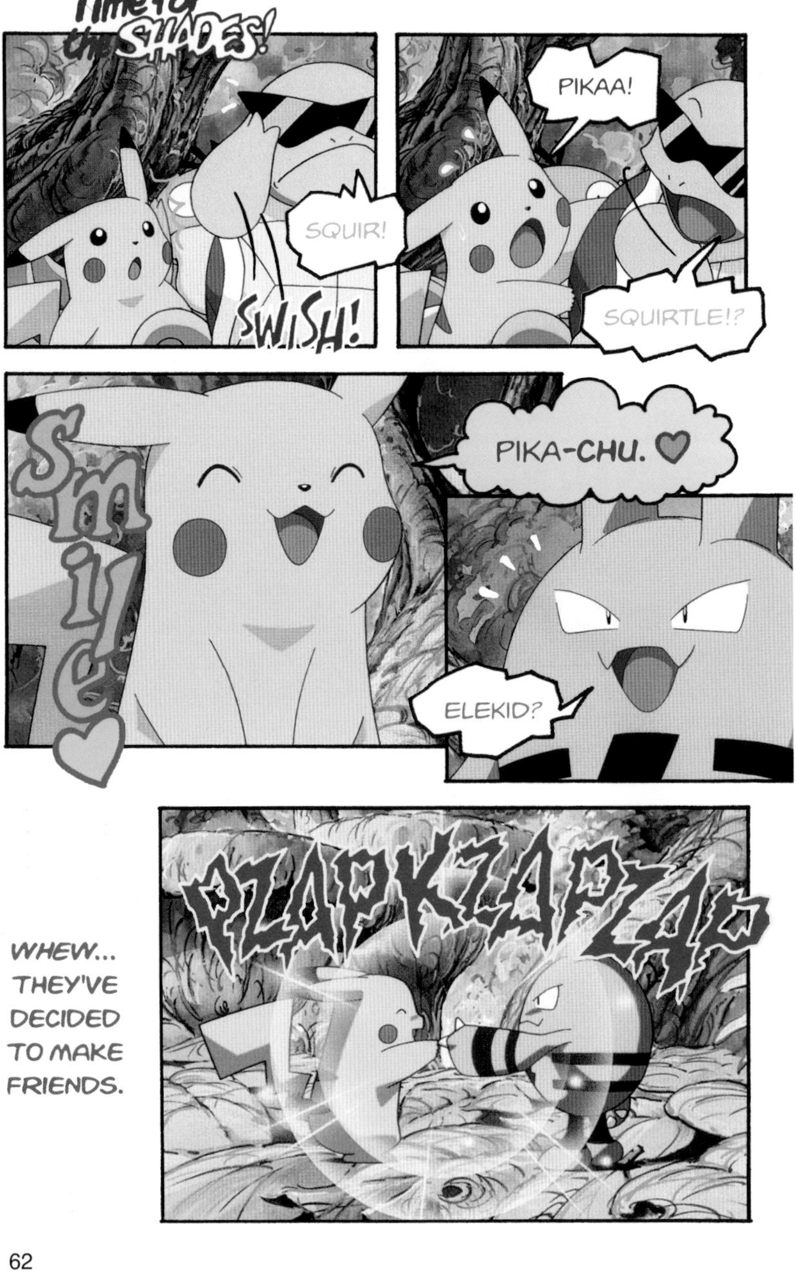

Time for the SHADES!
SWISH!
SQUIR!
PIKAA!
SQUIRTLE!?
Smile
PIKA-CHU. ♥
ELEKID?
PZAPKZAPZAP
WHEW... THEY'VE DECIDED TO MAKE FRIENDS.

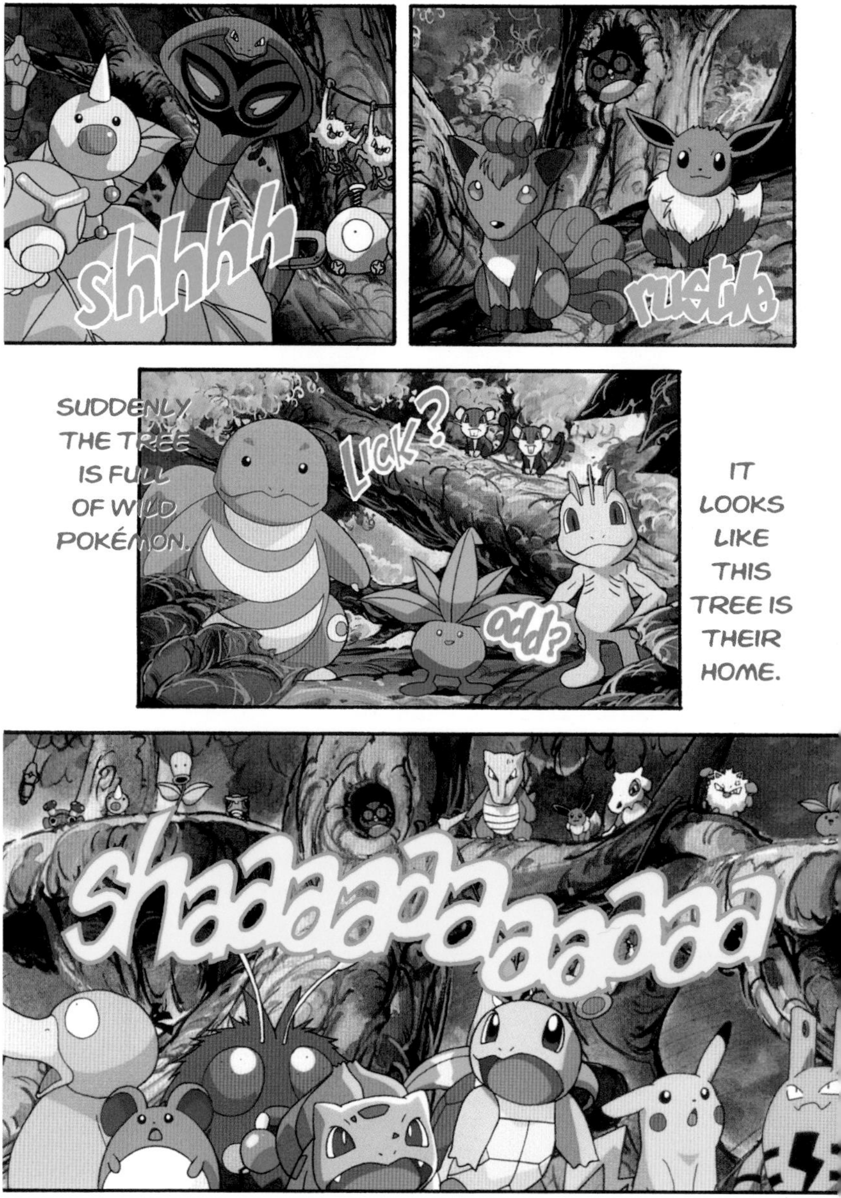
shhhh
rustle
SUDDENLY THE TREE IS FULL OF WILD POKÉMON.
LICK?
odd?
IT LOOKS LIKE THIS TREE IS THEIR HOME.
shaaaaaaaaaaa

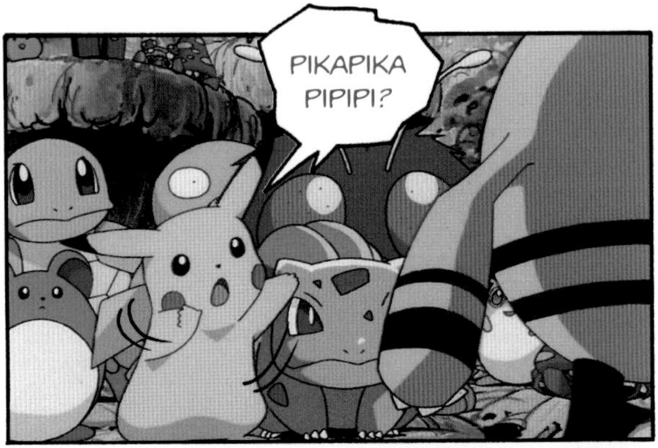
PIKAPIKA
PIPIPI?

"HAVE YOU SEEN TOGEPI?" ASKS PIKACHU.

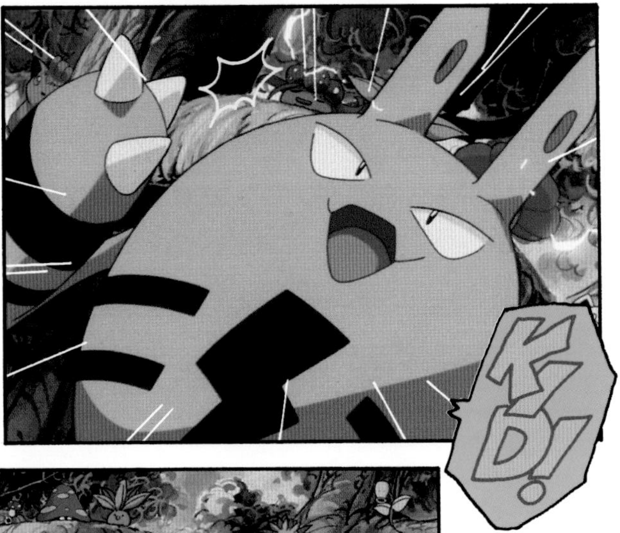
KID!

"A LITTLE EGG? I'VE SEEN IT!" ELEKID SAYS.

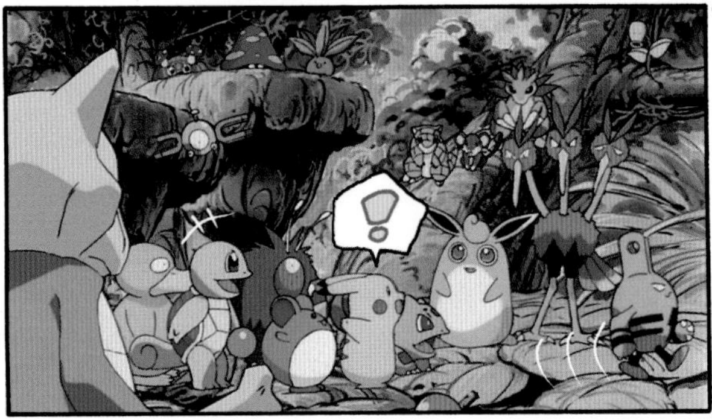
!

ELEKID AGREES TO BE THEIR GUIDE!

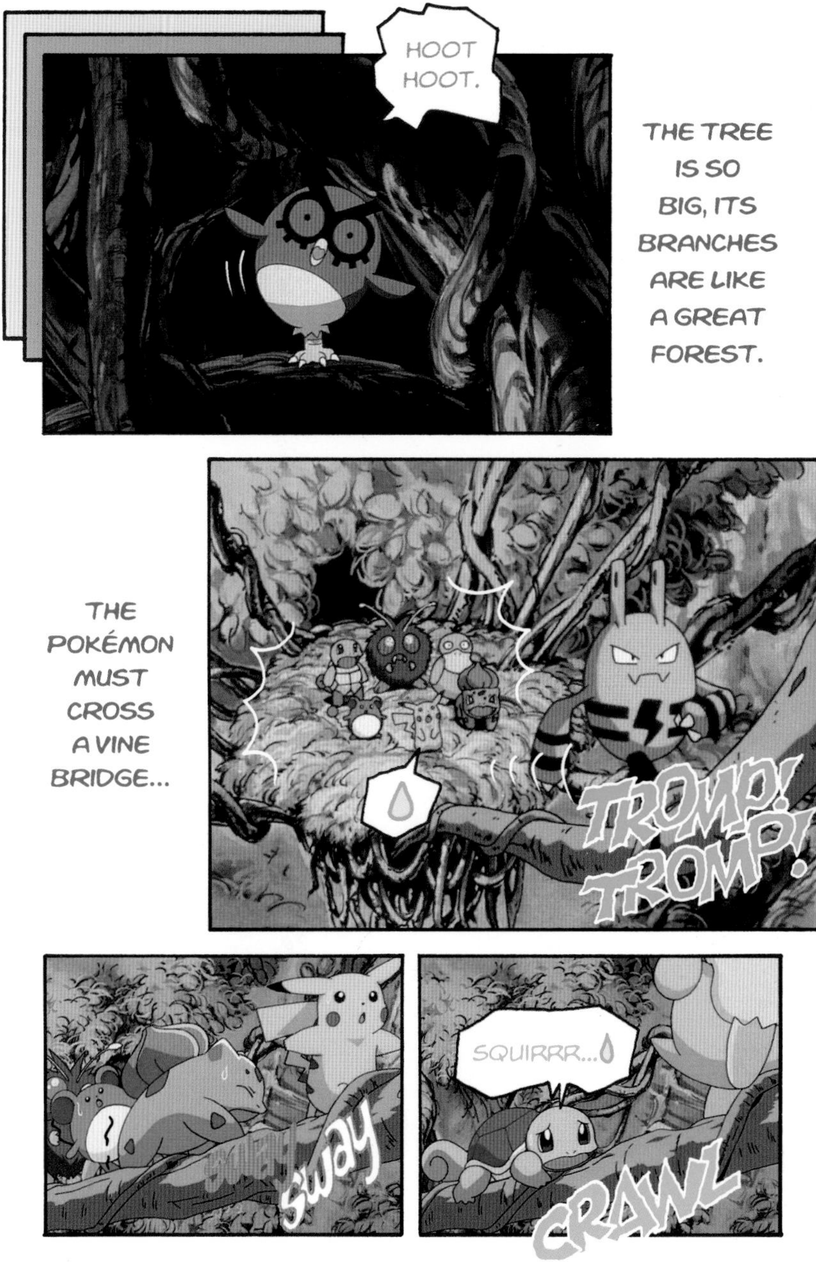
HOOT HOOT.
THE TREE IS SO BIG, ITS BRANCHES ARE LIKE A GREAT FOREST.
THE POKÉMON MUST CROSS A VINE BRIDGE...
TROMP! TROMP!
SWAY
SQUIRRR...
CRAWL

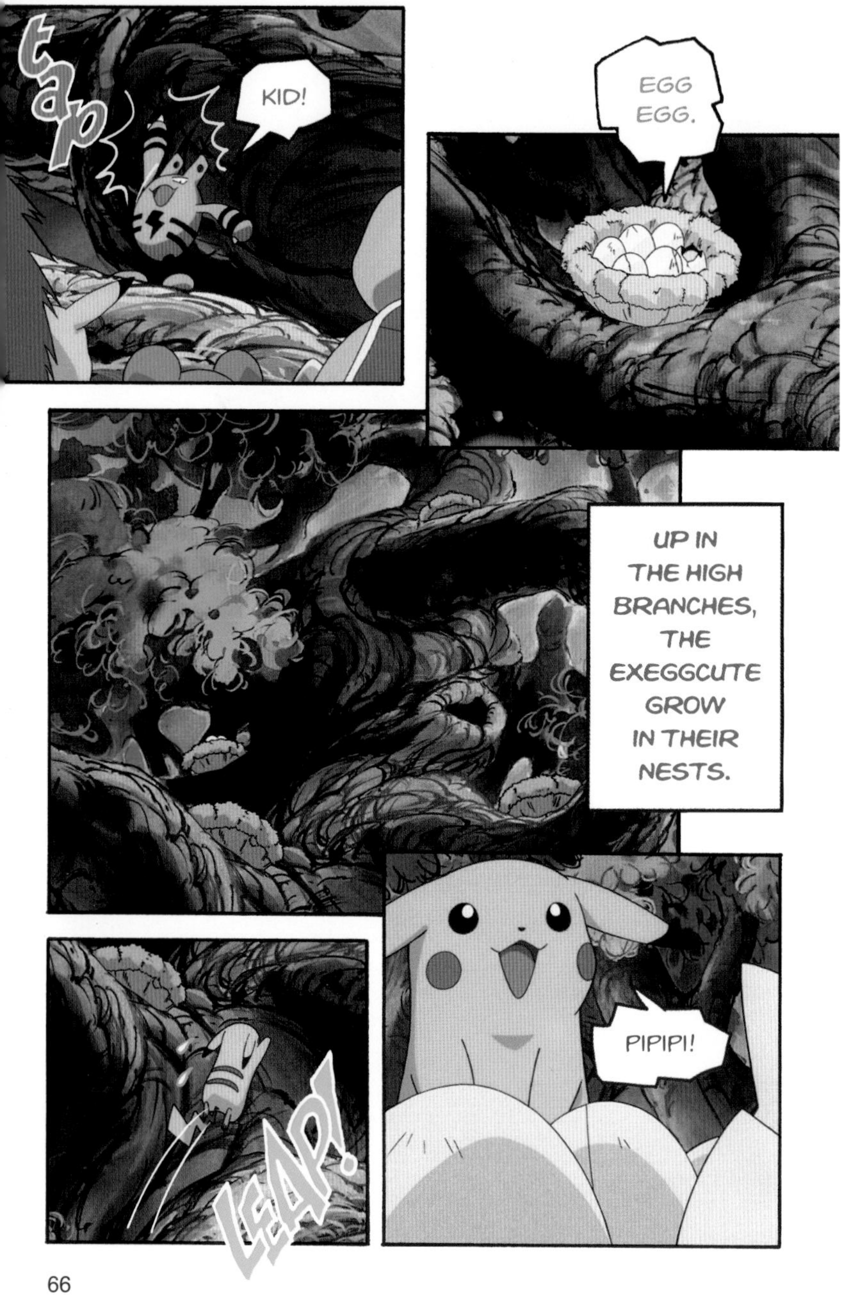
tap
KID!
EGG EGG.
UP IN THE HIGH BRANCHES, THE EXEGGCUTE GROW IN THEIR NESTS.
LEAP!
PIPIPI!

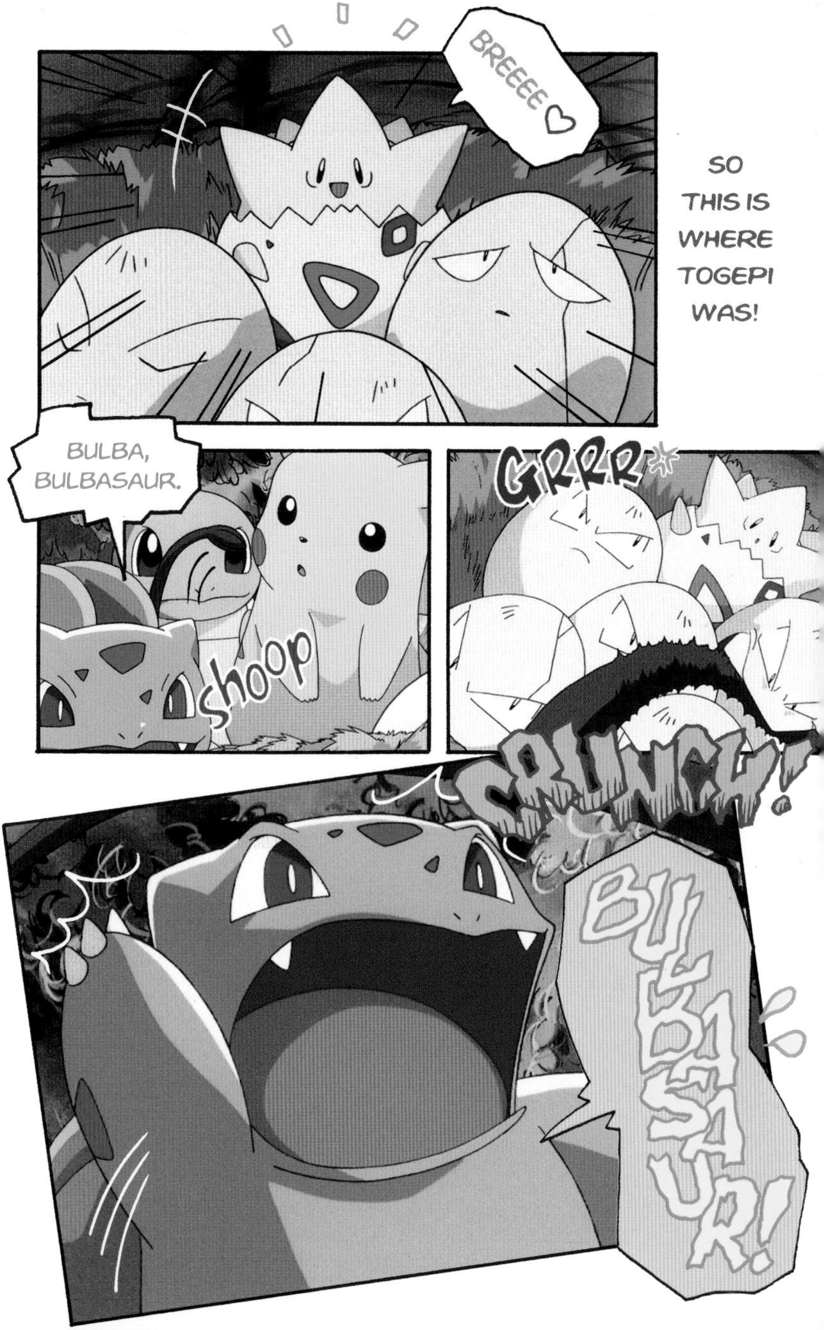
BREEEE ♡
SO THIS IS WHERE TOGEPI WAS!
BULBA, BULBASAUR.
shoop
GRRR
CRUNCH!
BULBASAUR!

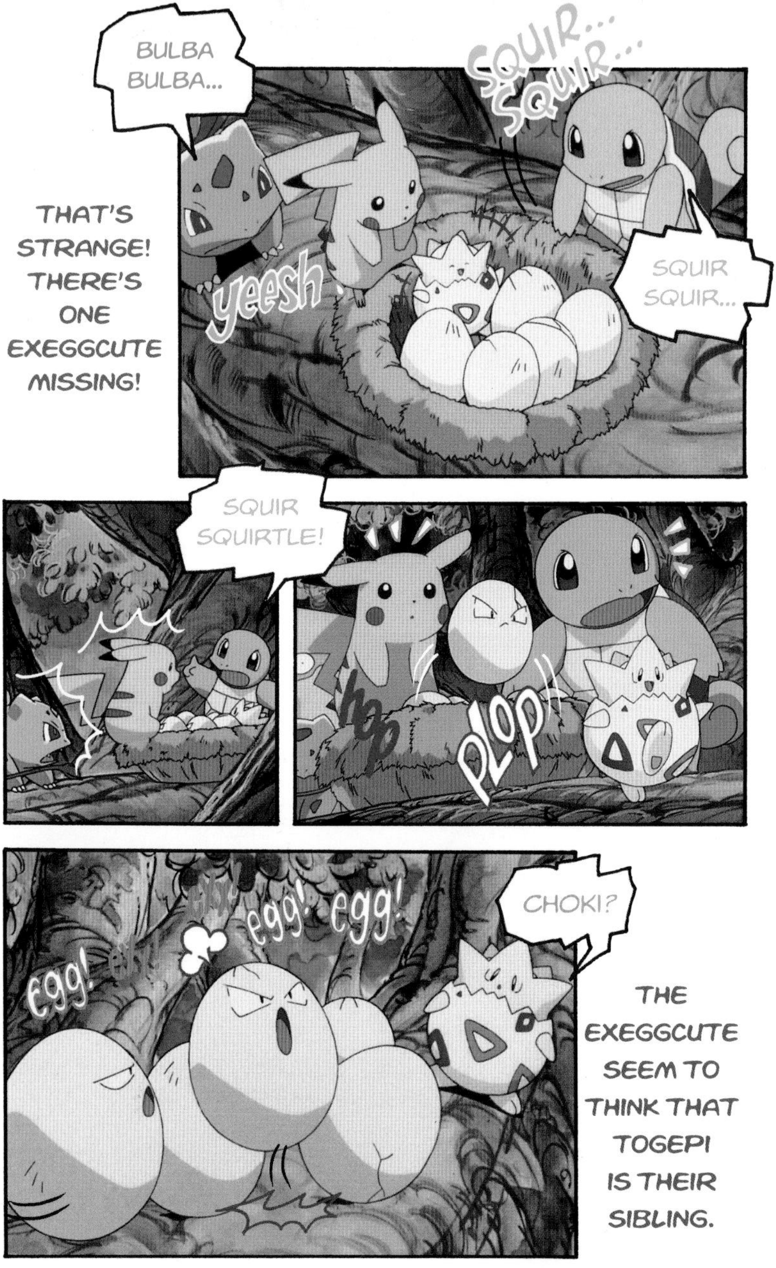

BULBA BULBA...
SQUIR... SQUIR...
THAT'S STRANGE! THERE'S ONE EXEGGCUTE MISSING!
yeesh
SQUIR SQUIR...
SQUIR SQUIRTLE!
hop
PLOP
egg!
egg! egg!
CHOKI?
THE EXEGGCUTE SEEM TO THINK THAT TOGEPI IS THEIR SIBLING.

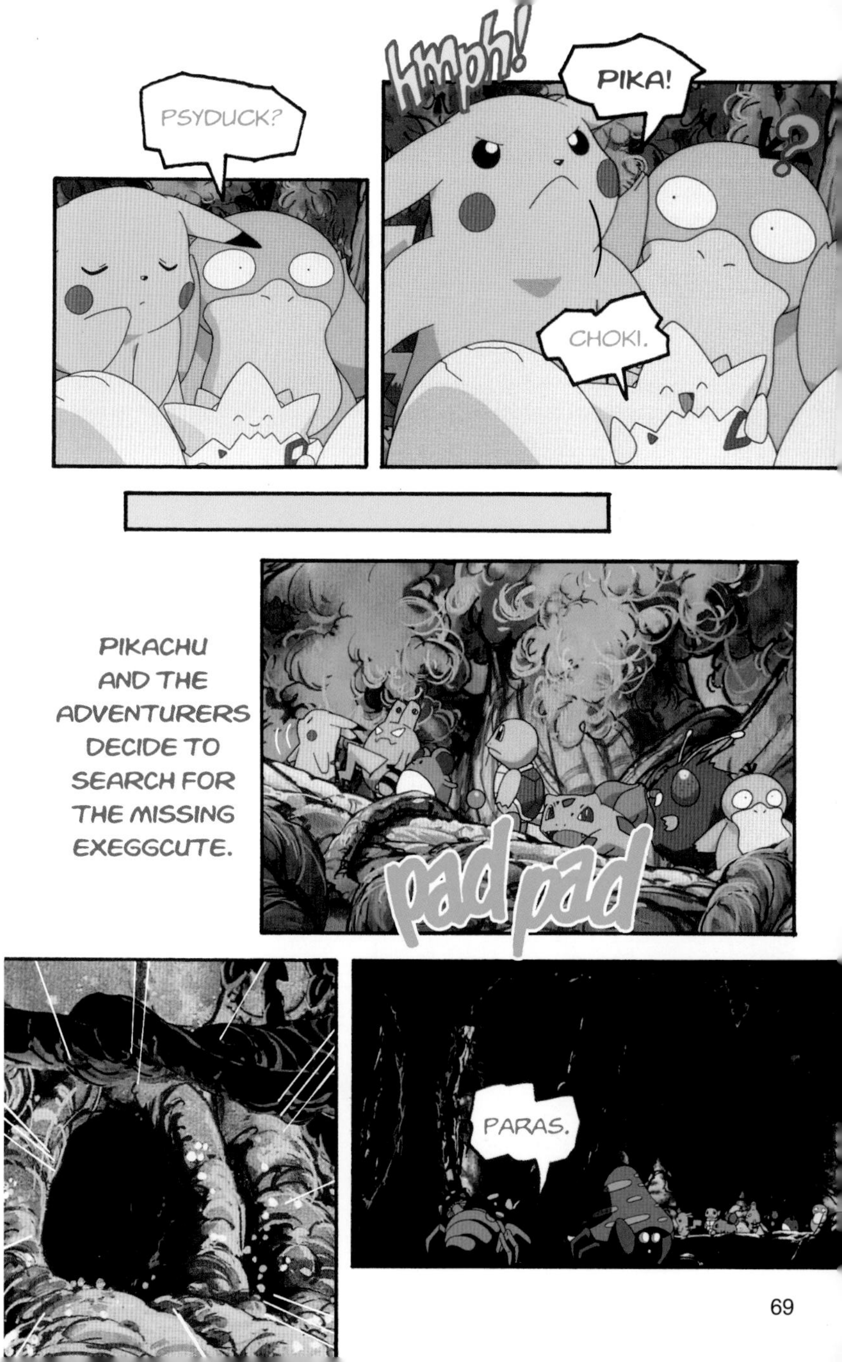
PSYDUCK?
hmph!
PIKA!
CHOKI.
PIKACHU AND THE ADVENTURERS DECIDE TO SEARCH FOR THE MISSING EXEGGCUTE.
pad pad
PARAS.

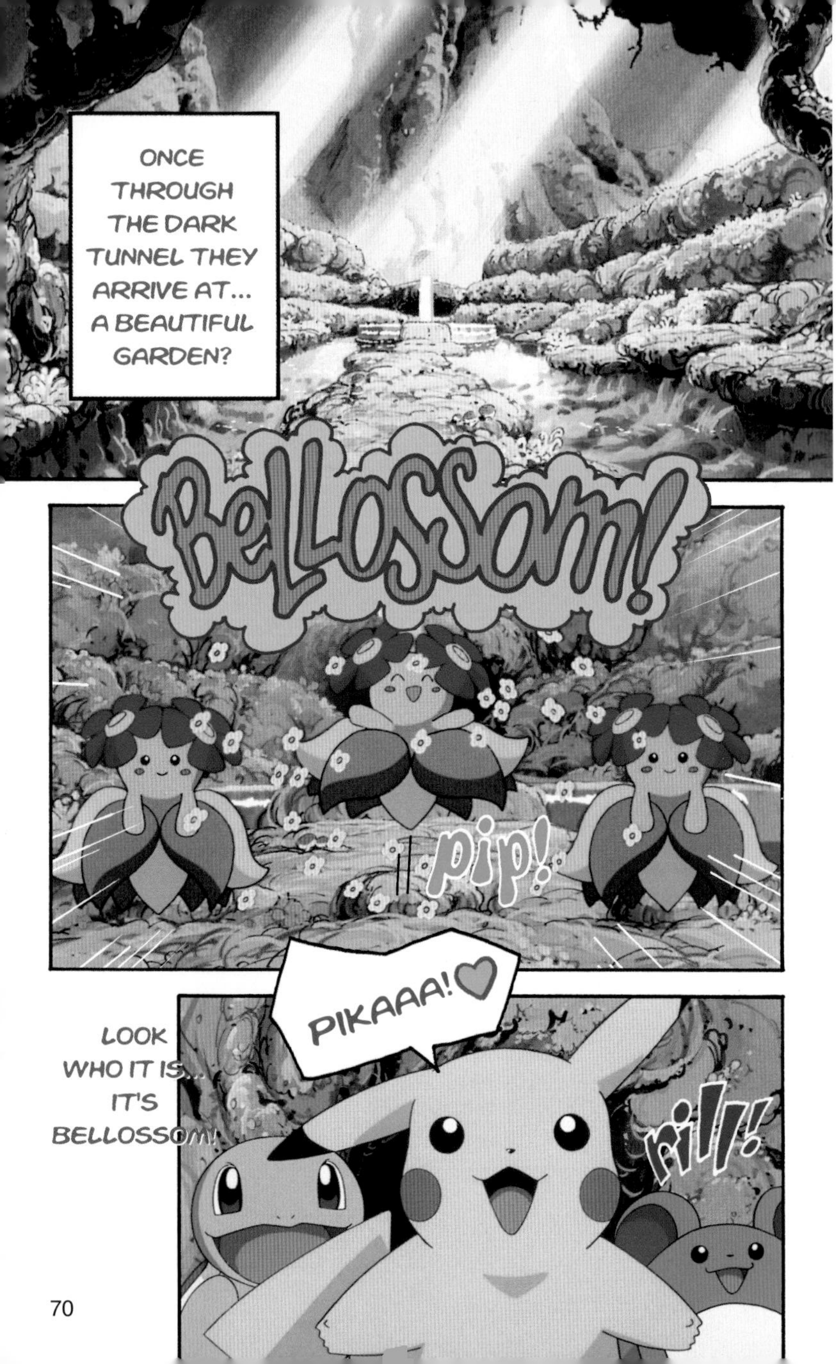
ONCE THROUGH THE DARK TUNNEL THEY ARRIVE AT... A BEAUTIFUL GARDEN?
BELLOSSOM!
PIP!
PIKAAA!♥
LOOK WHO IT IS... IT'S BELLOSSOM!
RILL!

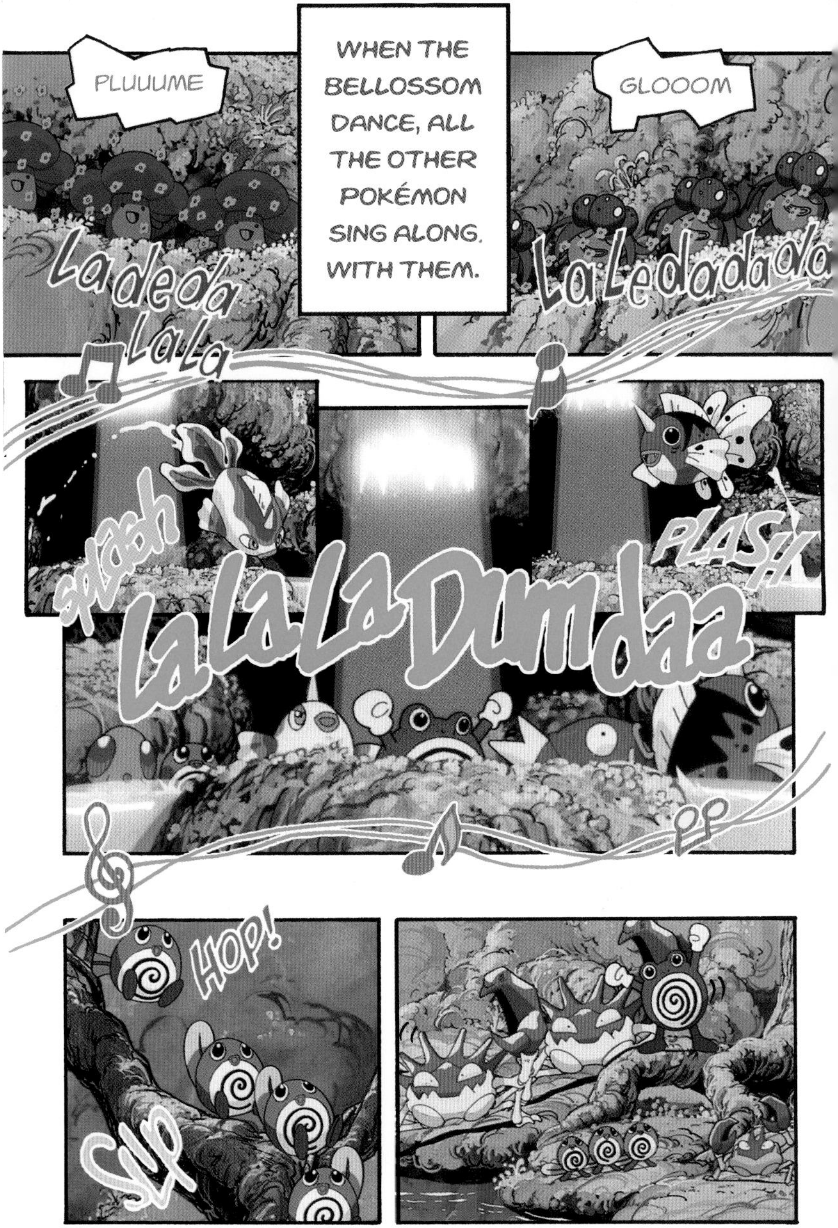
WHEN THE BELLOSSOM DANCE, ALL THE OTHER POKÉMON SING ALONG WITH THEM.
PLUUUME
La de da La La
GLOOOM
La Le da da da
splash
PLASH
La La La Dum daa
HOP!
SLIP

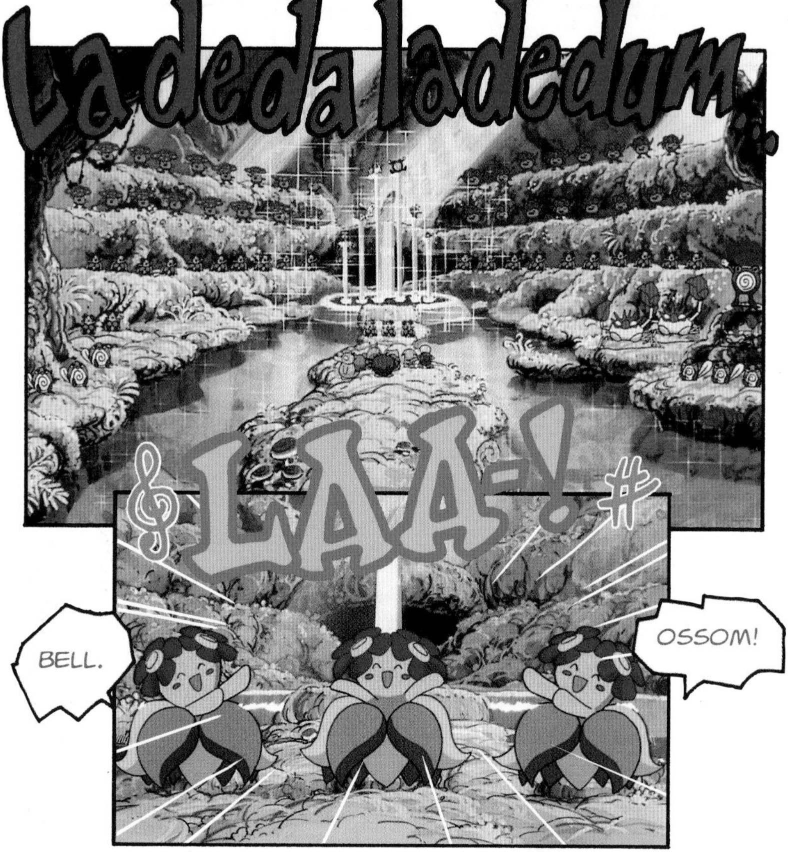
La deda ladedum...
LAA-!
BELL.
OSSOM!

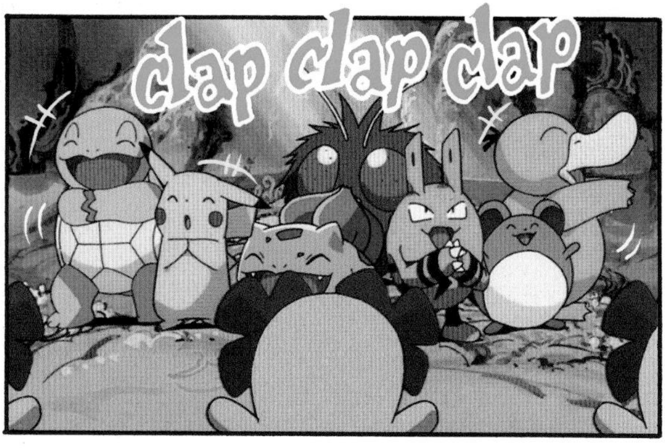
clap clap clap

WHAT A WONDERFUL DANCE...TOO BAD THEY CAN'T STAY.

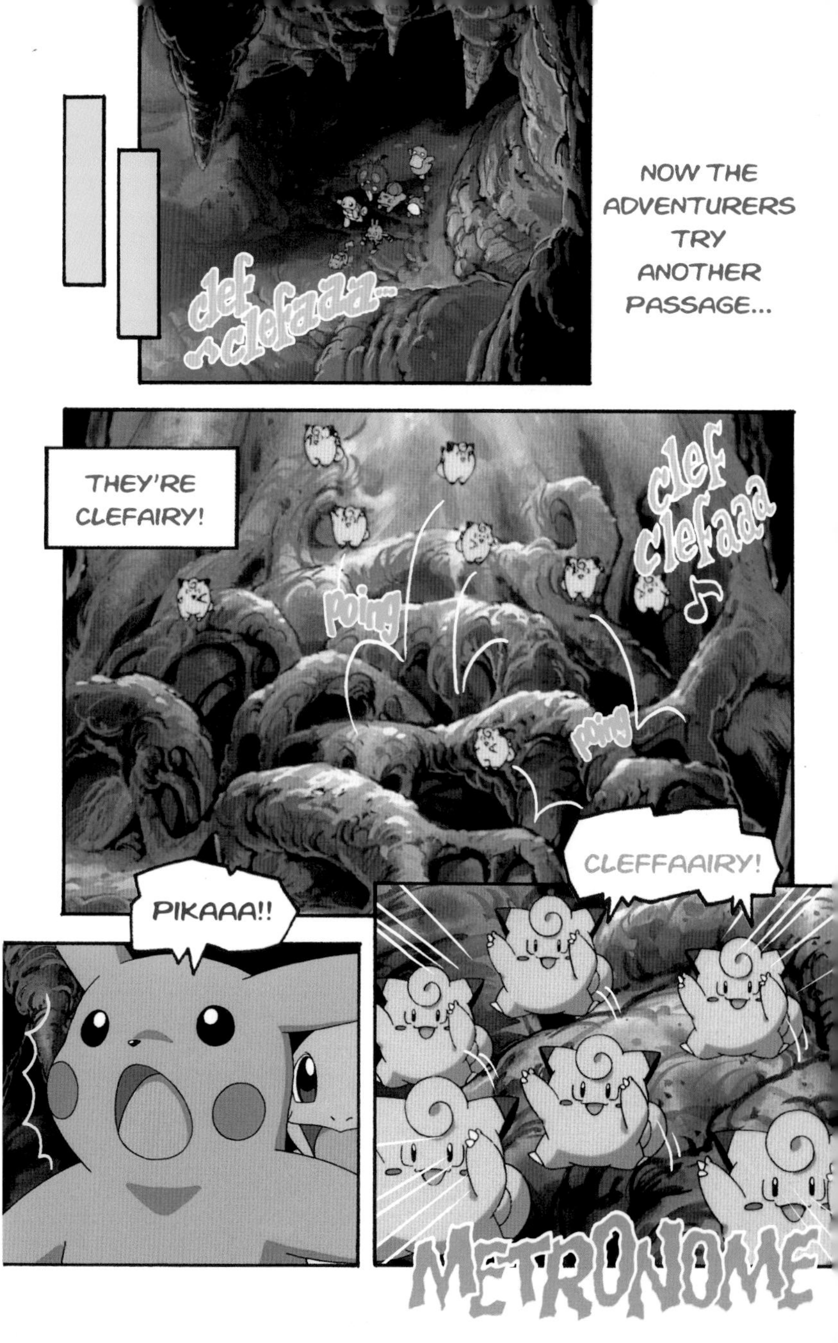
clef ~clefaaa...
NOW THE ADVENTURERS TRY ANOTHER PASSAGE...
THEY'RE CLEFAIRY!
clef clefaaa
poing
poing
CLEFFAAIRY!
PIKAAA!!
METRONOME

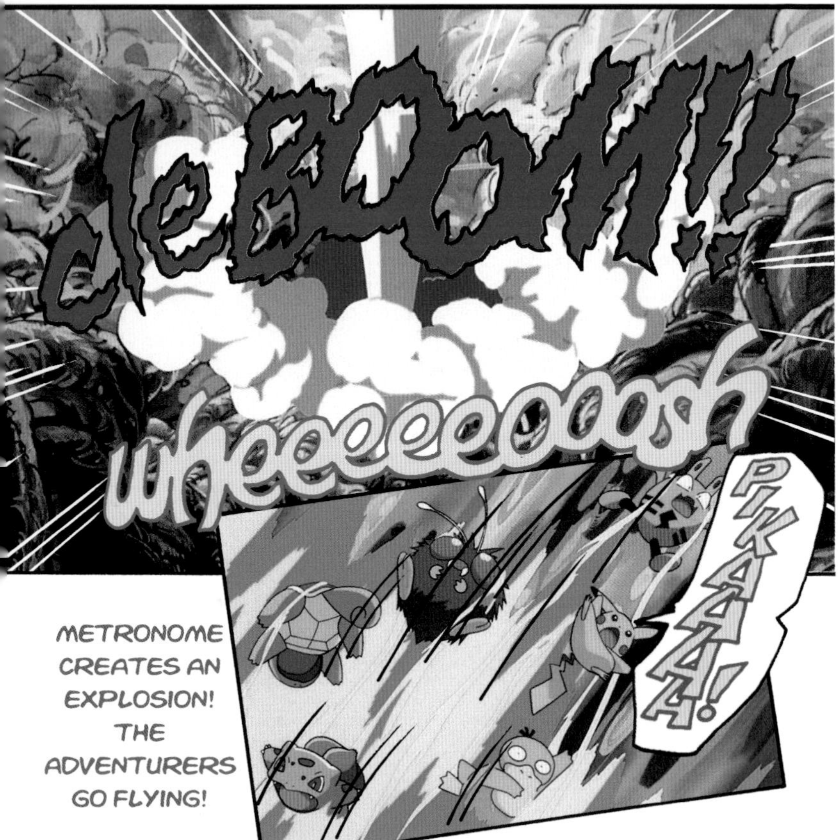
cleBOOM!!
wheeeeeooosh
PIKAAAA!
METRONOME CREATES AN EXPLOSION! THE ADVENTURERS GO FLYING!

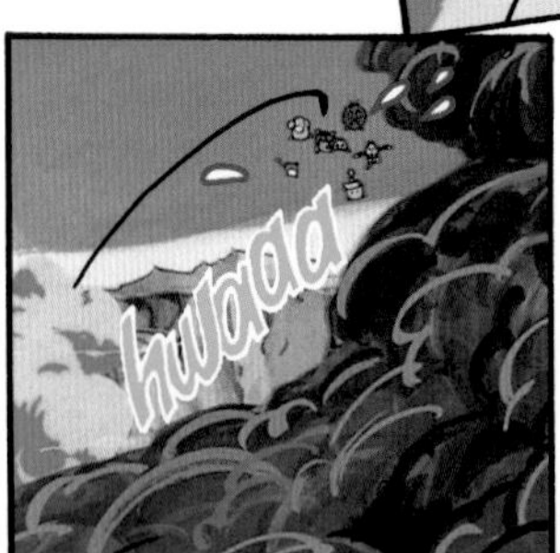
hwaaa

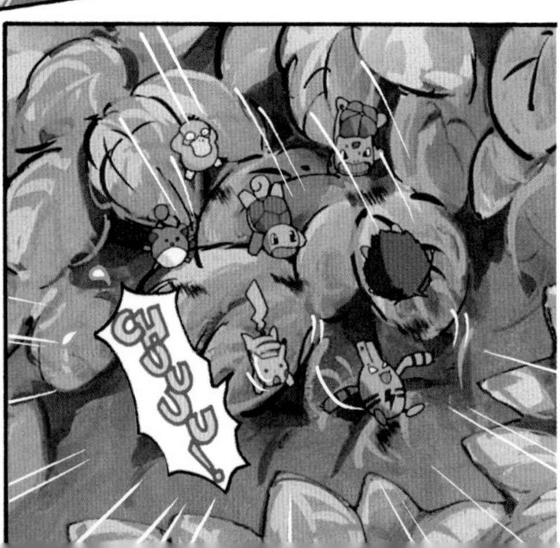
chuuuu!

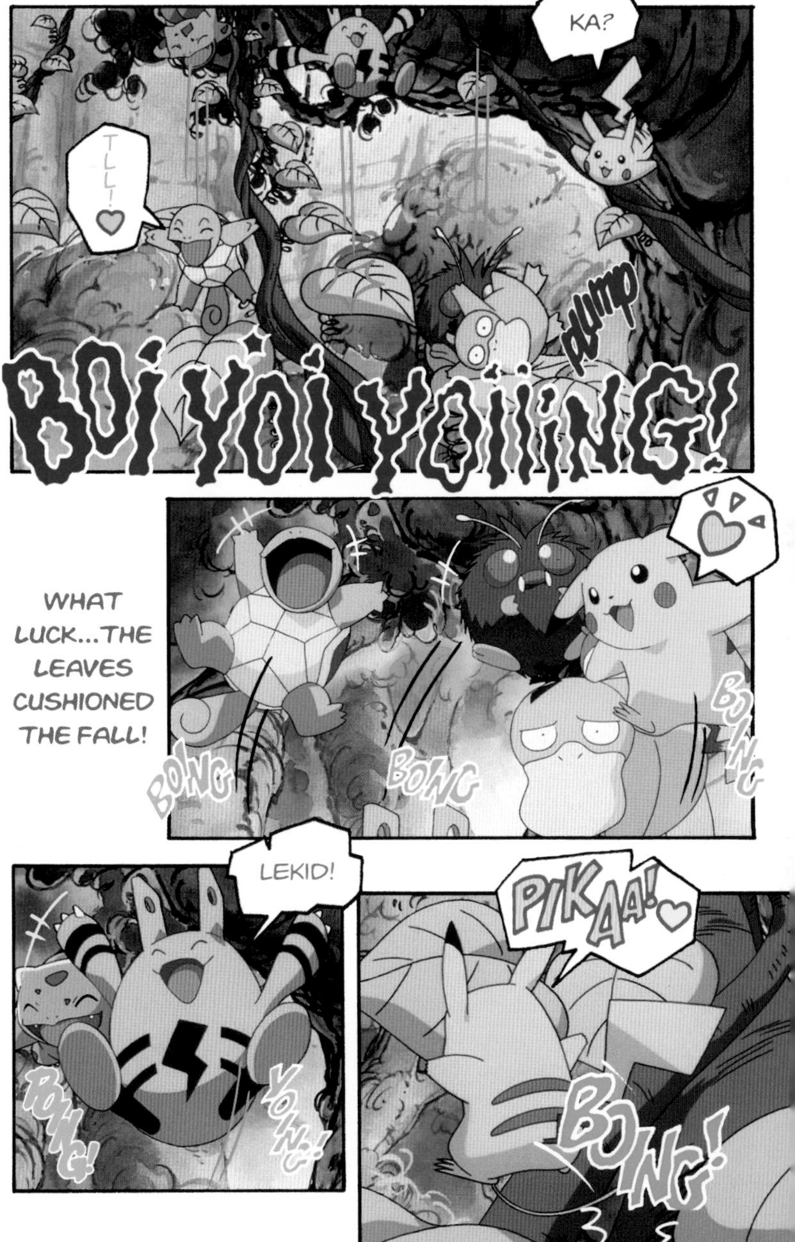
KA?
TLL!
plump
BOI YOI YOIIING!
WHAT LUCK...THE LEAVES CUSHIONED THE FALL!
BOING
BOING
BOING
LEKID!
BOING!
YOING!
PIKAA!
BOING!

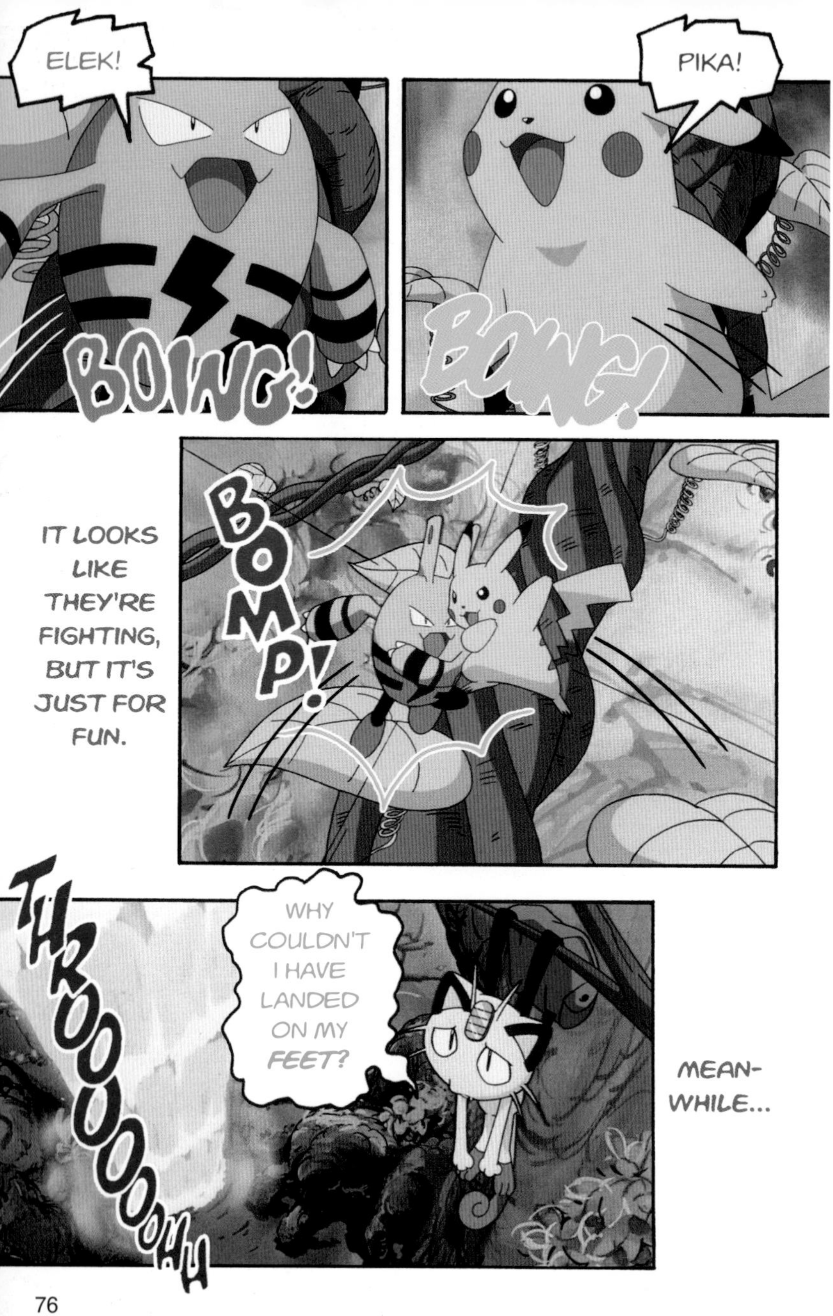
ELEK!
BOING!
PIKA!
BOING!
IT LOOKS LIKE THEY'RE FIGHTING, BUT IT'S JUST FOR FUN.
BOMP!
THROOOOOOOOHH
WHY COULDN'T I HAVE LANDED ON MY *FEET*?
MEAN-WHILE...

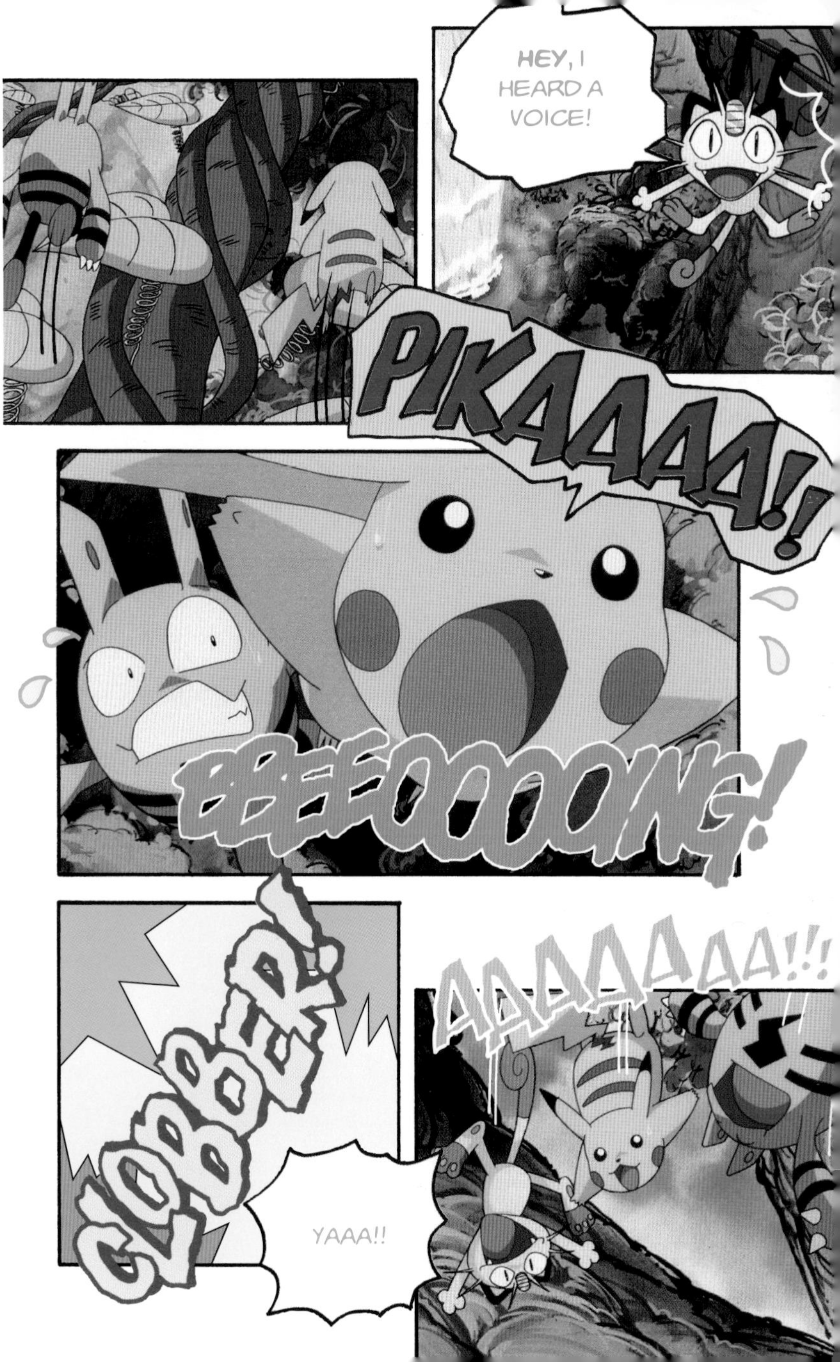
HEY, I HEARD A VOICE!
PIKAAAA!!
BBEEOOOOING!
GLOBBER!
YAAA!!
AAAAAAA!!!

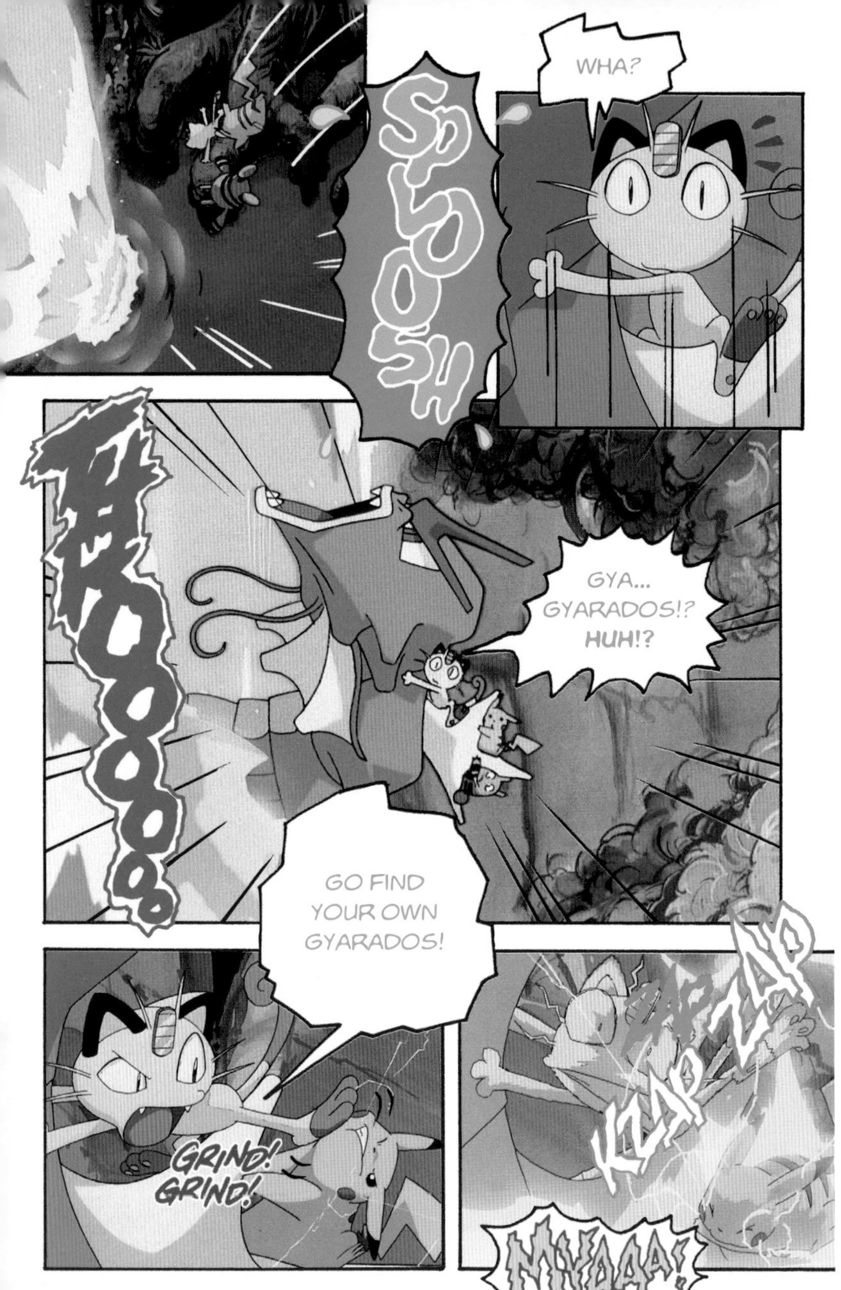
SPLOOSH
WHA?
FWOOOOOO
GYA... GYARADOS!? HUH!?
GO FIND YOUR OWN GYARADOS!
GRIND! GRIND!
ZAP ZAP
KLAP
MYAAA!

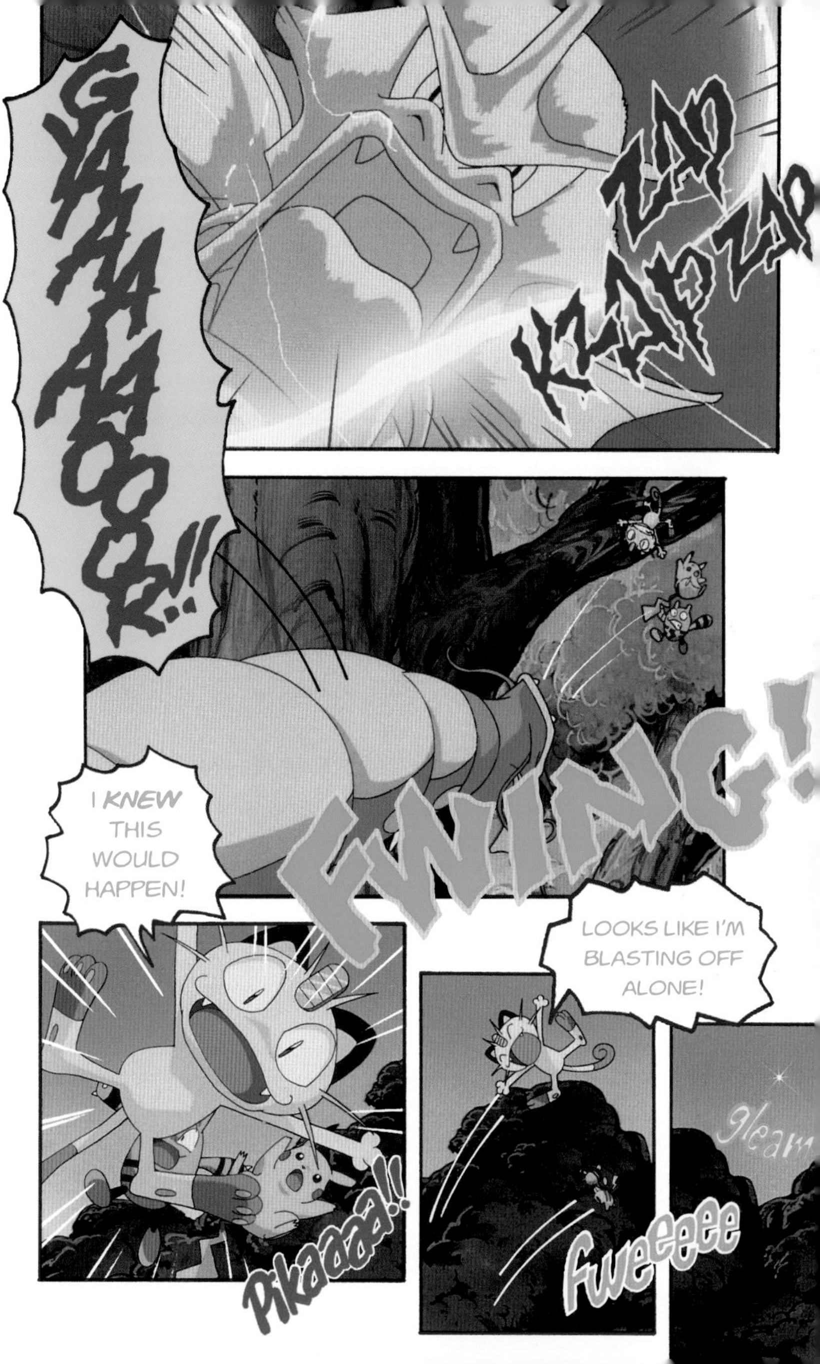
ZAP
KZZAP ZAP
GYAAAAOOOR!!
FWING!!
I KNEW THIS WOULD HAPPEN!
LOOKS LIKE I'M BLASTING OFF ALONE!
Pikaaaa!!
Fweeeee
gleam

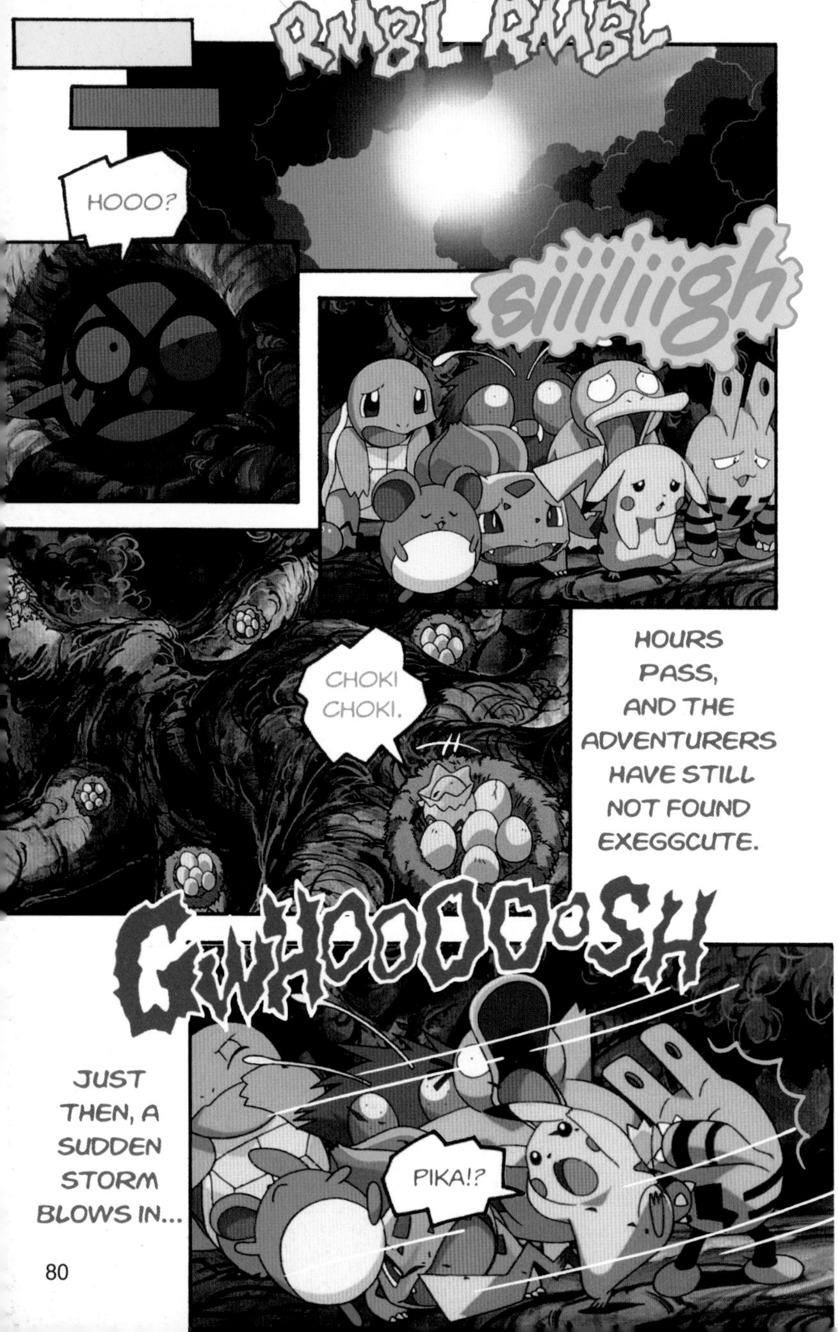
RMBL RMBL
HOOO?
siiiiiigh
HOURS PASS, AND THE ADVENTURERS HAVE STILL NOT FOUND EXEGGCUTE.
CHOKI CHOKI.
GWHOOOOOSH
JUST THEN, A SUDDEN STORM BLOWS IN...
PIKA!?

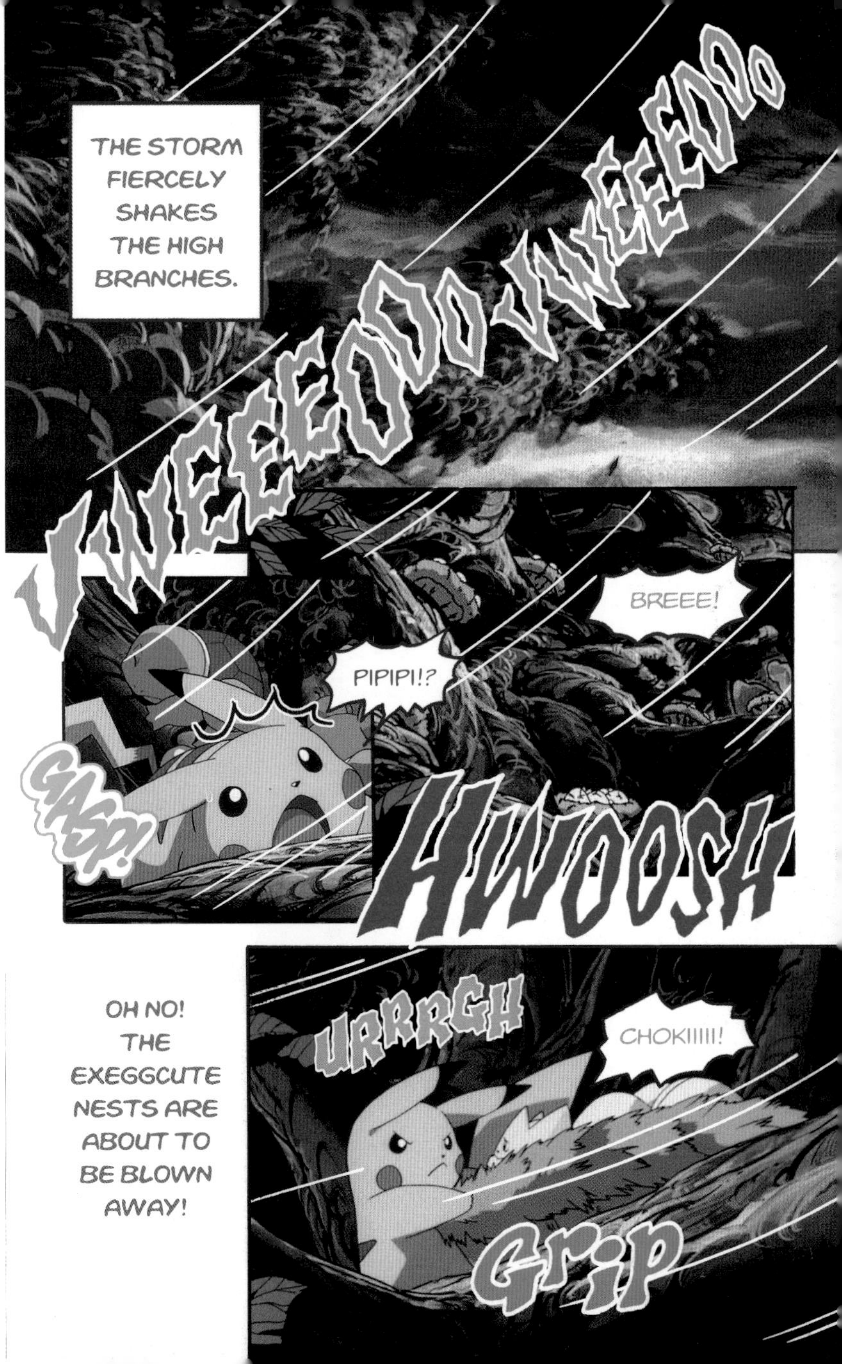
THE STORM FIERCELY SHAKES THE HIGH BRANCHES.
VWEEEOOO VWEEOOO
BREEE!
PIPIPI!?
GASP!
HWOOSH
OH NO! THE EXEGGCUTE NESTS ARE ABOUT TO BE BLOWN AWAY!
URRRGH
CHOKIIIII!
Grip

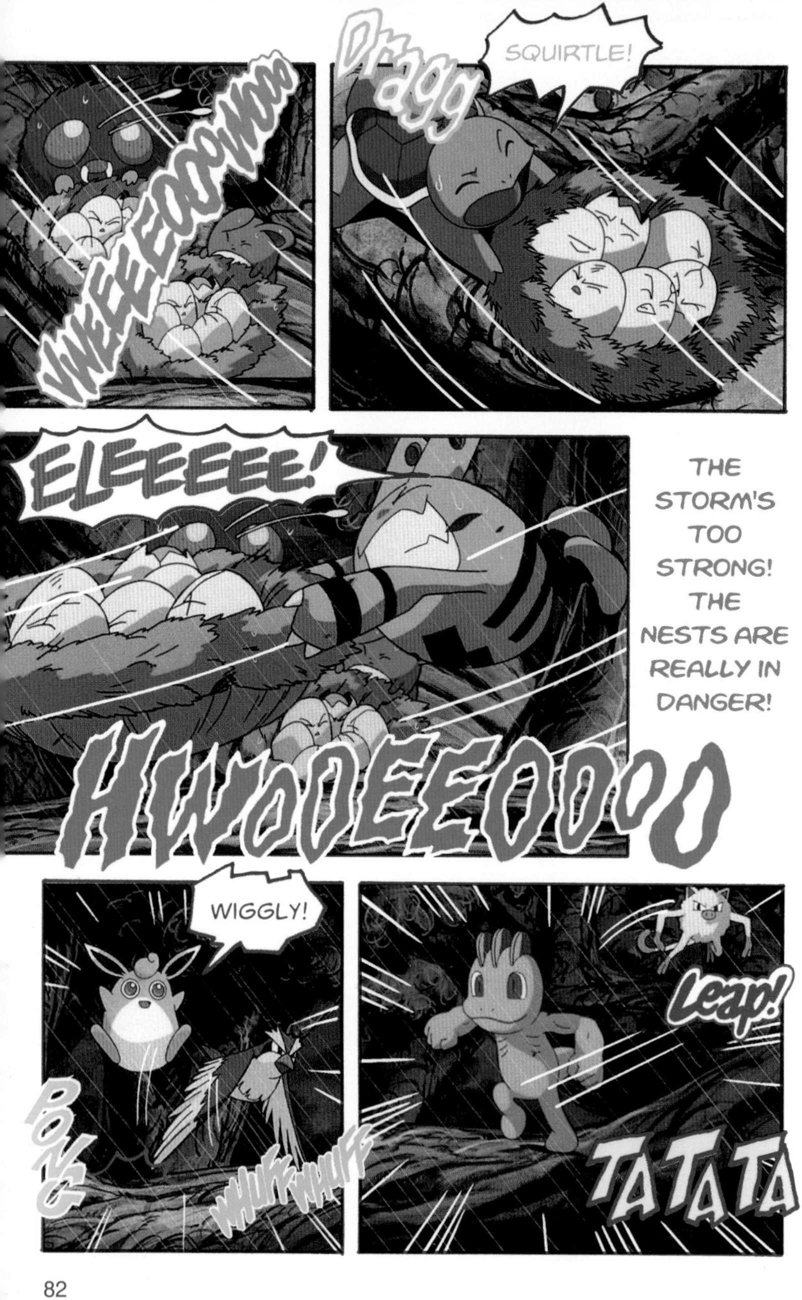

VWEEEEOOOWOOO
Dragg
SQUIRTLE!
ELEEEEE!
THE STORM'S TOO STRONG! THE NESTS ARE REALLY IN DANGER!
HWOOEEEOOOO
WIGGLY!
PONG
WHUFF WHUFF
Leap!
TATATA

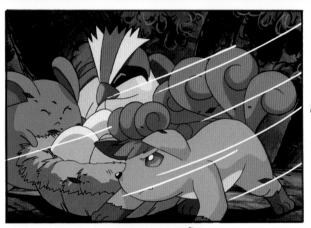

THE
WILD
POKÉMON
HAVE
COME TO
HELP!

HOWEVER,
THE STORM
ONLY GETS
STRONGER...

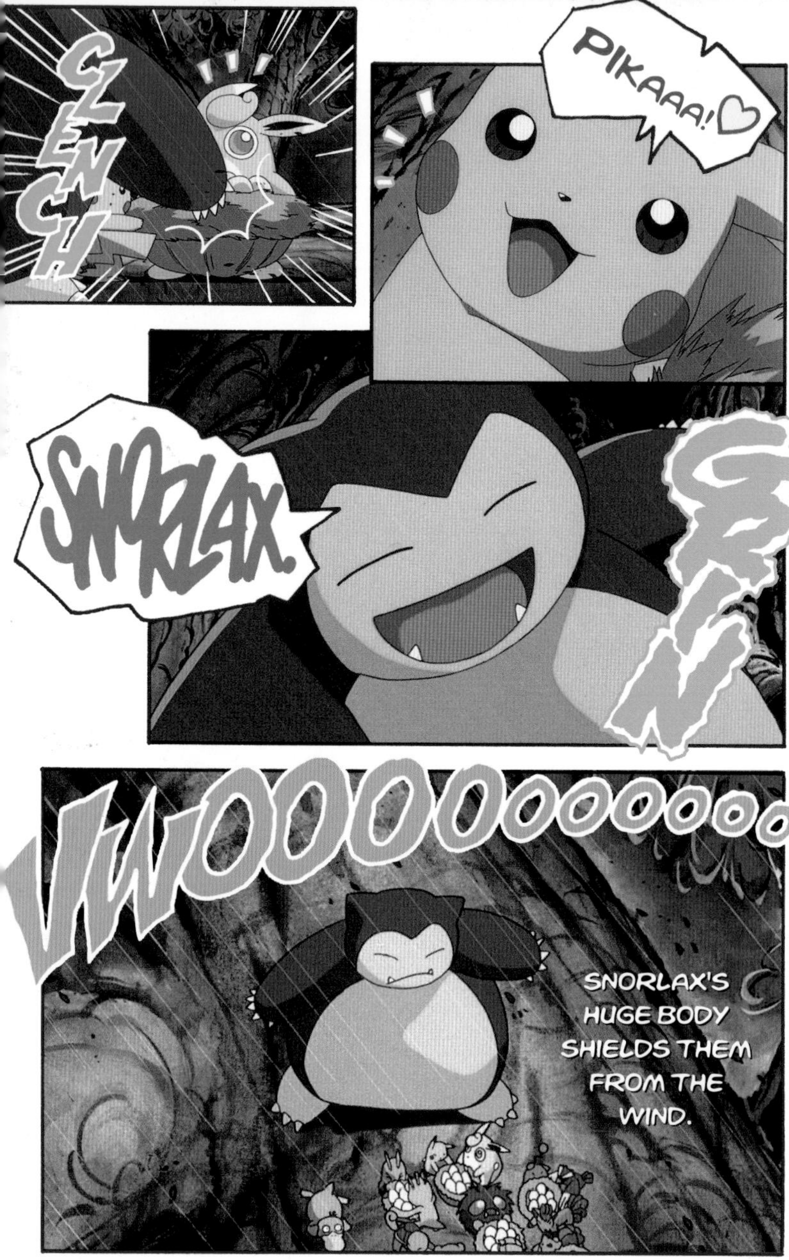
CLENCH
PIKAAA!♡
SNORLAX.
GRIN
VWOOOOOOOOOO
SNORLAX'S HUGE BODY SHIELDS THEM FROM THE WIND.

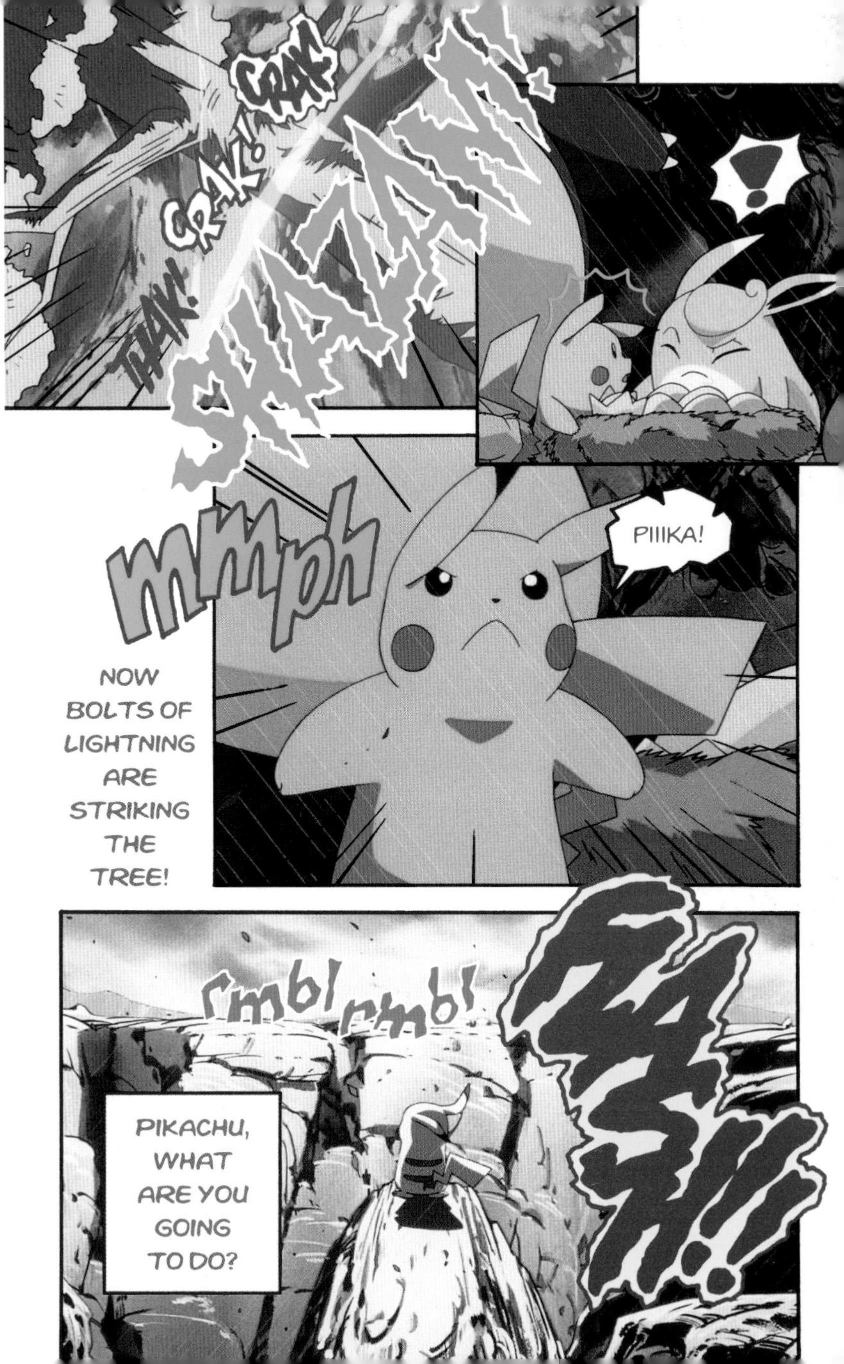
CRAK!
CRAK!
THAK!
SKAZAM!
!
mmph
PIIIKA!
NOW BOLTS OF LIGHTNING ARE STRIKING THE TREE!
rmbl rmbl
PIKACHU, WHAT ARE YOU GOING TO DO?
ZAAP!!

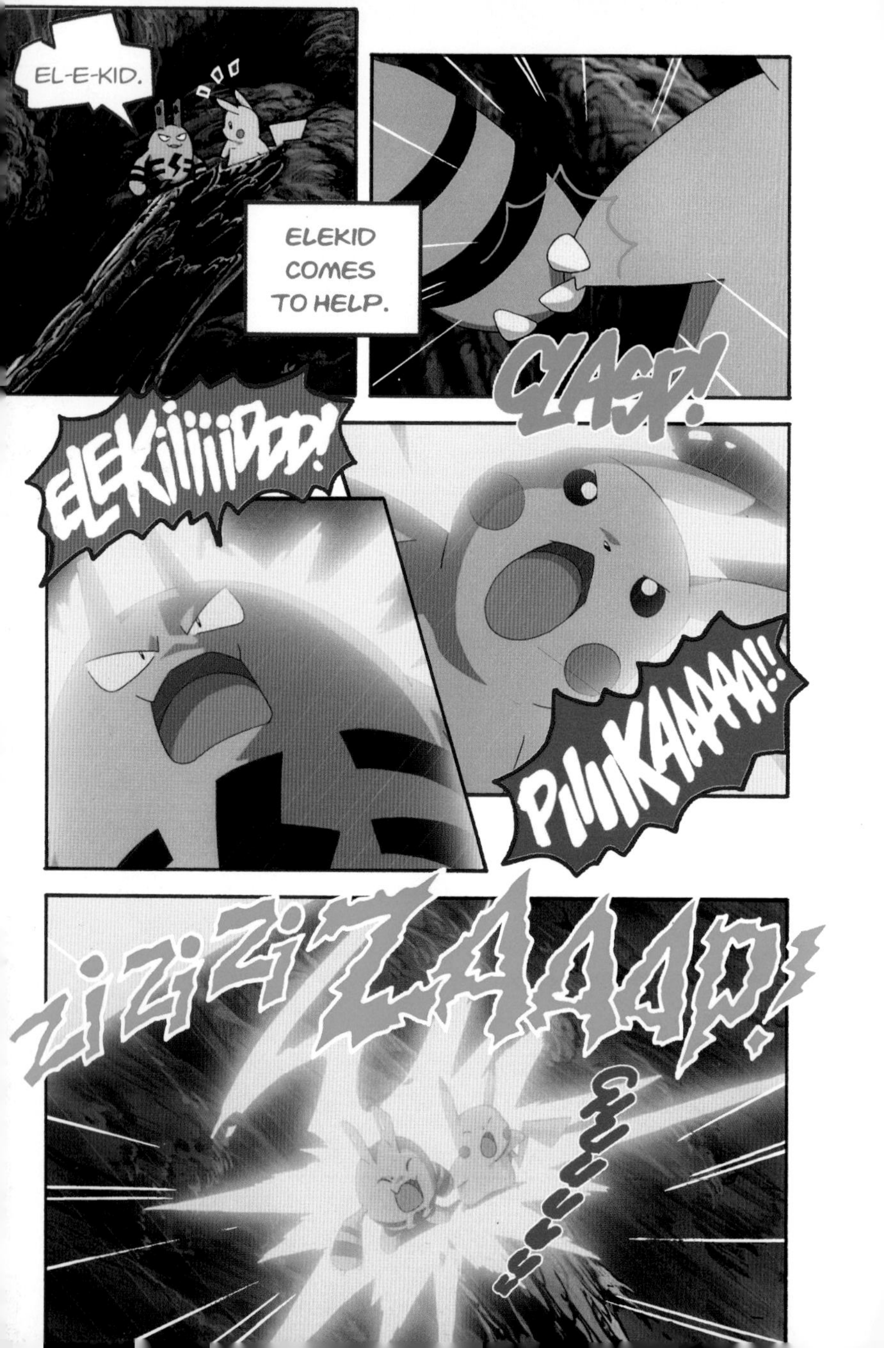
EL-E-KID.
ELEKID COMES TO HELP.
CLASP!
ELEKIIIIIDDD!
PIIIIKAAAAA!!
ZIZIZIZAAAP!

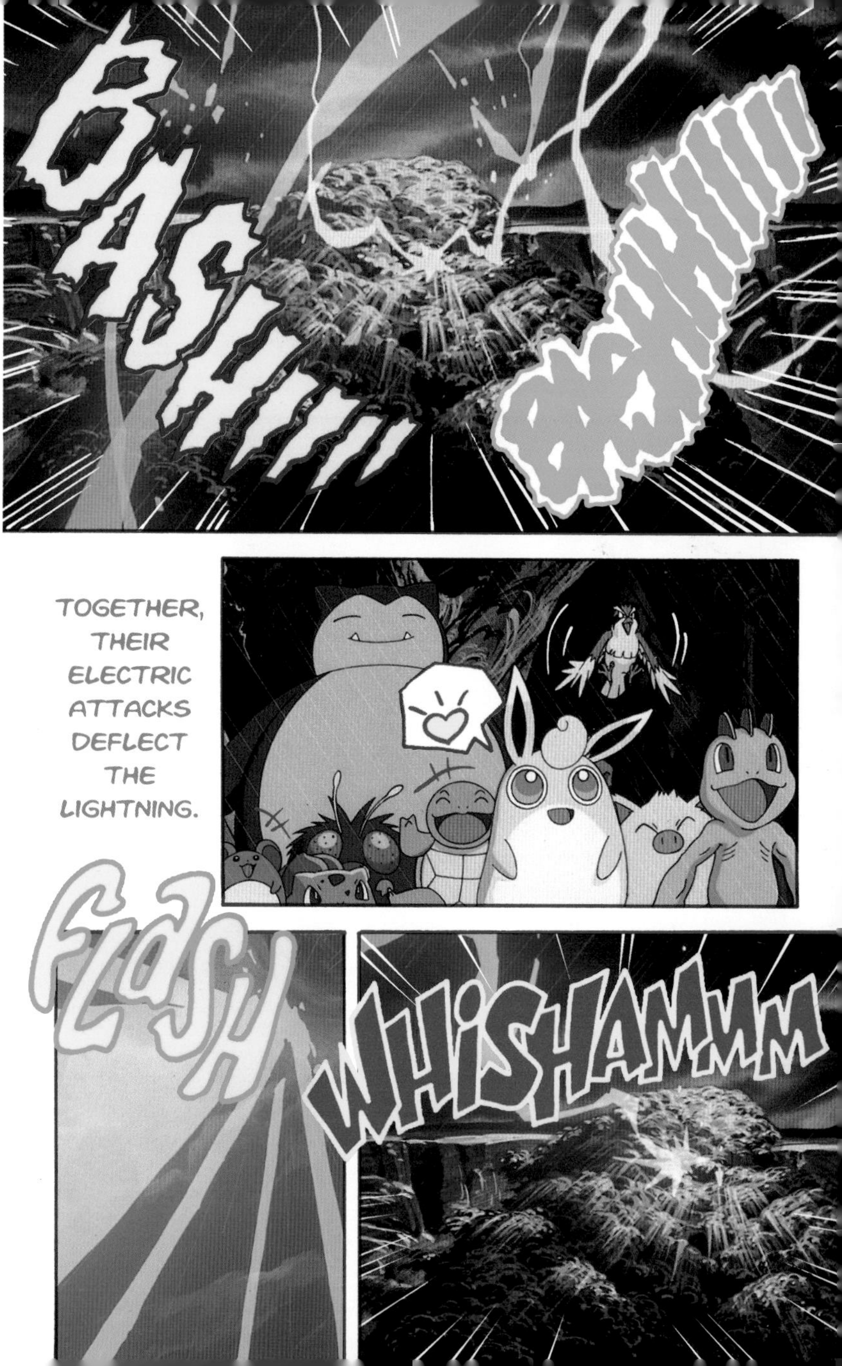
BASH!!!!
TOGETHER, THEIR ELECTRIC ATTACKS DEFLECT THE LIGHTNING.
FLASH
WHISHAMMM

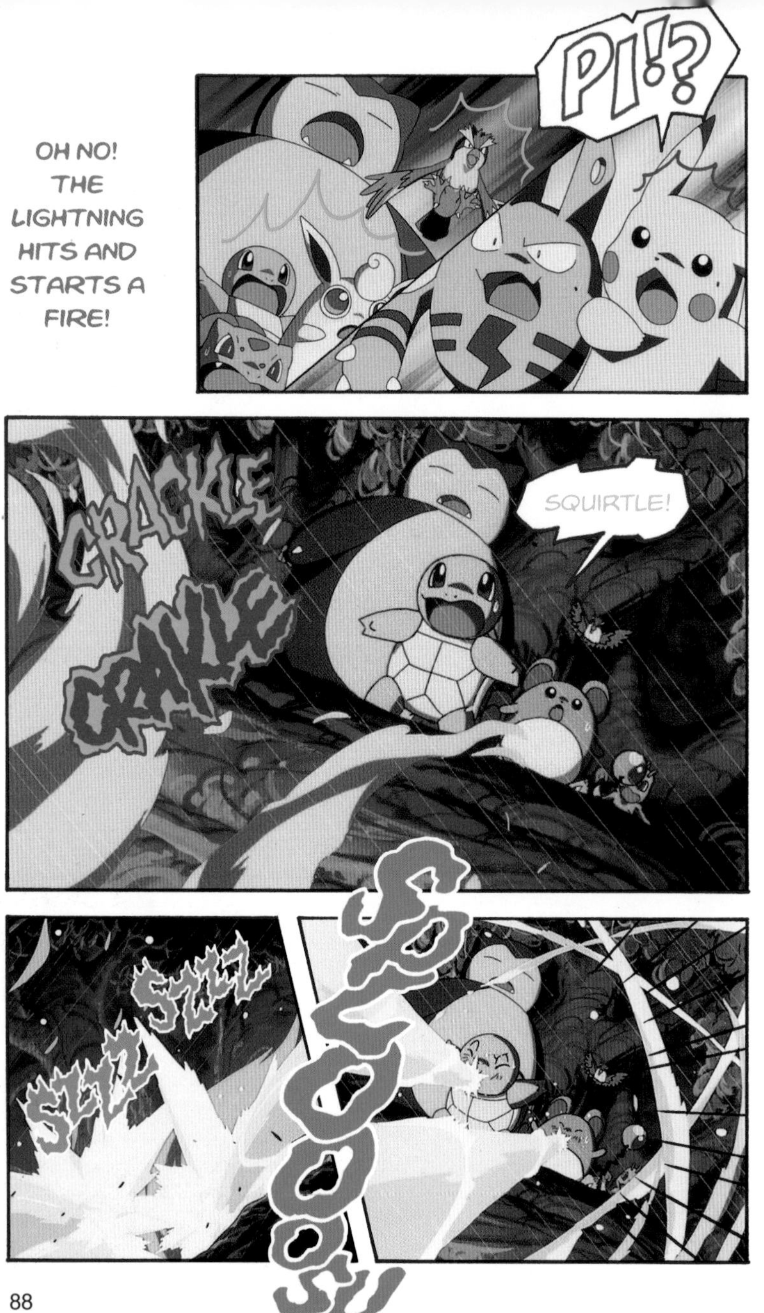
OH NO! THE LIGHTNING HITS AND STARTS A FIRE!
PI!?
CRACKLE
CRACKLE
SQUIRTLE!
SZZZ
SZZZ
SPLOOOSH

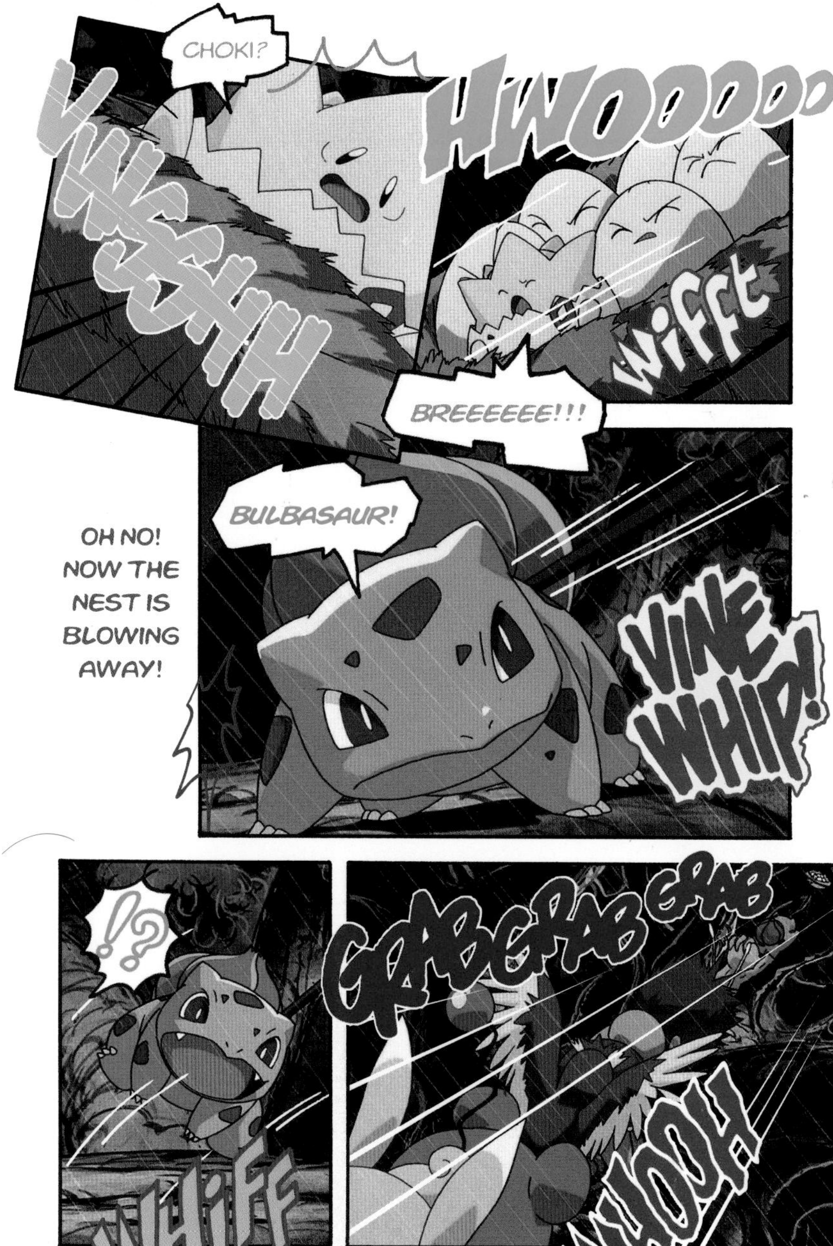
CHOKI?
wifft
BREEEEEE!!!
BULBASAUR!
OH NO! NOW THE NEST IS BLOWING AWAY!
VINE WHIP!
!?
WHIFF
GRAB GRAB GRAB
WHOOH

THE POKÉMON FORM A CHAIN, BUT THE WIND IS JUST TOO STRONG!

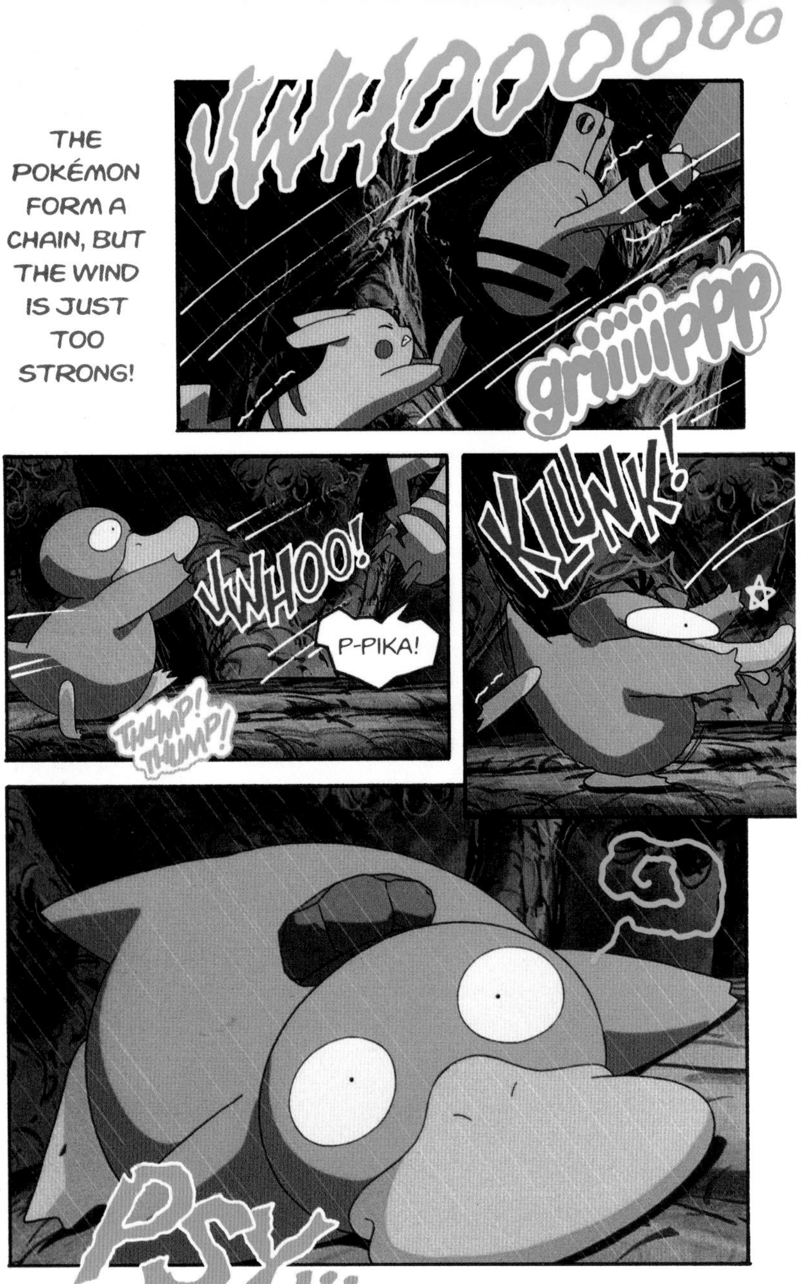
VWHOOOOOoo
griiiiippp
VWHOO!
P-PIKA!
THUMP! THUMP!
KLUNK!
PSY...

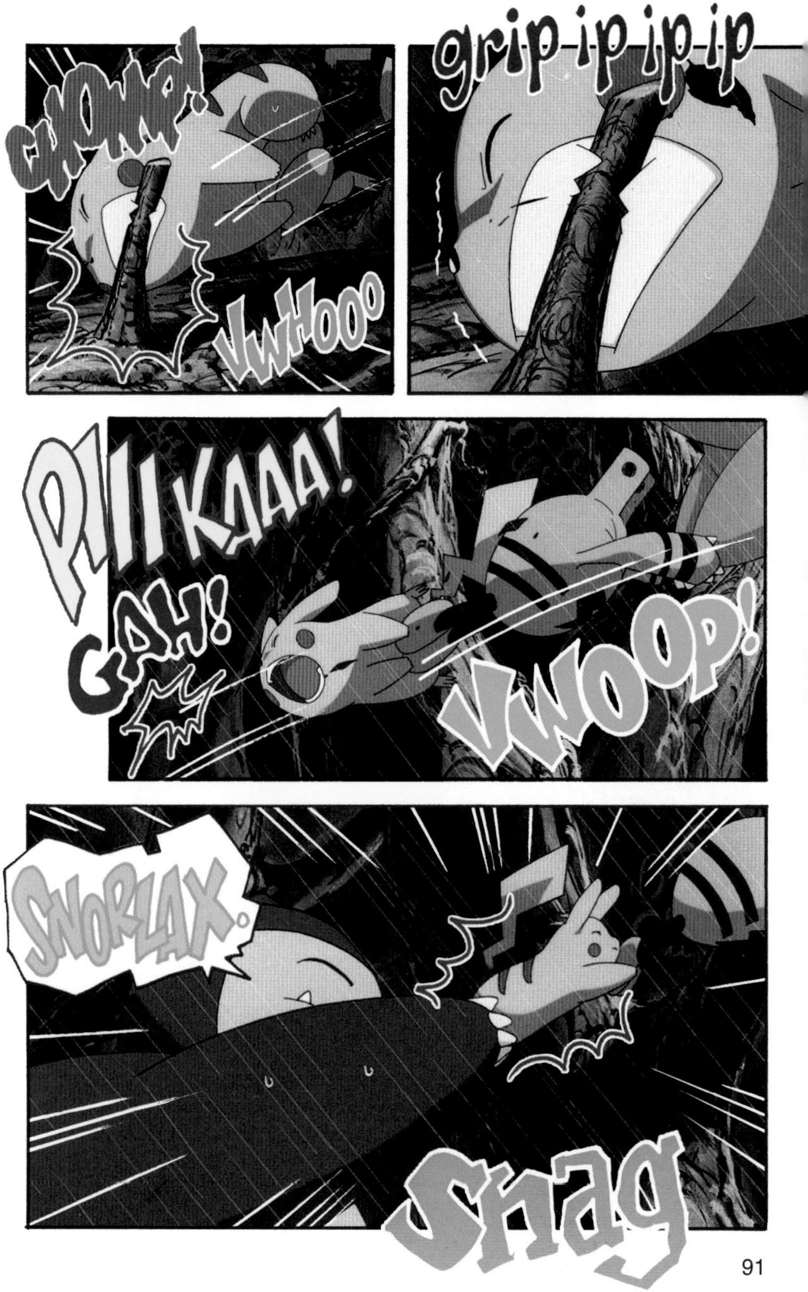
CHOMP!
VWHOOO
grip ip ip ip
PIIIKAAA!
GAH!
VWOOP!
SNORLAX.
Snag

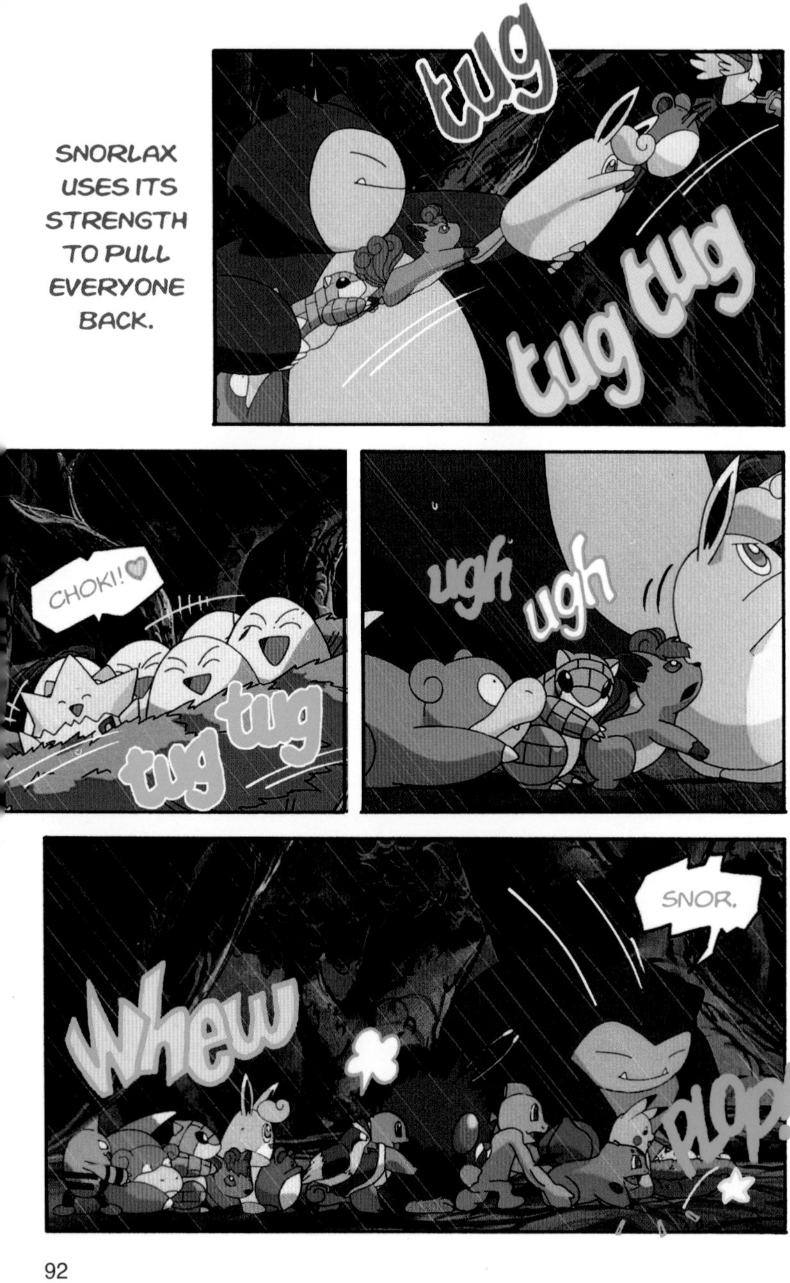
SNORLAX USES ITS STRENGTH TO PULL EVERYONE BACK.
tug
tug tug
CHOKI!♡
tug tug
ugh ugh
Whew
SNOR.
PLOP!

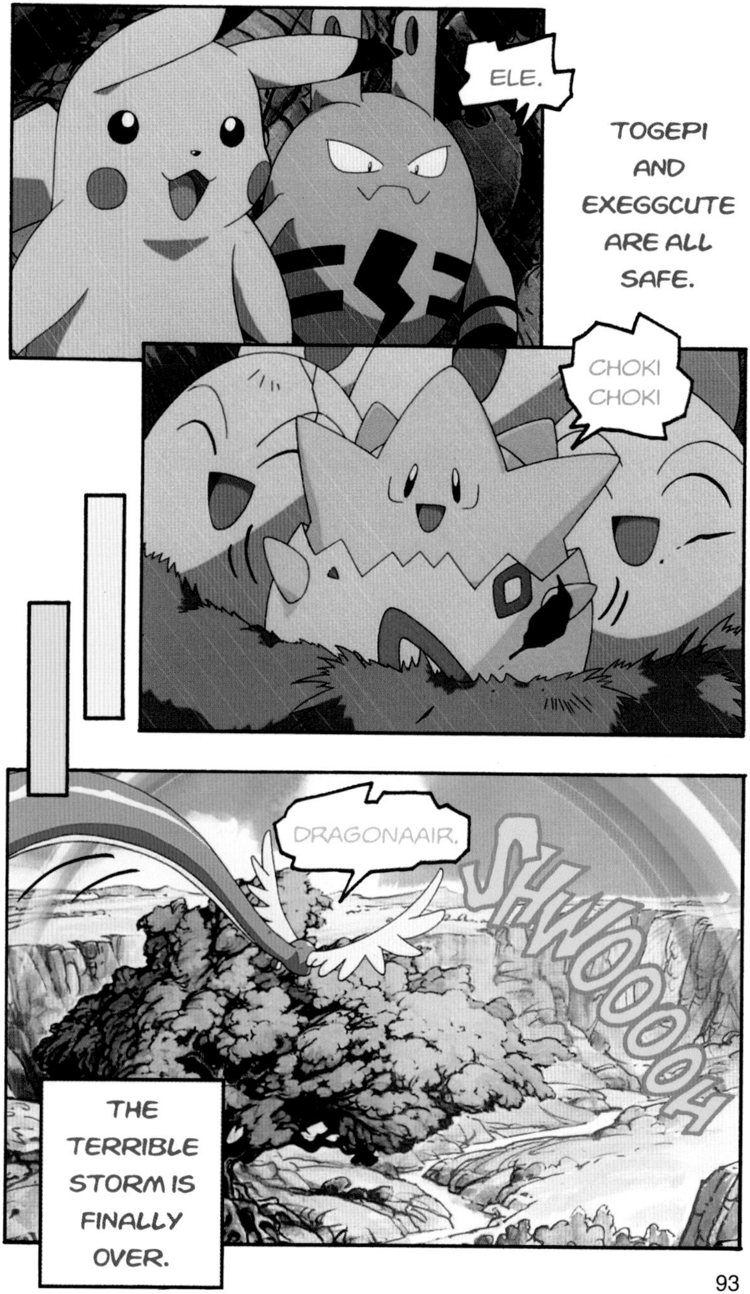
ELE.
TOGEPI AND EXEGGCUTE ARE ALL SAFE.
CHOKI CHOKI
DRAGONAAIR.
SHWOOOOH
THE TERRIBLE STORM IS FINALLY OVER.

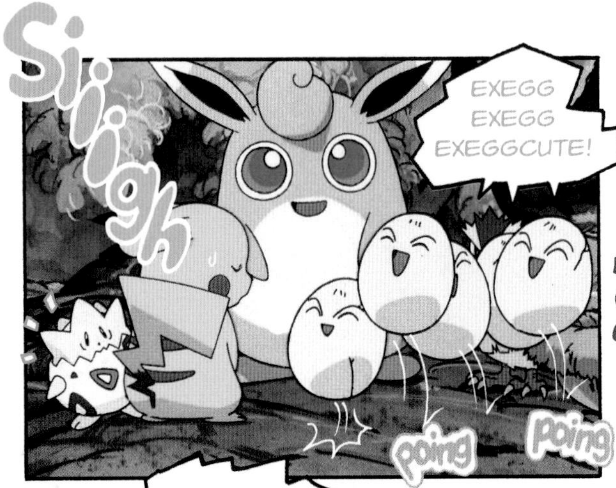
Siiiigh
EXEGG
EXEGG
EXEGGCUTE!
poing
poing

BUT WAIT...
ONE OF THE
EXEGGCUTE
IS STILL
MISSING.

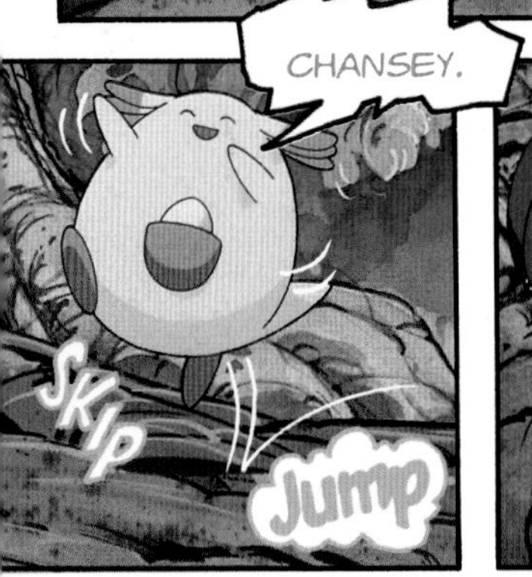
CHANSEY.
SKIP
Jump

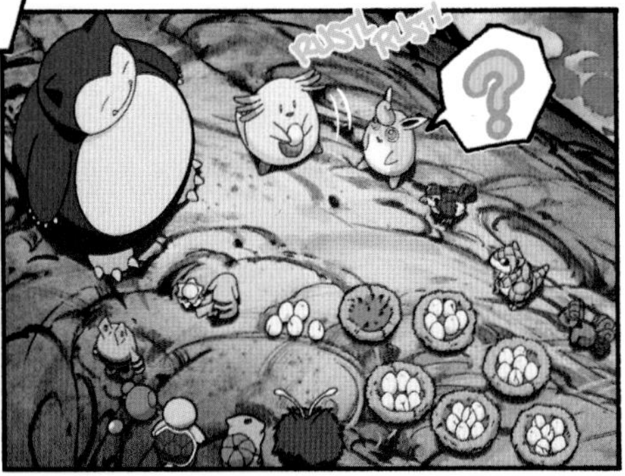
RUSTL RUSTL
?

WOW!
CHANSEY
HAD BEEN
TAKING
CARE
OF IT!

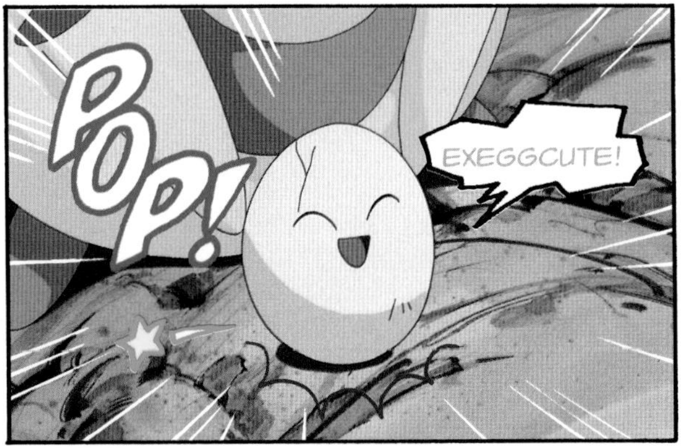
POP!
EXEGGCUTE!

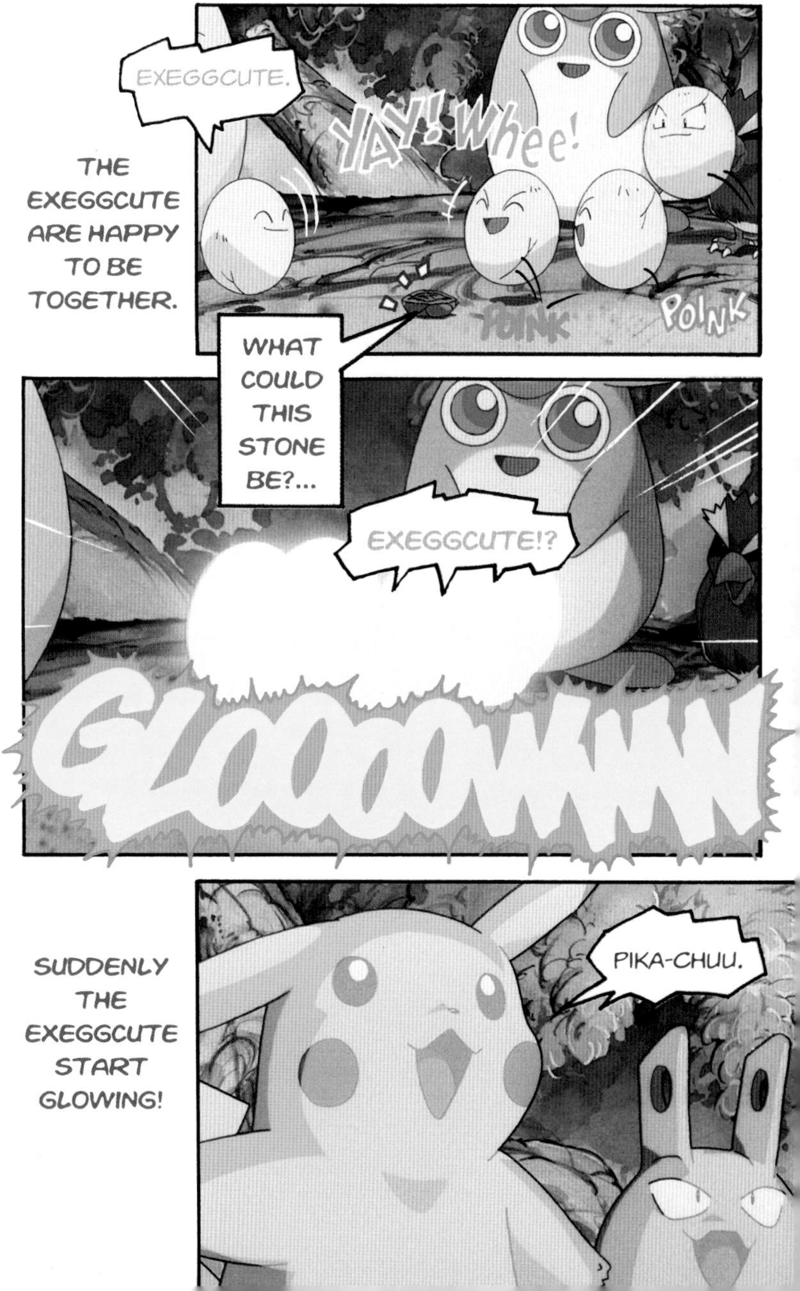
EXEGGCUTE.
YAY! Whee!
THE EXEGGCUTE ARE HAPPY TO BE TOGETHER.
POINK
POINK
WHAT COULD THIS STONE BE?...
EXEGGCUTE!?
GLOOOWWN
SUDDENLY THE EXEGGCUTE START GLOWING!
PIKA-CHUU.

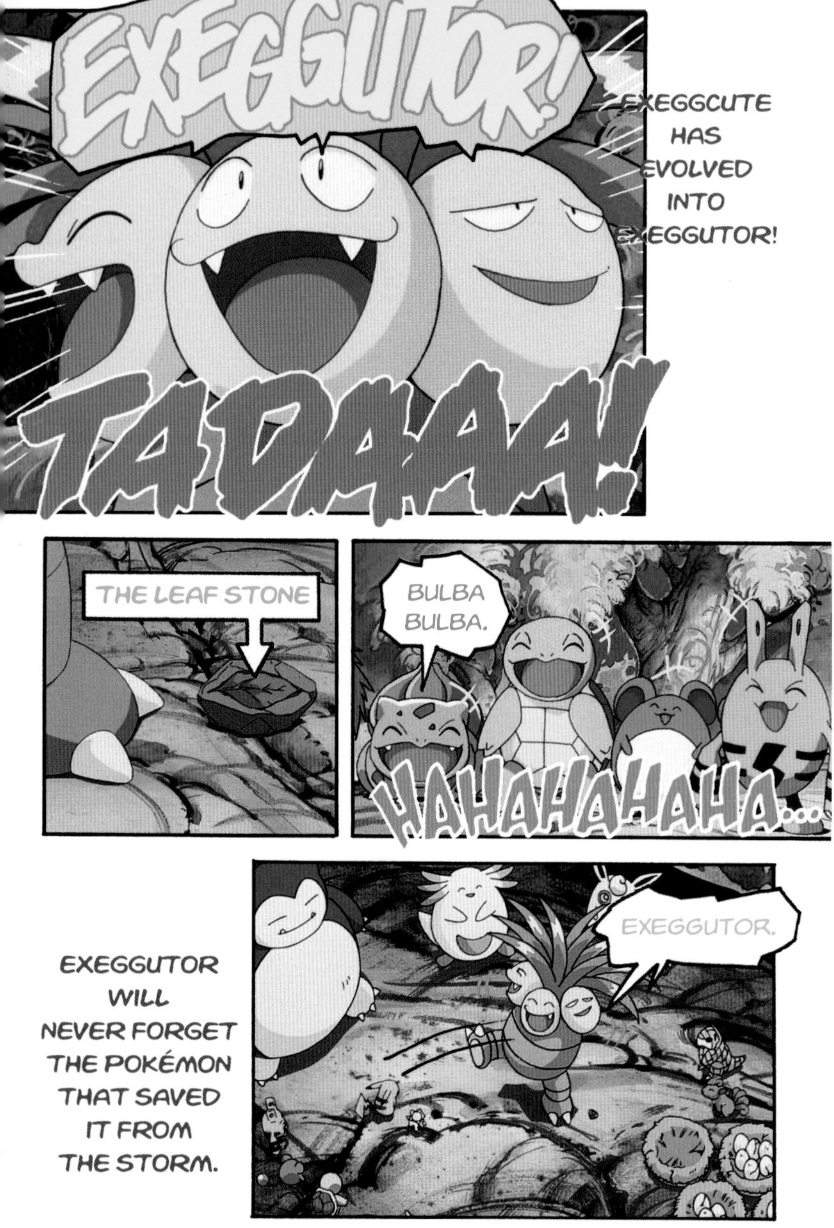
EXEGGUTOR!
EXEGGCUTE HAS EVOLVED INTO EXEGGUTOR!
TADAAA!
THE LEAF STONE
BULBA BULBA.
HAHAHAHAHAHA...
EXEGGUTOR WILL NEVER FORGET THE POKÉMON THAT SAVED IT FROM THE STORM.
EXEGGUTOR.

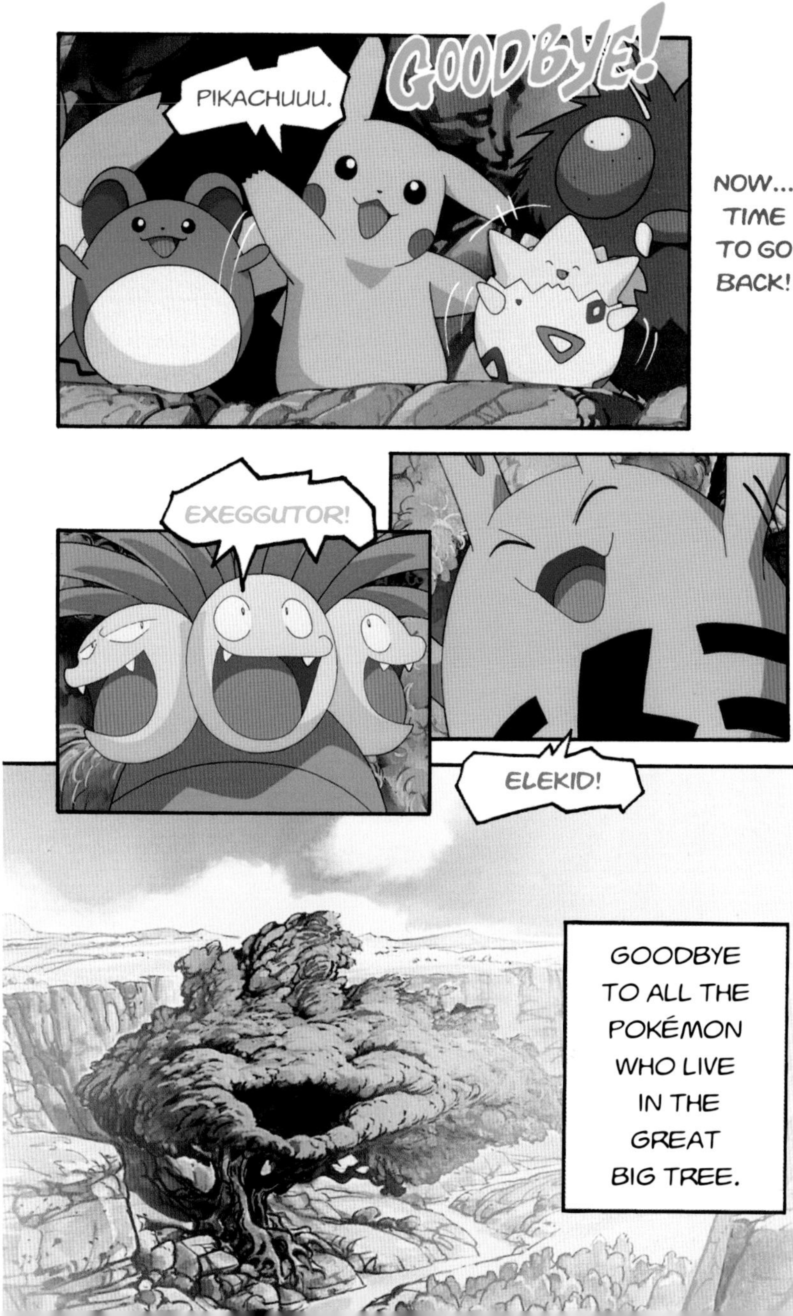
PIKACHUUU.
GOODBYE!
NOW... TIME TO GO BACK!
EXEGGUTOR!
ELEKID!
GOODBYE TO ALL THE POKÉMON WHO LIVE IN THE GREAT BIG TREE.

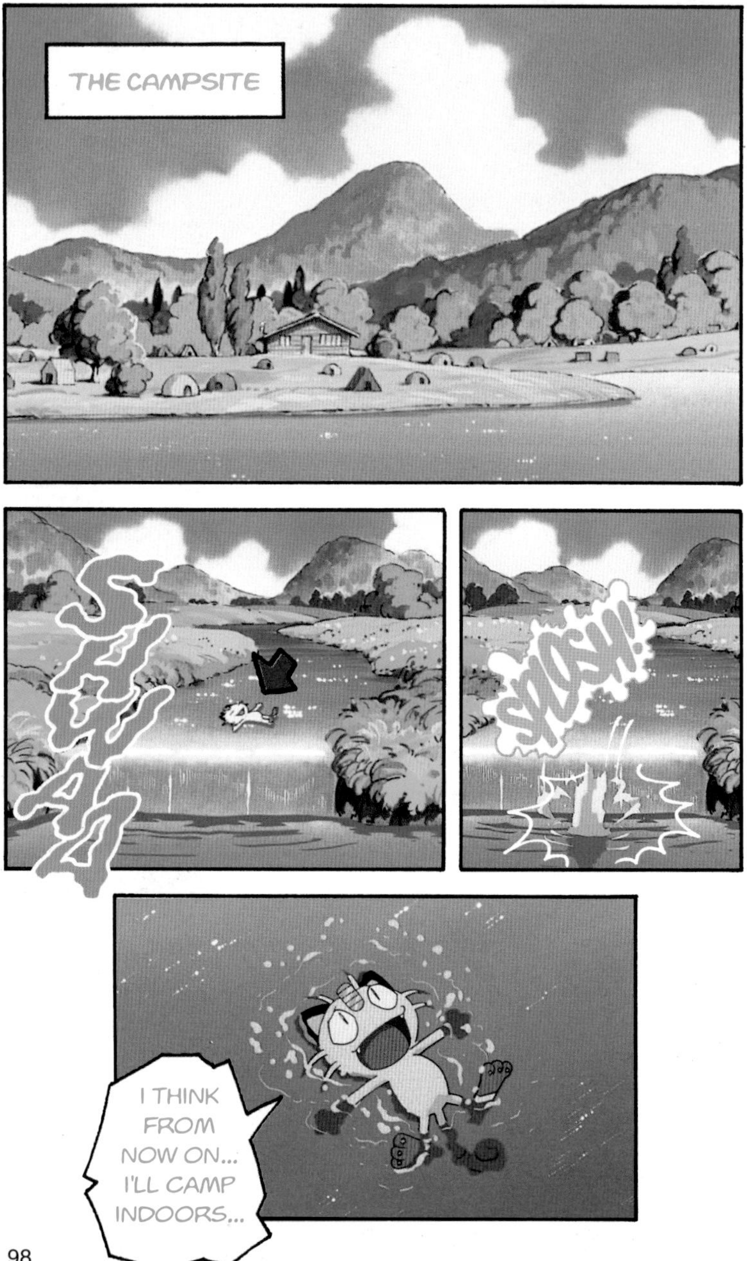
THE CAMPSITE
SHWA
SPLOSH!
I THINK FROM NOW ON... I'LL CAMP INDOORS...

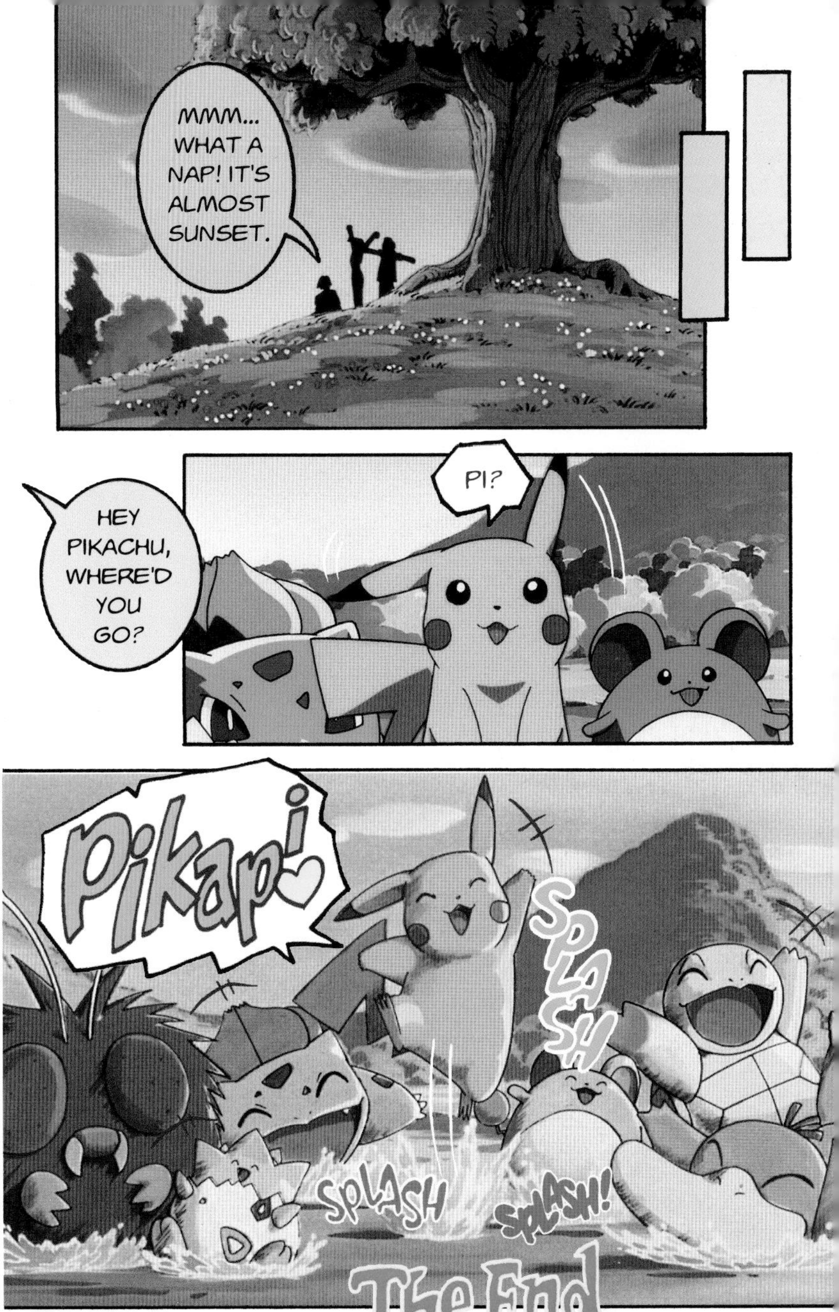
MMM... WHAT A NAP! IT'S ALMOST SUNSET.
HEY PIKACHU, WHERE'D YOU GO?
PI?
Pikapi
SPLASH
SPLASH
SPLASH!
The End

Ledyba

Five Star Pokémon

Height: 3´3˝ / Weight: 24 lbs.

A Bug-type Pokémon similar to a ladybug. Its wings are so strong, it can easily fly around with a small Pokémon (such as Pikachu) on its back. A kind and peaceful, although timid, Pokémon.

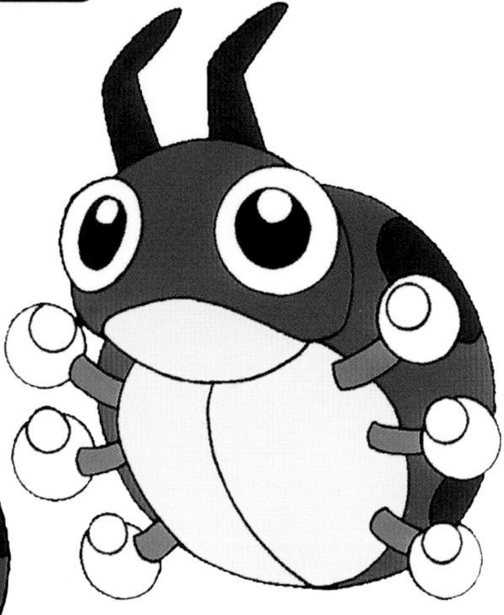

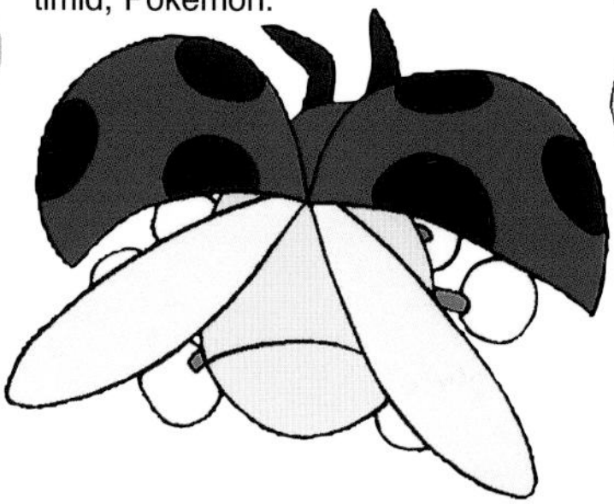

Pokémon No.

165

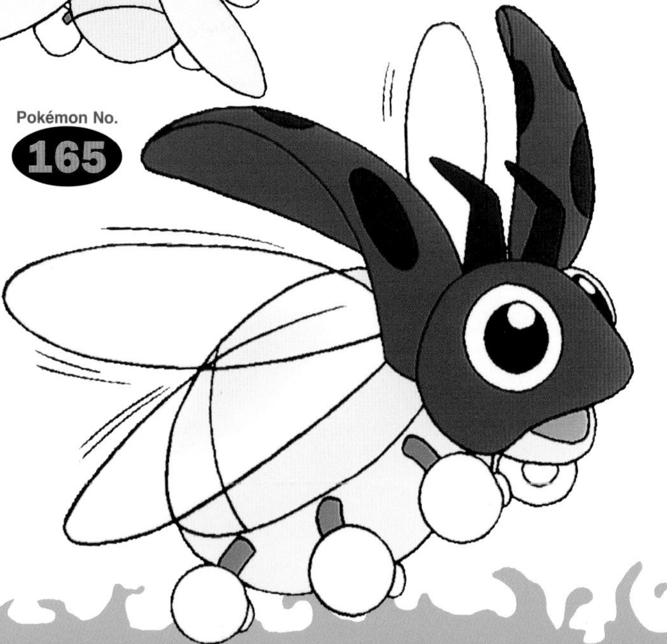

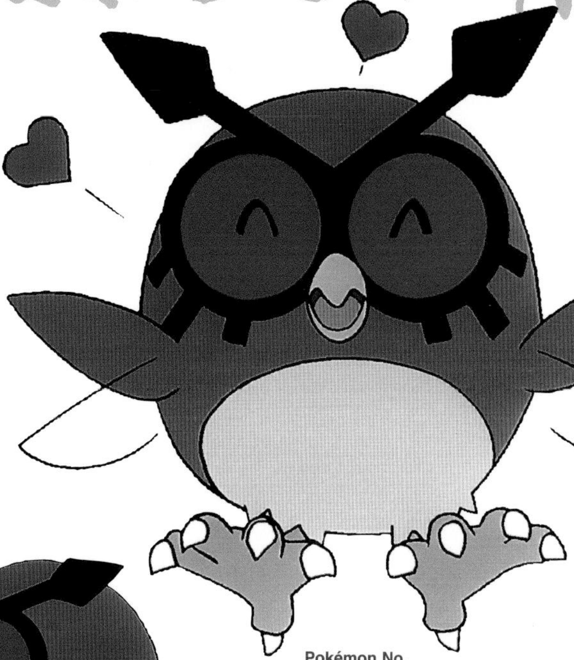

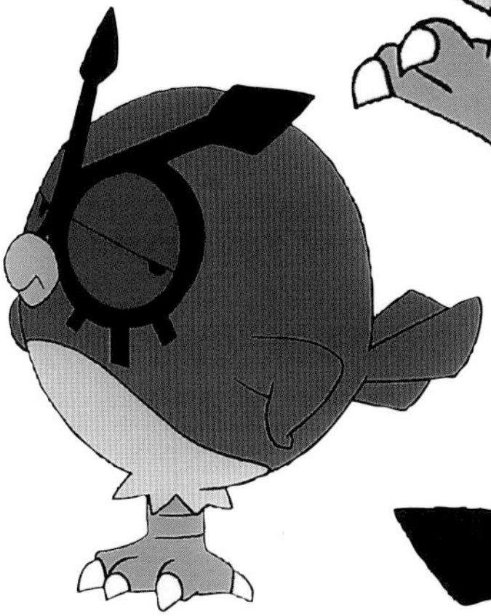

Pokémon No.

163

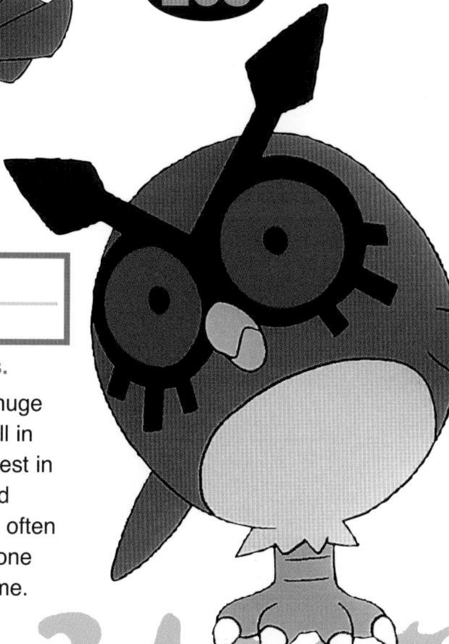

Hoothoot

Owl Pokémon

Height: 2´4˝ / Weight: 47 lbs.

A Flying-type Pokémon with huge eyes which allow it to see well in the dark forest. It makes its nest in the hollows of large trees, and when perched on a branch, it often seems as though it only has one leg. It has perfect sense of time.

Bellossom

Flower Pokémon

Height: 1´4˝ / Weight: 13 lbs.

Beautiful Bellossom loves to dance, and the flowers on its head whirl in time with its dancing. When Pikachu and its friends met the Bellossom, they all began to dance, and the other Pokémon joined in, turning the forest clearing into a giant symphony.

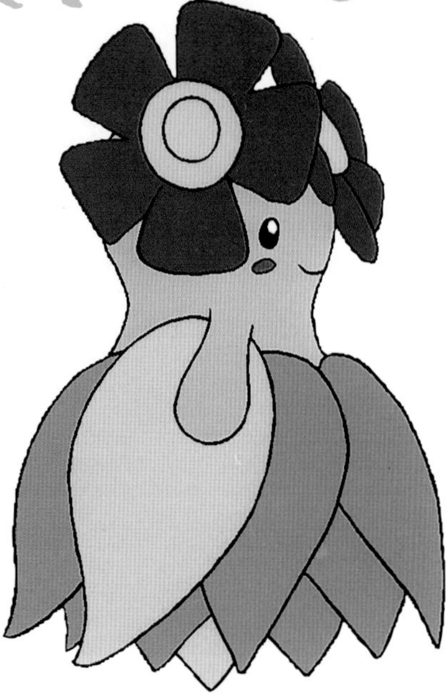

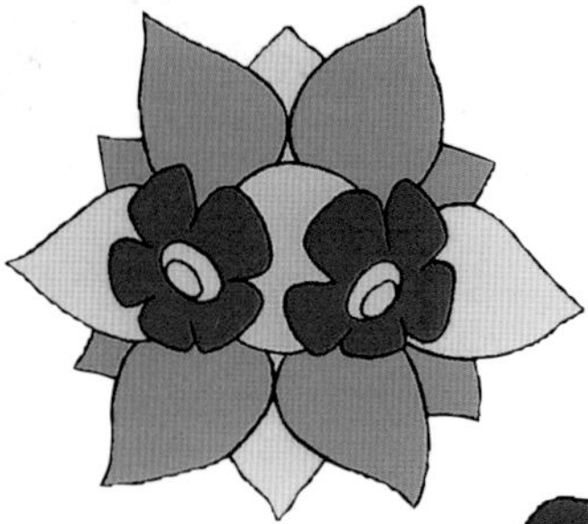

Pokémon No.

182

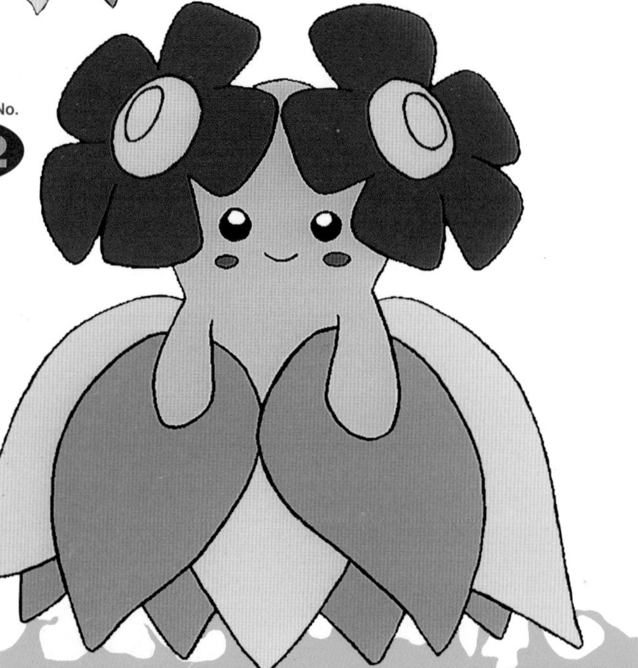